MW00436810

INTERMEDIATE THERMODYNAMICS

A Romantic Comedy

SUSANNAH NIX

Haver Street Press

INTERMEDIATE THERMODYNAMICS. Copyright © 2017 by Susannah Nix

FIRST EDITION: September 2017

ISBN: 978-0-9990948-1-5

Printed in the United States of America

Haver Street Press | 448 W. 19th St., Suite 407 | Houston, TX 77008

Edited by Julia Ganis, www.juliaedits.com

Ebook & Print Cover Design by www.ebooklaunch.com

Chapter One

*T*he dryer was full of clothes.

Goddammit.

Esther Abbott blew her bangs off her forehead and glared at the offending clothes with her hands on her hips. She *hated* touching other people's clothes. Laundry was an unpleasant enough task without having to manhandle a stranger's grungy socks and intimate underthings. But it was either that or wait for the offender to retrieve his own laundry. As much as she disliked touching other people's stuff, she valued her own time and convenience more.

She plunged her hands into the dryer, grimacing. Ugh. It wasn't even warm, which meant it had been in there for a while. At least it was dry laundry. It would be even grosser if it was wet clothes that had been left in the washing machine all day.

Esther knew exactly who the guilty party was. The abundance of plaid shirts was a dead giveaway. There was only one person in the building who wore this much flannel.

Jonathan Brinkerhoff.

The guy in apartment six, right next door to her. The guy with the annoying wind chimes on his balcony that kept her awake whenever it was windy. (Spoiler alert: Los Angeles was *always* windy.) The guy who liked to sit on said balcony and smoke, sending noxious clouds of cigarette toxins drifting into her apartment whenever she left her balcony door open. The guy who couldn't park his stupid Lexus between the lines of his assigned space next to Esther's, which made parking her Prius a feat of heroic dexterity.

Everything about Jonathan annoyed her, from the stupid knit beanies he always wore to his vintage-framed glasses and dumb scraggly beard. But she particularly hated the way he left his clothes in the laundry machines for hours at a time, as if he were the only one in the world who might need to use them. As if he didn't live in an apartment building with eighteen units all sharing the same two machines.

One of the other, *nicer* neighbors—like Mrs. Boorstein, the fifty-something accountant in twelve—might have folded Jonathan's clothes for him and left them in neat piles on the table. But Esther wasn't nice. Not to people who didn't deserve it. She had no patience for incompetence or selfishness. People who broke the laundry room social contract shouldn't get free laundry folding as a reward for their bad behavior. The dude should consider himself lucky she was only dumping his clothes on top of the dirty machine instead of straight onto the floor. And how much did she hate that she now knew what brand of underwear he wore? A lot. She hated it a lot.

"Oh, hey, those are mine," Jonathan said, walking in right as Esther was hugging an armful of his boxer briefs to her chest.

Of course.

She felt a flush of embarrassment, which made her even more irritated. It was *his fault* she had his underwear in her hands. If you left your laundry lying around for hours, you deserved to have strangers pawing through your underdrawers. Those were the rules of the laundry room. Everyone knew that.

"Lemme just grab those," Jonathan said, advancing on her.

Esther dropped his briefs on the dryer and stepped out of the way so he could retrieve the rest of his clothes.

"I got caught up writing and totally forgot all about these," he explained, dropping a sock on the floor as he scooped his clothes out of the dryer. He hadn't brought a basket with him, so he had to pile everything awkwardly in his arms. What was wrong with him? How could one person be so bad at everything? "I've been working on a screenplay, and when I'm in the zone I lose all track of time."

Esther's molars ground together. She already knew he was a screenwriter, because he'd worked it into the conversation *every single time* she'd talked to him. It wasn't as if they even talked that much. They'd had maybe a half dozen conversations, and this was the third time he'd mentioned he was a screenwriter.

Esther was an aerospace engineer—*literally* a rocket scientist— but you didn't hear her bringing it up at every opportunity with every random person she happened to interact with. Even though being a rocket scientist was way cooler than being a screenwriter. Los Angeles was crawling with screenwriters. You couldn't spit out a wad of gum without hitting two of them.

He wasn't even a *real* screenwriter. He was in the graduate screenwriting program at UCLA—a fact he'd mentioned *twice* before—so he was just a student. If he'd ever sold a script or had anything produced, he for sure would have brought it up in conversation by now. Probably several times.

"All yours," he announced, like he was being magnanimous by not parking his laundry in the machine the rest of the day. He collected his clothes from the top of the dryer, dropping another sock in the process, and started for the door.

"You dropped some stuff," Esther said.

He stopped and spun around, looking helplessly from the precarious bundle of clothes in his arms to the socks on the floor. "Do you think you could, uh…?"

She stooped to grab his socks off the floor—more ugh—and balanced them on top of the laundry he was holding.

"Thanks," he said. "You know you shouldn't use fabric softener."

"What?"

He indicated her bottle of fabric softener with his chin. "The waxy buildup that stuff leaves behind affects the fabric's natural ability to absorb moisture. I use a chemical-free laundry powder that's biodegradable and doesn't leave a residue."

Unbelievable. The guy who didn't even know basic laundry room etiquette was lecturing her about her fabric softener.

She gave him a thin-lipped smile. "You know everything's a chemical right? Even water. There's no such thing as chemical free."

His forehead creased, making his eyebrows draw together. "I meant bad chemicals. Like the stuff they put in commercial cleaning products."

"Okay." At this rate, Esther's molars were going to wear down to the size of Tic Tacs. "Thanks for the tip."

"See ya," Jonathan said, looking pleased with himself as he left.

Rolling her eyes, she cleaned the lint trap on the dryer—because *of course* he hadn't done it—and transferred her wet load out of the washer. She fed four quarters into the ancient machine and as it rumbled to life she set the timer on her phone for forty-five minutes. Because *she* was considerate of the other people she shared the laundry facilities with, and she knew how to use a damn clock.

As she was letting herself back into her apartment upstairs, her phone started blaring "Pocketful of Sunshine," the ringtone she'd assigned to her best friend.

Jin-Hee Kang, known as Jinny to everyone but her Korean parents, was the only person Esther knew who actually liked to talk on the phone anymore. The rest of her friends communicated via texting or social media. Not Jinny though. She liked to chat.

Esther kicked her apartment door closed behind her as she fished her phone out of the back pocket of her jeans. Her apartment reeked of cigarette smoke again. Jonathan must have come upstairs and gone straight onto his balcony for a smoke. "Hey, what's up?" she said into the phone as she trudged over to the balcony door and slammed it shut.

"What are you doing today?" Jinny asked.

It was Sunday, and the only thing Esther had on the agenda was laundry, cleaning out the cat litter box, and maybe burning through some of the TV shows stacking up on her DVR. She regarded her reflection in the glass door: the dull brown hair twisted into a messy bun, the zit forming on the tip of her long nose, the stretched-out tank top and cut-off jeans shorts that made up her laundry day uniform. "I've got high tea with Prince Harry and the Queen later, but I can push it if I have to."

"I need a pool hang. Can I come over?"

"Sure."

Esther lived in the Palms neighborhood of Los Angeles, in an older courtyard building with a pool. Jinny lived nearby in Mar Vista, in a newer, bigger building that didn't have a pool or a courtyard, so when the weather was nice she liked to come over to Esther's and hang out. The weather was nice about eighty percent of the time in Los Angeles, which meant they spent a lot of weekends sitting by the pool in Esther's courtyard.

"With mimosas," Jinny added.

"Uh oh. What happened?" Whenever one of them was having a crappy week, they'd make up a pitcher of mimosas and sip them from champagne flutes by the pool.

"I'll tell you when I get there."

Esther pulled open her fridge to take stock. "I've still got a bottle of champagne left over from last time."

"Good," Jinny said. "I'll be there in thirty with the OJ."

Chapter Two

*J*inny showed up at Esther's apartment exactly thirty minutes later in a blue sundress and matching flip-flops, carrying a jug of Simply Orange and a box of doughnuts.

"Oh god," Esther said, lifting an eyebrow at the doughnuts. "Is someone dead?"

Jinny plopped her things on Esther's Ikea dining table. "Only my self-respect." She was twenty-four, like Esther, but her small stature and flawless complexion made her look much younger. She was always being carded at bars and hit on by creepy guys who thought she was a high school student.

"What does that mean?" Esther asked.

Jinny's lips pursed into a Cupid's bow. "If I tell you, you have to promise not to be mad."

"Why would I be mad?" Esther asked with a feeling of dread.

"I sort of kinda slept with Stuart."

"What?"

Stuart was Jinny's ex-boyfriend—her very recently ex-boyfriend. They'd only broken up a week ago, and it had been all Esther could do to refrain from throwing a party to celebrate. The guy was a grade A dick, and he'd been a dick even before he'd cheated on Jinny.

Esther had *tried* to like him. She'd even managed it for a while. He was charismatic and attractive, and even if he wasn't exactly Jinny's intellectual equal, it was easy to see what she liked about him. At first.

Then Esther had begun to notice little things that set her teeth on edge. Like the habit he had of resting his hand on the back of Jinny's neck and steering her around in front of him. It was trivial, but it rubbed Esther the wrong way. Like Jinny was a pet he was parading around. Then she started to notice how he was always asking Jinny to get him things—another drink, something to eat, the phone he'd left in the next room—but never reciprocated. And how often he talked over Jinny, and the way he'd put her down subtly with backhanded compliments he always passed off as jokes.

The first time Esther saw him tell Jinny to lighten up after she got annoyed by one of his little "jokes" at her expense, Esther knew. Stuart was Bad News.

Maybe he wasn't abusive—yet—but the potential was there. He had all the makings.

The only fight she and Jinny had ever had was a few months ago when Esther had told her what she thought of Stuart. That he was a narcissistic, emotionally abusive asshole who would end up hurting her if she didn't get the hell away from him.

To say it hadn't gone over well would be an understatement. Jinny had told Esther to mind her own fucking business and refused to speak to her for an entire week. The fight had only ended when Esther apologized and promised to be nicer to Stuart. It had seriously rankled to do it, but what other option did she have? Abandon Jinny to that asshole? You couldn't tell people things they didn't want to hear. Jinny had been too infatuated to see what kind of man he really was.

Until she'd found out he was cheating on her with one of the women he worked with. Esther had been proud of how quickly and decisively Jinny had kicked him to the curb. Only, apparently it wasn't so decisive after all.

Jinny shook her head. "I knew you'd be mad."

Esther took a breath and did her best to sound calm and supportive. "I'm not mad. But I do have questions. Number one: how do you *sort of* sleep with someone?"

Jinny's eyes skated away, embarrassed. "You regular-sleep with them and then kind of regret it after but not totally."

This was bad. Very, very bad. "But he cheated on you. I thought you were done with him?"

"I was. I mean, *I am.* I definitely am. Done with him. For good." She bobbed her head, trying to seem convincing. Unconvincingly.

"Except for the part where you slept with him."

Jinny turned away to examine the doughnuts. "Yeah, except for that part."

"So again I ask, what happened?"

Jinny sighed as she picked up a chocolate-glazed. "You know how he's been texting me?"

Esther scowled. "I told you you should have gotten a restraining order."

"He was being all sweet and apologetic!" Jinny said around a mouthful of doughnut.

"You didn't fall for that, did you?" Of course she had; she always fell for that. Stuart had played her like a bass guitar.

"No! I was very firm with him. But then last night his texts started getting all sexy, and we may have ended up sexting a little bit—"

Esther squeezed her eyes shut. "Gross."

"And it got me all worked up—"

"Double gross."

"And then he showed up at my door and—"

"Okay, fine, I get the gist. No need for further details." *Like a bass guitar.* Stuart was a parasite. He'd always find a way to attach himself to his host.

Jinny stuffed the rest of her doughnut in her mouth and went to the fridge for the champagne. "Look, he can be really convincing, okay? It's hard to say no to him."

"But you're going to say no the next time, right?" Esther said as she got down two champagne flutes.

"Absolutely. Grab the OJ." Jinny shouldered the tote she kept packed with pool-day essentials—towel, sunglasses, sunscreen, and trashy magazines—and picked up the box of doughnuts.

Esther perched her sunglasses on top of her head and carried the OJ and champagne flutes out of the apartment. "If you take him back, he'll cheat on you again. Once a cheater, always a cheater."

Jinny followed with the champagne and doughnuts. "I *know*."

Esther regarded her with a healthy dose of skepticism. Jinny was a recidivist. She'd keep going back to Stuart every time she felt lonely. If someone else didn't come along to distract her—fast —she might very well give in and take Stuart back for real. She'd done it before, with her last boyfriend. That one had taken three tries to shake, and he hadn't been nearly as beguiling as Stuart.

"How did you leave things with him?" Esther asked as they clomped down the stairs.

Like a lot of the older buildings in the neighborhood, the apartments were all on the second floor, arranged in a rectangle around a central courtyard. Underneath the apartments were the laundry room, mailboxes, storage, and off-street resident parking. The courtyard was by far the nicest part of Esther's building—thanks entirely to the efforts of Mrs. Boorstein, who liked to garden and kept the beds full of attractive flowers and vegetation at no cost to their cheapskate landlord.

"I made it clear it was just a one-time thing," Jinny said as they emerged into the courtyard.

Sunlight reflected off the surface of the pool, which was a

cloudy aquamarine color today. They never actually got in the water, because the last person who'd swum in it had come down with an ear infection. Even if the two things weren't related, Esther wasn't taking any chances.

She set the glasses and OJ down on a rusty metal table in the shade. While Jinny dragged one of the lounge chairs closer to the table, Esther filled the two glasses half full with champagne and topped them off with orange juice. She passed one to Jinny. "Do you want him back?"

Jinny accepted the glass, avoiding Esther's eyes as she settled into the lounge chair. "We were together for six months. I love him."

"Enough to forgive him for cheating?"

Jinny looked down at her lap, frowning as she rearranged her skirt over her legs. "Did I tell you he cried when I broke up with him?"

"No." *Good.* The asshole deserved to cry. Esther hoped he cried himself to sleep every goddamn night.

"Yeah, I almost felt bad."

"Don't you dare feel bad. He cheated on you. Also, he was a jerk."

Jinny tugged the hair elastic off her wrist and fastened her shoulder-length black hair into a ponytail. "He wasn't that bad."

Esther stared at her over the top of her champagne flute. "He missed your birthday to go surfing in Mexico."

"That was one time. And he felt really bad about it."

"He didn't do anything for you for Valentine's Day either. And when he won those free concert tickets, he took one of his surfing buddies instead of you."

Jinny sighed and sipped her mimosa. "Yeah, okay. He kind of sucked."

At least she was admitting it. Esther slipped off her flip-flops and pulled another chair closer so she could put her feet up on it. Her stocky legs were cadaverously pale, an effect that was only enhanced by the blue polish on her toes. "You can do so much better," she said, pulling her sunglasses down over her eyes.

Jinny scowled as she fished a magazine out of her tote bag. "That remains to be seen."

For such a beautiful, awesome person, Jinny had crazy low self-esteem. It didn't help that Stuart had zeroed in on her insecurities with expert precision, feeding them for his own purposes. She hadn't been able to see how badly he treated her, because on some level she didn't seem to believe she deserved to be treated better.

Esther *really* hated that guy. "You were always way too good for him. Honestly, I never understood what you saw in him."

Jinny peered at her over the top of her sunglasses. "Um, he's a total hottie?"

"*You* are a hottie, friend. You basically had nothing common, beyond the fact that you're both good-looking."

"We both work in tech fields."

Esther snorted into her mimosa. "The Apple Store does not count as a tech field."

"He totally fixed my iPad!"

"He's into all this outdoorsy stuff like cycling and hiking and camping, and you hate the outdoors."

"I don't hate the outdoors." Jinny waved her hand, encompassing the courtyard around them. "I'm outdoors right now."

"Lounging by a pool drinking mimosas does not count as outdoorsy."

"Whatever."

"All I'm saying is don't go for second best, baby."

Jinny raised her sunglasses and squinted at her. "Are you quoting Madonna at me right now?"

"It's a very appropriate song. Madge knows what's up."

"Your buddy Madge was married to Sean Penn, so let's not pretend her judgment is infallible."

A door slammed overhead, and they both glanced up as

Jonathan came out of his apartment. Awesome. How many times was Esther going to see this guy today?

His footfalls echoed around the courtyard as he plodded down the stairs. When he saw them, he halted and offered a half-hearted nod. "Hey."

Esther nodded back, just as half-heartedly.

"Hi!" Jinny called out, waving.

Jonathan nodded again, plunged his hands into his pockets, and continued on to his car.

Esther had never once seen the guy smile. The closest he'd ever come was a pained sort of grimace.

"He's cute," Jinny whispered when he was out of sight.

Esther gave her a sidelong glance. "Who?"

"Him. Your neighbor. Whatshisname."

"Jonathan? Ugh. No. He's not." Pretentious, beanie-clad, farmer's-market-shopping hipsters weren't Esther's type. Objectively, she supposed he might be considered attractive—so long as he didn't open his mouth and start talking. He was just so damn annoying, it was impossible to separate his looks from his personality.

"*Yeah*, he is," Jinny insisted. "He looks like a young Jake Gyllenhaal. Don't tell me you haven't noticed."

"He does *not* look like Jake Gyllenhaal." Esther didn't even like Jake Gyllenhaal, but she felt this was an unfair aspersion against him that required her defense.

"Come on, he's got that great, thick, wavy dark hair—"

"Which is always covered by those dumb beanies he wears."

Jinny sniffed. "I like a man in a beanie."

Of course she does. Stuart wore beanies all the time. So did half the men in LA under thirty, but still. Esther felt justified in her loathing of them.

"Plus, he's got those soulful blue eyes," Jinny added.

Soulful? What was she talking about? Esther wrinkled her

nose. "You can't even tell what his eyes look like under those hipster glasses."

"I love those glasses! Guys in glasses are super hot. Oh!" Jinny reached over and smacked Esther on the arm. "You know who else he looks like? Dev Patel."

Esther stared at her. "Dev Patel is Indian."

"I know that. Duh."

"And looks nothing like Jake Gyllenhaal *or* Jonathan, both of whom are white."

Jinny laid her magazine aside and leaned back, crossing her legs. "It's the hair. Jonathan has the same great hair Dev Patel has. The kind you want to run your fingers through." She wiggled her fingers for emphasis. "And that beard. God, I love a beard."

Stuart had a beard. Although his hair was golden brown instead of Jonathan's darker, almost-black-brown.

Esther's eyes narrowed as she tried to decide whether Jinny was actually interested in Jonathan or projecting Stuart onto him. "How long have you felt this way about my neighbor?"

Jinny shrugged and reached for her mimosa. "I've always thought he was cute." Her phone vibrated beside her, and she picked it up. "Ugh. I wish Stuart would just leave me alone."

Esther frowned. "What does he want?"

Jinny set her phone down without replying. "Forgiveness. Reconciliation. More sex. Take your pick."

"I'm telling you, you should get a restraining order."

"Thanks, your honor, but I don't need a restraining order. It's just Stuart."

Stuart, who'd been gaslighting Jinny for the better part of six months. Who had her convinced she was dating above her level and should be grateful for his half-assed attentions. Who steered her around like a child.

Esther eyed her suspiciously. "You're considering it, aren't you? Taking him back."

Jinny didn't say anything.

Jonathan reappeared in the courtyard with a forty-pound bag of mulch balanced on his shoulder. He skirted around the edge of the pool and dumped it onto the ground by Esther's chair, next to a bed of freshly planted begonias.

"What are you doing?" she asked, peering at him over her sunglasses.

"Mrs. Boorstein asked me to pick up some mulch for the new plantings." He wiped his hands on his jeans and headed back toward the carport.

Jinny leaned over and smacked Esther on the arm again. "He helps little old ladies with gardening? That is so sweet!"

Esther wasn't sure Mrs. Boorstein would appreciate being called a little old lady, but she had to agree it was kind of sweet.

They heard the sound of a trunk slamming, and Jonathan reappeared with another bag of mulch hoisted on his shoulder. He dropped it next to the first one, then bent over to slide it a few feet to the left, spacing them out at either end of the bed.

His backside was right in Esther's eyeline, and she had to admit it wasn't the worst view she'd ever seen. Fine. So he had a decent body. *He irritates the hell out of you, remember?*

Jinny smacked her on the arm a third time and Esther jerked her gaze away, flushing slightly.

"Nice ass," Jinny mouthed silently, tilting her head in Jonathan's direction.

Esther shook her head, recovering herself enough to roll her eyes. "I didn't know you helped with the gardening," she said when Jonathan straightened, removing his ass from her field of vision.

"Just with the heavy stuff. Mrs. B doesn't trust me to touch the plants." He reached up to brush a piece of mulch off his shoulder. "She said she'd be down in a bit to spread the mulch. Will you tell her I'll be upstairs if she needs any more help?"

There was another piece of mulch caught in his beard. Esther considered pointing it out to him, but decided against it. "Sure," she said.

He gave another nod and shuffled off, up the stairs and into his apartment.

Jinny's phone vibrated with another text message. She picked it up and stared at the screen, frowning.

"Stuart again?" Esther asked with a feeling of unease.

"Yeah." Jinny powered the phone off and shoved it inside her tote.

"You should ask Jonathan out," Esther said.

Jinny gave her a quizzical look. "I thought you hated him."

"I didn't say *I* should date him. You're the one who thinks he's cute." He might be annoying, but as far as Esther could tell, he wasn't a manipulative bastard. He'd definitely be an upgrade from Stuart.

Jinny shook her head. "I'm not asking him out."

"Why not?"

"Because he doesn't even know who I am. I'm not walking up to a total stranger and asking him out on a date."

"I could set you two up."

Jinny's expression darkened. "Don't you dare. You know how I feel about blind dates." She'd spent her high school years only being allowed to go on dates arranged by her mother, and it had permanently soured her on being fixed up.

The timer on Esther's phone went off, and she fished it out of her pocket to silence it. "Gotta grab my laundry." She stood up and pointed her phone at Jinny. "You know what he looks like, so it wouldn't be a blind date."

"Arranged dates. Whatever." Jinny made a face. "You can't force love. You have to let it find you."

Esther rolled her eyes as she headed to the laundry room. "If you say so."

Jinny was a romantic, but Esther didn't buy into any of that crap.

She didn't believe in fate or love at first sight or happily-ever-afters. There was no such thing as soul mates, no fairy godparents watching over anyone, and no prince coming to sweep you off your feet. She reserved her faith for things that could measured with empirical evidence and behaved predictably, according to the laws of nature.

Fairy tales were all well and good in books, but it was dangerous to put your faith in fiction. Look what had happened to Esther's mother. She'd thought she was living a perfect, fairy-tale life until her prince had up and left her, and she'd been completely unprepared to cope with reality. Fifteen years later, she was still drifting along, waiting for the next prince to show up and save her.

Forget princes. You had to make your own luck in life. If you wanted something, you couldn't sit back and wait for it to fall into your lap. You had to go out and make it happen.

Chapter Three

*T*wo days later, Jinny was still waffling on Stuart. Esther knew she was still texting with him. Who knew how much longer she'd be able to hold out with Stuart wheedling her and tempting her with the power of his magical dick? Esther had a sinking feeling they'd be back together by the weekend.

She'd been racking her brain for a way to keep them apart, but so far she'd come up empty. If she pushed too hard, Jinny might get pissed and dig her heels in. That was what had happened the last time Esther had tried to talk some sense into her about Stuart. It needed to be handled delicately—and quickly, before it was too late.

Esther was still musing on it when she got home from work on Wednesday. As she walked past Jonathan's apartment, she heard his deadbolt unlock and quickened her steps, digging around in her bag for her keys. Maybe she could get inside before he came out and tried to start up another conversation—

"Hey," he said, stepping out of his apartment behind her.

Dammit.

Esther threw a polite smile over her shoulder. "Hi."

Was it too much to hope that he had somewhere to be and no

interest in chatting? She fumbled for the key on her key ring and shoved it into the lock.

"Hey, I've got something for you," he said.

She froze with her hand on the doorknob. *So close.*

Pasting a smile on her face, she turned around. "Oh, yeah?"

"Hang on," he said, holding up a finger, and disappeared inside his apartment.

Great. What was this about? She couldn't think of anything he might have that she wanted. And how long was she supposed to stand out here in the breezeway waiting on him anyway? All she wanted to do was go inside her apartment, kick off her clunky oxfords, peel off the tights she'd been wearing all day, and drink a beer. Was that too much to ask at the end of a long, annoying work day?

He had another five seconds, and then she was going inside.

Five…four…three…two…

Jonathan reappeared, holding a handful of envelopes and a magazine. "Here, the mailman put some of your stuff in my box by mistake."

Oh. He was actually being neighborly.

"Thanks." Feeling a little ashamed, Esther shuffled forward to accept the mislaid mail. She'd been wondering where this month's *Astronomy* magazine had gotten to. It was nice of him to hang on to her mail for her; plenty of assholes would have dumped it in the trash to save themselves the trouble of redelivering it.

"Not exactly light reading." He shoved his hands in the back pockets of his jeans. "Are you like an astronomer or something?"

"Aerospace engineer. Astronomy's just for fun."

He nodded. "That's cool. You must know a lot of science, then."

"A little, yeah."

He nodded again and shifted his weight. "Could I ask you favor?"

Nooooo.

"So, you know how I'm a screenwriter..."

Please, no.

"I've been working on this sci-fi script for one of my classes, and I've got the essence of the story all laid out, but I could really use some help with the science aspects. Just to make it more realistic—well, not realistic, exactly, but plausible, at least."

Why was she being punished? What had she ever done to deserve this?

"Would you mind taking a look at it for me? And maybe giving me some notes? Just on the science part. What do you say?"

Shit. Was there any way to get out of this without being rude? "I don't really know anything about writing movies," she hedged. "Isn't there someone in your program...?"

He shook his head. "You don't need to know anything about screenwriting, I've got that covered. But the only person I know with any science under their belt is my buddy Greg, who was premed for a semester before he switched to English. He's shit with physics though, and I need someone who knows about things like gravity and propulsion and asteroids. That's you, right?"

Esther swallowed. "Um..." She felt her phone vibrate in her bag—*thank god, an interruption.* "Sorry," she muttered. "I just need to check..."

It was a text from Jinny: *Stuart's begging me to take him back. Tell me not to get back together with him.*

"One sec," Esther said to Jonathan, mashing her thumbs against the screen as she typed her reply.

DO NOT GET BACK TOGETHER WITH CHEATING JERKFACE STU.

"Everything okay?" Jonathan asked.

"Yeah. Just trying to avert a catastrophe." Esther looked up from her phone, into Jonathan's eyes.

His *soulful* eyes.

Jinny thought he was cute. Jinny *liked* him.

If he asked her out, she'd say yes. And if she went out with him, maybe she'd forget about Stuart. She'd remember there were other men in the world, and she didn't have to settle for one who was an asshole.

Jonathan was awkward and a little irritating, sure, but he actually seemed pretty nice. She'd never seen him say or do anything purposefully unkind, and he didn't have the social skills to be manipulative. A lot of his mansplaining seemed to be his clumsy way of trying to be helpful, which could be considered sort of sweet from a certain perspective. He was the kind of guy who helped old ladies with gardening. How bad could he be?

"So, about my script..." Jonathan said, rubbing the back of his neck.

"I'll do it if you do something for me," Esther told him.

His eyebrows scrunched together. "Okaaay. What?"

"You have to ask my friend Jinny out."

His mouth opened and then closed again. His eyebrows had joined into a solid stripe, like a dark, furry caterpillar. "Um..."

"You don't have a girlfriend, do you?"

"No, but—"

"Jinny's really nice and totally normal and beautiful." This was all true. Socially awkward writer boy would be lucky to go out with someone as great as Jinny. And it would do Jinny good to date a guy as nice as Jonathan seemed to be.

He looked skeptical. "Then why does she need you to get dates for her?"

"Because she just broke up with a jerk and I'm afraid she's going to take him back."

"Isn't that her choice to make?"

A noble sentiment, but this was a desperate situation that called for desperate measures. "I'm not trying to take away her choice. I'm trying to give her *another* choice. To show her there are other guys out there who like her, and she doesn't have to date a creep." Esther narrowed her eyes at him. "You're not a creep, are you?"

"No!" he said, then frowned like he wasn't sure. "I mean, I don't think so?"

She pointed a warning finger at him. "I know where you live, remember, so if you hurt her—"

He held up his hands, palms out. There were black ink stains all over his fingers. "I haven't agreed to go out with her yet. I don't even know who she is."

"She's the one who's always hanging around the pool with me. You saw her last weekend, remember?"

"Oh, yeah." His mouth curved into something that almost resembled a smile. "Yeah, she's cute."

Got ya! It was perfect. Jinny liked him, and he liked her. She was doing them both a favor by setting them up. She was being a good Samaritan. "So you'll do it, then?"

He frowned again and rubbed his hand over his jaw. Up close, his beard looked a lot less scraggly. And his eyes actually were a gorgeous shade of blue. "It seems kind of sketchy. Why do I have to ask her out? Couldn't you just fix us up on a blind date or something?"

Esther shook her head. "She hates blind dates. She'd never agree to it."

"But I don't even know her. Won't she think it's weird that a stranger is asking her out, out of nowhere?"

Clearly, this guy did not get out much and had no idea how often men propositioned women they didn't know. Which, again, was sort of sweet. Naive, but sweet. He was like a character from a Jane Austen novel who needed a formal introduction before he could commence his courtship. "You've seen each other around plenty of times. It's not weird."

"What if she says no?"

She nearly had him on the hook. He just needed a little nudge. "She won't say no, because she thinks you're cute too."

"Really?" His eyes lit up like a Christmas tree, which was pretty damned adorable. Fine. Jinny was right. He was cute.

"Yes, really."

"She told you that?"

"She told me that."

Doubt crept into his expression again. "It still seems weird."

Oh, my god. What was it going to take to get him to say yes? Blackmail? Because Esther could do blackmail if she had to. "Do you want me to read your script or not?" The carrots weren't working; it was time for a little stick.

His frown deepened. Then he nodded. "Yeah, okay. I'll do it, I guess."

Yes! Not as much enthusiasm as Esther would have liked, but it was good enough. "You have to take it seriously and give her a real chance though. No blowing her off after one date."

He scratched the back of his head. "What constitutes a real chance?"

Esther pursed her lips as she considered the question. How much dating did Jinny need to do to get over Stuart? A single date might not be enough. It had to be enough to put Stuart out of her mind for good. "Three dates," she finally decided.

Jonathan's eyes widened. "*Three?* No way."

"That's the deal. Take it or leave it." If it was only one date, he might half-ass his way through it. But if he knew he had to go out with her two more times, he'd make more of an effort. Theoretically.

"I'll do two."

"Three," Esther repeated. Now that she'd gotten him to agree to the plan, she had the upper hand. She wasn't budging.

His mouth settled into a scowl. "You have to give me real help with the script, then. Not just scribble down a few notes, or mark the stuff that's inaccurate. You have to work with me and help me come up with ways to make the science work with the story."

Lord. The things Esther was willing to do for Jinny. She'd better appreciate this. "I'll science the shit out of that script for you. Do we have a deal?"

"Yeah." He nodded. "Okay."

Esther stuck out her hand. After a moment's hesitation, Jonathan took it.

It was official. They were doing this.

"We have to move fast," she said, "before Jinny goes back to Stuart."

"How fast?" Jonathan asked.

Esther grinned at him. "What are you doing tonight?"

All the color drained out his face. "Tonight?"

Chapter Four

*I*t took a bit of finagling to pull it off.

Jonathan couldn't just call Jinny to ask her out, because he didn't have her number. As far as Jinny knew, he didn't even know her name, much less her phone number. So he had to ask her out in person. Which meant they had to arrange an "accidental" meeting.

You would think a screenwriter would be able to come up with a simple meet-cute, but he was worse than useless in this department.

"Why don't you just give me her number so I can call her?" he said, shrugging. "I don't see why it has to be so complicated."

"Because this can't look like a set-up," Esther reminded him. "How is she supposed to think you got her number, if not from me?"

He shrugged again.

Useless. Fortunately, Esther was a master strategist. She'd been kicking her older brother's ass at Risk since she was seven years old. She had this.

MY PLACE STAT, she texted Jinny. *I'm ordering from the Hawaiian place.*

Jinny loved the Hawaiian place, and they didn't deliver to Mar Vista.

On my way, Jinny texted back almost immediately. *Order me the kalua pork ramen.*

ONCE SHE WAS sure Jonathan knew what he was supposed to do, Esther shooed him out of her apartment so she could finally take off her damn tights. She changed out of the loose floral dress she'd worn to work and into a pair of sweatpants and her favorite University of Washington T-shirt. Shaking her long, wavy hair out of its neat work bun, she sank down on the couch and twisted it into a looser, messier bun.

Her big, black-and-white tuxedo cat, Sally Ride, jumped into her lap to demand head scratches. Esther obliged her, stroking the purring cat while she waited for Jinny to arrive.

Five minutes later, there was a knock on the door, and Sally hightailed it to the bedroom.

"Take my phone," Jinny said, thrusting it at Esther as she walked past her into the apartment.

"Okay." Esther stared at the phone as she closed the door "Why?"

The phone vibrated in her hand with a new text message from Stuart: *Let me come over tonight baby. I miss my ickle lover bunny.*

Gross.

"That's why," Jinny said, helping herself to a beer from the fridge. "Don't let me answer it."

Esther set the phone facedown on the table by the door. "He wants a booty call tonight? It's a weeknight."

"People have sex on weeknights, you know." Jinny twisted the cap off her beer and took a swig.

"Sounds exhausting. I barely have enough energy to feed myself when I get home from work."

Jinny flopped onto Esther's red Ikea sofa with her beer.

Esther's entire apartment had been furnished at Ikea. She'd basically just copied one of the model living rooms from the showroom.

"This is torture," Jinny groaned. "I'm trying to resist him, but every time he texts, it reminds me how much I miss him. He's slowly wearing me down."

Sometimes Esther couldn't understand Jinny at all. Sure, Stuart was hot, and maybe he was as good in bed as Jinny claimed. But no matter how good he might be, or how much she might think she loved him, Esther couldn't imagine ever forgiving a man who'd cheated on her.

"You could block him," she suggested, sitting at the other end of the couch and pulling her legs up under her.

Jinny took another swig of beer. "I thought about it. But I can't stand the thought of cutting him off like that. Knowing he's still texting, but not knowing what he's saying." Her eyes drifted to the phone on the table, like she wanted to go over there and look at it.

Jesus, she was really far gone. Thank god Esther had run into Jonathan tonight. Not a minute too soon.

Sally reemerged from the bedroom and came over to the couch to sniff Esther's toes. Esther reached down to scratch the top of her head. "You *know* what he's saying though. You don't need to read his texts to know what he wants."

"I kind of like the attention," Jinny admitted. "After what he did, he deserves to grovel. And I deserve to enjoy his groveling." She leaned over to pet Sally, who glided just out of reach. "Why doesn't your cat want to be my friend?"

Esther shrugged. "She doesn't like anyone but me. She's choosy."

"Are you saying I'm not good enough for your cat?"

"No, I'm saying she knows where her food comes from and doesn't have time for anyone who doesn't keep her in the gourmet salmon bits to which she's accustomed."

"That's fair," Jinny said. "I'll give you a pass, Sally."

There was another knock on the door, and Sally bolted for the bedroom again. Esther got up, signed the receipt for the food, and carried it to the dining table.

"God, it smells so good," Jinny said as she helped Esther unpack the food. "I'm famished. Turning down sex is hard work."

"I'm sure," Esther said sourly as she went into the kitchen for utensils and napkins.

Jinny peeled open one of the containers. "You ordered the kettle corn, right?"

"Of course. I'm not an amateur."

They'd barely started eating when there was yet another knock on the door. Right on cue.

"Listen for our food to be delivered," Esther had told Jonathan. *"Once the delivery guy leaves, wait two minutes, then come over with the mail."* She'd given him back her misdelivered mail, so he could bring it over while Jinny was there.

"Did the delivery guy forget something?" Jinny asked, taking stock of the food containers.

"I don't think so." Esther headed for the door. "Maybe I signed the wrong receipt." She pulled it open and pretended to be surprised. "Oh! Jonathan. Hi."

"Hey," he said without much enthusiasm.

She raised her eyebrows, waiting for him to explain why he was here. *Don't screw this up, you idiot.*

"Hey," he mumbled again. *Smooth.* "The—uh—the mailman left these in my box by mistake." He held out her mail.

"Thanks!" Esther said, trying to sound friendly. "I guess he got our boxes mixed up, because I've got some of yours too. Come on in." She stepped back and waved him over the threshold.

Hands shoved deep in his pockets and slouching like a kid being dragged to church against his will, Jonathan shuffled into the apartment. So far, he was really not selling this.

Esther pretended to rifle through the stack of mail piling up on the Ikea bookcase by the door. "I know I set it down around here somewhere...aha! Here we go. Sorry, I was going to bring it over earlier, but then Jinny came over and I sort of forgot. This is my friend Jinny, by the way," she added, waving her hand like it was an afterthought. "Jinny, Jonathan. Jonathan, Jinny."

"Hey," Jonathan mumbled.

Come on, Esther thought. *Try harder.* This wasn't going to work if he kept acting like he didn't want to be there.

Jinny stepped forward and stuck out her hand. "Hi, nice to meet you." Thank god one of them had social skills.

Jonathan stared at her hand for a second, like he didn't know what he was supposed to do with it. And then finally—*finally*—some kind of automatic response kicked in, and he stepped forward to take it. "Oh, yeah. I've seen you around before."

"Tell her you've seen her around before," Esther had coached Jonathan earlier. *"She'll be flattered that you noticed her."*

Jinny's smile got wider. "I'm here a lot. I like Esther's pool. Esther's okay too, but mainly it's the pool that's the draw."

Jonathan nodded, relaxing a little. "Yeah, it's pretty nice. I hope you don't get in it though, because of the bacteria."

"Esther or the pool?" Jinny asked, straight-faced.

Jonathan laughed. "The pool. I don't really know anything about Esther's bacteria situation."

Hey, what do you know? The guy could smile after all.

"That's funny," Esther said. "I can tell you're a writer. Did you know Jonathan's a screenwriter?" she said, turning to Jinny.

"Really?" Jinny said, doing a good job of acting impressed. "That's cool."

"It smells really good in here," Jonathan said. "Are you guys about to eat?"

Esther nodded. "We ordered from Mahalo. It arrived right before you did."

"Their kettle corn is out of this world."

"Yeah, it is. You want some?" Esther offered.

Jonathan shook his head, doing a passable job of looking tempted. "Nah, I don't want to crash your dinner."

"It's fine, I always order way too much." Esther went into the kitchen to get more utensils. "You should have some ribs to go with your corn."

"Yeah, okay," Jonathan said. "Thanks."

"You want a beer?" Esther pulled open the fridge. "You can't eat ribs without beer."

"Sure."

Jinny came into the kitchen. "What are you doing?" she whispered.

"Getting him a beer."

"But you don't even like him."

"Yeah, but you do." Esther shrugged. "Maybe you were right. Maybe I was too harsh on him before. He's my neighbor—I should be more neighborly, right?" She thrust the beer and a fork and plate at Jinny. "Take these to him."

Esther hung out in the kitchen, pretending to tidy up while Jinny went back out to Jonathan.

"Here you go," she said, handing them to him. "Dig in."

"Thanks," he said. "So, uh, do you live near here?"

Nice, Esther thought, eavesdropping on them. That was a perfectly decent conversation starter. Maybe he was getting better at this stuff.

"Not too far," Jinny said. "Over in Mar Vista."

"Oh, yeah, it's nice over there."

"It's all right. I like coming over here though. I mean, obviously, since I'm here all the time."

"So, how do you two know each other?"

"Don't talk about yourself too much," Esther had warned him. *"Ask her questions, try to get to know her. Make it clear she's the one you like."*

While Jinny was telling Jonathan the story of how she and Esther had become friends, Esther rejoined them in the dining room. She sipped her beer and ate her food, only jumping into the conversation occasionally, letting the two of them do the majority of the talking.

Ten minutes later, she decided things were proceeding well enough that it was time to move on to the next stage of the plan. "Anyone want another beer?" she asked, going to the fridge.

"I'll take one," Jinny called out.

"Thanks, but I'm still working on mine," Jonathan said.

While she was in the kitchen, Esther set a four-minute timer on her phone. Then she grabbed two beers and took them into the dining room.

When her timer went off, she pretended to be surprised. "Oops, that's my laundry! Gotta run downstairs and put my clothes in the dryer. Be right back."

"I can't be gone longer than five minutes without it looking weird, so that's all the time you'll have," she'd told Jonathan earlier. *"That's your window to ask her out. Don't miss it."*

Grabbing a handful of quarters out of the bowl, she let herself out of the apartment. When she got downstairs to the laundry room, Brent, the stoner musician who lived in fourteen, was there, transferring his clothes from the washer into the dryer.

"You need the machine?" he asked, glancing at her over his shoulder.

"Nope." Esther hopped up onto the folding table and pulled up a game on her phone.

He gave her a puzzled look.

"I'm just hanging out," she explained.

"In the laundry room?"

"I've got people in my apartment and I needed to give them a few minutes alone."

"Okay, whatever." Brent went back to putting his clothes in the dryer, and Esther went back to playing on her phone. "Later," he said on his way out.

"Yep, see ya," Esther replied.

When five minutes had passed, she went back upstairs to her apartment.

Jonathan and Jinny were standing a lot closer together than when she'd left. They both had their phones out, like they were exchanging numbers. Even better, they were both smiling.

"Get your laundry squared away?" Jinny asked, setting her phone down.

"Yep."

"All right, well, I'm gonna go," Jonathan said. "Thanks for the beer and the ribs." He glanced at Jinny shyly. "I'll text you."

Jinny nodded. "Cool."

"Don't forget your mail," Esther said.

"Right, my mail. Thanks." He grabbed it off the table and let himself out of the apartment.

"What was *that*?" Esther asked Jinny when he was gone. As if she didn't know.

Jinny bounced on her toes, practically glowing. "He asked me out!"

Esther grinned. "And you said yes?"

"Of course I said yes!"

"That's awesome. Good for you!" Feeling extremely pleased with herself, Esther began gathering up the leftovers and carrying them into the kitchen. She'd done it. *Jonathan* had done it.

"Can you believe he asked me out?" Jinny said, following her.

Esther pulled open the fridge and shoved the other takeout containers around to make room. "Of course I can believe it. You're beautiful and awesome. Who wouldn't want to ask you out?"

"Yeah, but I was just talking about how cute he was the other day, and then tonight he asked me out, out of nowhere. It must be fate or something."

"Must be," Esther agreed.

Chapter Five

---

*W*hen Esther told people she was a rocket scientist, they tended to imagine she spent her days walking the floor of a gigantic manufacturing facility, wearing one of those white cleanroom suits with the hats and the footies, carrying a clipboard as she stared at a fully-assembled spacecraft—like one of the background extras in *The Right Stuff*.

The reality was that she sat in a cubicle in a drab office building in El Segundo and spent a truly ridiculous amount of her day using Microsoft Office. The Sauer Hewson Aerospace facility where she worked had started life as an automobile plant in the nineteen forties before being sold and acquired by a half dozen different aircraft companies, most of which no longer existed. In the golden age of space exploration, some of the components of the Apollo service modules had been manufactured there. These days, the site was focused exclusively on satellites, which were a little less cool than the Apollo program—but between satellite television, radio, broadband, and mobile voice and data, they were big business.

"You're twelve minutes later than usual," Yemi said when Esther got into work the next morning. He was a design analyst who sat at the cubicle behind Esther. He was Nigerian, wore glasses with thick black frames, and could calculate square roots up to six digits in his head.

"There was a traffic light out on Overland," Esther said as she docked her laptop. It usually took her thirty minutes to drive to work during morning rush hour, but today she'd underestimated how stupid people could be in the face of a blinking red light treated as a four-way stop.

Yemi turned back to his own computer. "You should take the freeway." His accent was almost undetectable; he'd been born in Abuja, but his family had come to the U.S. when he was ten. The only time his accent came out was when he was talking to one of his parents on the phone.

"You know I don't like sitting in traffic." Esther reached up to check the bun she'd twisted her hair into this morning. She wore her hair in a bun almost every day, but she'd been in a hurry this morning and was afraid it might be lopsided.

"On average, you'll spend five percent longer waiting at traffic lights than it would take you to get through rush-hour congestion on the 405. Your aversion to freeways is irrational and inefficient."

"I'll take it under advisement," Esther said, smiling.

Some people found Yemi's directness off-putting, but it was one of the things she liked best about him. He didn't dissemble or try to hide what he was thinking. His honesty and practicality made him an outstanding analyst. She liked working with him, because she never had to waste time cutting through the bullshit or trying to figure out what he really meant when he said something. He always told you clearly and concisely what was wrong, and what you needed to do to fix it.

Esther spent a few minutes skimming through her email before opening up Excel and diving back into the spreadsheet she'd been working on Friday. When her phone vibrated with a new text message two hours later, she was so deep in concentration she nearly jumped out of her seat.

It was Jinny, asking when she wanted to take lunch. They worked at the same office, but Jinny was a network systems engineer on the deep space telescope project, and her cubicle was clear on the other side of the building, so they had to coordinate their lunch breaks via text.

Esther stretched her arms out and rolled her head from side to side, working the kinks out of her neck. "Hey." She spun around and kicked the back of Yemi's chair.

He was squinting at a heat map on his screen. "Hmmmm?" he replied without looking at her.

"Lunch?"

"It's only ten o'clock."

"I'm asking what time you want to take it." Esther waved her phone next to his ear. "Jinny wants to know."

He tore his eyes away from the screen and swiveled to look at her. "I don't care."

"I know you like to have a schedule."

"As long as I know what the schedule is, I don't care what it is."

"What's the special today?" Yemi always knew the cafeteria schedule. He memorized it every month when it came out.

"Lasagna."

"Better go at eleven forty-five, then." The lasagna was one of the cafeteria's better offerings. There would be a crowd, and sometimes they ran out.

"Fine." Yemi had already gone back to work.

Esther texted Jinny the time, got an affirmative confirmation, and plunged back into her spreadsheet. An hour later, Esther startled again when Jinny showed up at her cubicle.

"Pssst," Jinny said behind her.

Esther dragged her attention away from the PowerPoint deck she'd been squinting at and swiveled her chair around. "Hey!"

"What do you think of this dress?" Jinny asked, twirling to

show off the floral halter dress she was wearing. There was still a tag hanging on it.

"I think you look amazing," Esther told her.

Jinny looked down as she fluffed the skirt. "I ordered it last week and it just came today." She had all her packages delivered at work so they wouldn't get stolen from her apartment building lobby. "I'm thinking of wearing it on my date with Jonathan." She looked up, biting her lip. "Too much?"

"No, definitely not." Jonathan's eyes were going to pop out of his head.

Jinny rested her hands on her hips, frowning. "Tell me the truth—do you think it's too soon to be dating after a breakup? It's only been a week."

"You're not a Victorian widow," Esther said. "You don't need to observe a formal period of mourning for the relationship."

"But I look so good in high lace collars and bustles," Jinny deadpanned before her expression settled into a frown again. "Seriously though, am I rushing things? Maybe I need to spend some time alone, get over Stuart a little before I jump back into the dating pool?"

It was a valid point, but knowing Jinny, "spending time alone" was liable to turn into "taking Stuart back." Rebounding as quickly as possible seemed like the safer course. She could always spend time alone *after* Jonathan had helped her get Stuart out of her system.

"Do you *feel* like you need to get over Stuart more?" Esther asked. "I mean, if you don't want to go on the date, that's one thing…but I thought you were excited about it."

"I am." Jinny twisted her lips to the side. "I was. I think I'm starting to have second thoughts."

"About Jonathan specifically? Or about going out with someone who's not Stuart?" Esther hadn't cooked up the Jonathan plan to push Jinny into a relationship she didn't want. If she genuinely didn't want to go out with him, that was one thing. But if she was using her attachment to Stuart as an excuse not to move on, that was something else entirely. Something she needed help getting past.

Jinny thought about it. "The second one. I'm pretty sure."

Esther nodded. "I think you should trust your first instinct, then. You don't owe Stuart anything. If you want to go out with Jonathan, go out with Jonathan."

Jinny broke into a smile. "You're right. A cute guy asked me out. I should enjoy it. Screw Stuart. He shouldn't have let all this go," she said, gesturing at herself.

"Exactly. Screw Stuart." *Only not literally*, Esther thought. *Please, stop screwing Stuart.*

"Hello," Yemi said, coming back to his desk.

Jinny turned. "Hi!"

Yemi stared at her. "You, um…" He reached up and adjusted his glasses. "You look very nice. Very…beautiful."

Jinny's smile got even brighter. "Thank you." She turned back to Esther. "That's two yays for the dress. I guess I'm wearing it Friday night."

"What's Friday night?" Yemi asked, dropping into his chair.

"Jinny has a date," Esther said.

He looked at Jinny, frowning. "I thought you and your boyfriend broke up?"

"Not with him," Jinny said. "With someone new. One of Esther's neighbors asked me out. A very cute neighbor."

"Oh." Yemi nodded and cleared his throat. "So…apparently the CEO is in the building."

Jinny groaned. "Fantastic."

Their company CEO was a woman named Angelica Sauer, and she was terrifying. She'd once stormed into a team leadership meeting, informed everyone they were incompetent, and had their catered lunches sent away because they "didn't deserve to eat" until they'd presented something worth her time.

As luck would have it, the El Segundo campus was the closest production facility to corporate headquarters in Glendale, so the CEO and other assorted executives graced them with semi-frequent unscheduled appearances. Whenever Angelica Sauer was on site, it made all the managers and team leads nervous. And when they got nervous, they made everyone else nervous.

Yemi nodded again. "Anil saw her at the security desk thirty minutes ago."

"Maybe she's gotten nicer since she got married," Jinny said. "Maybe she was only mean because she was sad."

Angelica Sauer had become CEO after her first husband, who had founded the company, died of pancreatic cancer a few years ago. But she'd just recently remarried—to the company's CFO. The Sauers apparently liked to keep the business in the family.

"I don't know," Esther said. "I think it might be her management style. That's probably how you have to be to run a company. CEOs aren't usually known for being warm and cuddly."

"Well, I better change and get back to my desk," Jinny said. "Got to look busy in case the big boss wanders by."

"So you're definitely still going out with Jonathan Friday?" Esther asked.

Jinny nodded. "Might as well, right?"

Good. Jinny wouldn't get back together with Stuart as long as she had a date with Jonathan on the horizon. At the very least, it would buy a few days.

Hopefully more.

"Hey," Jonathan said when Esther opened the door. He was holding a sheaf of papers bound with brass brads, which he held out to her. "Here's the script."

"Cool." Esther carried it into the apartment, leaving the door open for him. She tossed the script onto her Ikea coffee table without looking at it.

Jonathan followed her inside and closed the door behind him.

"You can redline that copy, or type your notes into another doc, whatever's easier for you."

Esther nodded. "Yep."

He shoved his hands in his pockets. "I did pretty well last night, huh?"

"You did okay." It wouldn't do to let him get cocky this early. "You're going to have to do better than okay on the actual date though. What are you wearing?"

His brows drew together. "I don't know. I hadn't thought about it. Clothes."

"You should make an effort. No flannel. And no beanie either."

"Seriously?" She wasn't sure whether he was offended she thought he needed to be told not to wear a beanie on a date, or offended that he shouldn't wear a beanie on a date.

"Seriously. What's your hair look like under there, anyway?" She reached up and plucked the beanie off his head. He was taller than he seemed, probably because he did so much slouching. Esther was five foot nine, and she had to reach pretty high to get at the beanie, which meant he must be six one or six two.

She frowned at the mop of unruly hair that spilled out. "Okay, well, fortunately for you, Jinny happens to like her men vaguely disheveled. Just...put some product in it or something. And wash it."

Jonathan snatched the beanie away from her and shoved it back on his head. "I'm not an idiot. I know to wash my hair before a date."

"Where are you taking her?" Esther asked.

"I was thinking Tap 21."

She wrinkled her nose. "Really?"

"What's wrong with that?"

"It's kind of boring. And full of posers."

"I eat there all the time."

"I rest my case. Rule number one: stay away from any place that calls itself a gastropub—all that means is mediocre overpriced burgers. You want somewhere with character, that tells her something about you. You should take her someplace unique. Someplace *you* love. What's your favorite place to eat?"

"In-N-Out?"

Esther rolled her eyes. "I said somewhere unique. Somewhere no one else would think of."

He thought about it. "Doozo's."

"What's that?"

"It's this Chinese noodle place on Venice. Kind of a hole in the wall, but they've got this cool, *Blade Runner* vibe and killer dumplings. And the old lady behind the counter likes me."

"That's perfect. Take her there."

He frowned, running his hand over his jaw. His face was heart-shaped, tapering to a pointed chin. He actually did look a little like Jake Gyllenhaal, if you squinted and didn't look too closely. "Isn't it weird to take an Asian girl to a Chinese restaurant?"

"She's not Chinese, she's Korean. And she loves Chinese food. It'll be fine."

He still looked uncertain. "Are you sure this whole thing is a good idea?"

Esther arched a threatening eyebrow at him. "Don't you dare chicken out on me." If he backed out now, Jinny would be so disappointed, she'd go running back to Stuart for sure.

Jonathan chewed on his lower lip. "It's just...won't she get pissed if she finds out you put me up to it and the whole thing's a sham?"

"It's not a sham. It's just a blind date...under slightly modified circumstances."

His weight shifted from one foot to the other as his eyes darted around her apartment. He looked like he wanted to pace, but was trying to restrain himself. "Is it really a blind date though, if only one of the people on the date knows it's a blind date and the other one thinks it's a date-date? Cause that seems a lot like a lie to me."

"Think of it like a hybrid date—half blind date, half date-date. But the principle is the same as a regular date. You're both trying each other on for size to see how you like the fit."

"Yeah," he said without enthusiasm.

"What's the matter? You liked her when you met the other night, right?" Esther was getting impatient with all his second-guessing. He'd already agreed to the arrangement. She shouldn't have to keep convincing him to go along with it.

He shrugged. "She seemed okay."

Okay? Yesterday she was cute. Esther huffed, gritting her teeth. "Don't overcomplicate it. You both like each other, and you're going on a date. It's as simple as that."

"I guess." He still looked unconvinced.

"Remember," she said, crossing her arms, "your script notes are at stake here."

He sighed, shoulders sagging. "Yeah, I know. Believe me." He nodded at the script sitting on the coffee table. "You think you'll be able to start on that tonight?"

"I don't know," Esther said. "Maybe. I don't want to rush through it. I want to give it the attention it deserves. You know, really take my time and dig into the details."

He nodded. "If you have any questions—"

"I'll write 'em down," Esther said, herding him toward the door. "We good?"

"Yeah. Okay." He nodded half-heartedly. "I'll see ya."

"Good luck on your date!" Esther called out as the door closed behind him.

LATER THAT NIGHT, Esther put on her favorite llama pajamas, settled into bed with Sally Ride curled up next to her, and flipped to the first page of Jonathan's script.

It shouldn't take any longer to read a screenplay than it would to watch a movie, right? So, like, two hours, give or take. Easy peasy. How bad could it be?

It was *bad*, she quickly discovered.

It was appallingly, *offensively* bad.

If Jonathan's script were made into a movie, it would easily be the worst movie Esther had ever seen.

It was like if Michael Bay and Uwe Boll decided to write a screenplay together, got in a fight partway through, and gave it to Darren Aronofsky to finish—drunk.

She only got halfway through before literally flinging it across the room in anger.

This was going to be way more difficult than she'd anticipated. She didn't know where start with her notes. The only way to fix the thing would be to scrub it from existence entirely. How did you put that into feedback?

Why had she agreed to do this? If time machines existed, she would go back twenty-four hours and punch herself in the face for making this stupid bargain.

Jinny had sure better enjoy her date with Jonathan. She'd better like it *a lot*.

Chapter Six

Friday night, while Esther was watching the clock and waiting for Jinny to call and tell her how the date had gone, she forced herself to finish reading Jonathan's script.

It was a Sisyphean effort. The thing was just so bad. *So* bad.

Esther didn't know anything about writing per se, but she knew movies. She was a huge fan of movies, and she'd read a lot of movie reviews. She knew what made for a good movie, and she knew what made for a bad one.

This was a bad movie.

Under ordinary circumstances, she would have made the task more bearable by texting Jinny snarky updates about how incredibly bad Jonathan's script was. But she couldn't text Jinny about it because Jinny was on a date with Jonathan at that very moment. Also, if Esther wanted Jinny to actually *like* Jonathan, she needed to protect her from ever knowing how bad this script was. At all costs.

Originally, Esther had figured she'd do a quick read, then go back through it more exhaustively a second time as she made notes. But after her last failed attempt at reading the thing, she'd realized a second full read-through would be intolerable.

So she started over from the beginning, taking notes as she went along.

She had a *lot* of notes. By the time Jinny called a little before ten o'clock, Esther had already filled ten pages of a Word document, and she was only two-thirds of the way through.

"Hey," Esther said, pushing her laptop aside and answering the phone. "Are you home already?" It was a little early to call it a night. She hoped that wasn't a bad sign.

"Yep," Jinny said. "He just dropped me off."

Esther sat up on the couch, propping her feet on the coffee table. "Well? How'd it go? Tell me everything."

Jinny made a noncommittal noise. "It was okay."

Uh oh. "Just okay?"

"I don't know. Maybe it's too soon to start dating again. Maybe I'm not over Stuart yet."

"That bad, huh?" *Dammit, Jonathan, you had one job.*

"It wasn't *bad*, exactly, but...you know that fluttery feeling you get in your chest around a guy you really like? I didn't get that, not once. I guess I was hoping for a little more chemistry."

Esther brushed a clump of cat hair off the couch. "Well, it's just the first date. Maybe you need to give it more time. Get to know each other a little better."

"Maybe," Jinny said without much conviction. "I felt the fluttery thing with Stuart the first time he talked to me though."

But Stuart is an asshole, Esther thought but didn't say.

"Where'd you go?" she asked instead, like she didn't already know.

"This noodle bar on Venice. It was good. And the lady behind the counter called him Jon Jon, which was adorable."

Nice. Score one for Esther's advice. "So far it doesn't sound bad."

"Yeah, but then he spent like half an hour talking about the original *Blade Runner*, and I didn't have the heart to tell him I didn't like the movie."

"Wait," Esther said, shaking her head to make sure she'd heard right. "How can you not like *Blade Runner*? And how did I never know this about you?" *Blade Runner* was one of Esther's top ten favorite movies. Her brother had taken her to see it at an art house revival when she was twelve, and she'd thought it was one of the coolest things she'd ever seen.

"It's so slow! And boring. I don't understand what the big deal is with that movie. The new one with Ryan Gosling was a little better, but still not great."

Esther was speechless. It was like hearing someone say the *Star Wars* prequels were better than the original trilogy. It was sacrilege. It should be grounds for a seventy-two-hour psychiatric hold.

"That movie influenced an entire generation of cinema," she said. "I feel like I don't even know you right now."

"Whatever," Jinny huffed. "I didn't want to hear about it for half an hour. He spent a lot of time talking. I barely got a word in edgewise the whole night."

Oh, no. That was definitely not good. "He was probably just nervous. Some people talk too much when they're nervous."

"I guess."

Esther leaned her head back and stared at the ceiling. "How'd you end things? Are you going out with him again?" If Jinny decided she didn't like him enough to go out with him a second time, the whole plan was busted.

"I don't know. He left it with a vague, 'We should do this again sometime.' Which could mean anything. I may never hear from him again."

She'd better hear from him again. He'd made a deal, and Esther planned on holding him to it.

"But if he asked would you say yes?" Esther pressed. She'd have to coach him more next time. Obviously, the guy needed even more help than she'd anticipated. But that was fine. She could work with that. She'd be the Henry Higgins to his Eliza Doolittle if that was what it took. She'd *Pygmalion* the shit out of him. As long as Jinny was willing to give him another chance.

"Mmmm. Probably. He's a good kisser, at least."

"Wait. He kissed you?"

"I kissed him. He was a little shy at first, but once he got into it, it was pretty great. Really great, actually."

"Huh," Esther said.

"Yeah, it makes me wonder what he's like in bed. Based on that kiss, I'd say pretty damn good."

"Wow. Okay." That must have been some kiss. Good for him. And for Jinny, apparently.

So the plan was still on track. Jonathan just needed to up his conversation game a little. No problem. They could work on that before the next date.

"It sounds like there was some chemistry after all," Esther said. "It must not have been completely terrible."

"No, not terrible," Jinny conceded.

"Well, I'm glad. Maybe your second date will be better." There was still time for them to actually hit it off. With a little coaching, Esther was convinced, Jonathan could make a good boyfriend for Jinny. And Jinny could be good for him too. They could be good for each other.

"If there is a second date," Jinny said. "He might not call."

He was definitely going to call. And the next time, he'd be a better date. Esther would see to that.

A LITTLE PAST noon the next day, Esther knocked on Jonathan's door. It took so long for him to answer it, she'd just about decided he wasn't home when she heard the deadbolt turn.

The door opened a crack and he squinted at her. "Oh. It's you." He sounded about as thrilled to see her as she was to be there.

"It's me," she said, and waited.

He pulled the door open wider—but not wide enough to invite her in—and ran his hand through his hair. He wasn't wearing a beanie for once, and he had a truly impressive case of bedhead. His half-hearted attempt to smooth the unruly locks only succeeded in making them fluffier.

"Did I wake you?" Esther asked. He had the rumpled, bleary-eyed look of someone who'd just crawled out of bed.

"No," he said, clearly lying. He was wearing sweatpants that hung low on his hips and a plain white T-shirt that was so stretched out it was nearly see-through.

"I can come back," she offered.

"No, it's fine." He stepped back and held the door open, waving her inside. "Come on in."

Esther stepped inside and peered around curiously. It was dark except for the slits of sunlight leaking in through the closed mini-blinds. The layout of his apartment was the mirror opposite of Esther's, and his furniture all looked like it had been rescued from a curb. There was a hideous plaid couch, a set of bookshelves constructed out of cinderblocks, and a cheap footlocker doubling as coffee table. An old Formica dinette table had been pushed against the wall to serve as a desk. It was stacked with precarious towers of books and papers and scripts, with a MacBook Air squatting in the center of it.

"I just came to see how last night went," she said.

"You want some coffee?" he asked, wandering into the kitchen. It was full of dirty dishes, at least half of which were coffee mugs.

"No thanks." If she had more than two cups a day, she got jittery, and she'd already had her allotment this morning.

Jonathan filled an electric kettle with water and switched it on. "I'm sure you already heard all about it from Jinny."

"Yeah, but I wanted to hear how you thought it went."

He shrugged. "It wasn't as bad as I was afraid it was going to be."

"That's a ringing endorsement." Esther watched him scoop coffee beans out of a brown paper bag into a burr grinder. There was a layer of coffee grounds all over the counter. "You grind your own beans?"

"Yeah. It's a fair-trade organic blend from a co-op in Peru that I special order from a small-batch local roaster."

Of course it was. And of course he did.

He switched on the grinder, which made an ear-piercing racket as it pulverized the beans. That explained the weird sound Esther heard coming through the wall from his apartment every day. She'd thought maybe he had a power tool fetish. Turned out it was a coffee fetish.

"I don't think Jinny liked me all that much," he said when the grinder was done.

At least he'd noticed. Esther supposed he deserved a few points for that. "What made you think that?"

"I don't know." He dumped the coffee grounds into a cone-shaped filter on top of a glass carafe. "She didn't talk much."

"Is that your coffeemaker?" Esther asked, leaning in for a better look.

"It's a Chemex," he said, as if it should be obvious.

"I don't know what that is."

He poured hot water over the coffee grounds and set the kettle back down, waiting for it to filter through. "The special filter and glass design make a purer cup of coffee than traditional drip coffeemakers."

Esther nodded with pretended interest as he launched into a lecture about ideal "brewology"—which was definitely not a word—and the importance of letting the grounds "bloom." *Christ.*

"Maybe you talked so much Jinny didn't have a chance to respond," she suggested when he'd finished explaining his absurdly fussy coffeemaker.

He looked up, his brow furrowing. "Is that what she said?"

"Not in so many words."

"So she didn't like me." He poured more water over the grounds and set the kettle down again. This thing had better make the best coffee in the world, because it seemed like the slowest, most inefficient way imaginable to make coffee.

"I didn't say that." Esther leaned against the counter, crossing her arms. "Okay, maybe she wasn't instantly wowed. But she didn't have a totally bad time."

His jaw clenched. "Great."

"You'll do better on the next one."

"Assuming there is a next one." He poured a little more water over the coffee grounds. Seriously, how long did it take to get a cup of coffee out of this thing?

"No wriggling out of this," Esther said. "Three dates—that was the deal."

"It just seems pointless if she doesn't like me."

"You're her rebound guy. You've got to go out enough times that she, you know, rebounds."

He nodded, tapping his thumbs on the edge of the counter as he watched the water drain through the coffee filter. "What if she says no to a second date?"

"She told me she'd go out with you again if you asked."

He looked up, surprised. "She did?"

"Yeah. She said you were a good kisser."

His expression turned smug. "Really?"

Esther rolled her eyes. "Yeah, really. You just need some coaching on the other stuff."

"What other stuff?"

"Talking. And maybe not doing so much of it. Show some interest in her. Ask her about her life, her likes and dislikes. Make an effort to get to know her, don't just tell her about yourself."

"I thought I had." Apparently the coffee was finally done, because he dumped the filter into the trash.

"What does she do for a living?" If he'd actually bothered to ask Jinny about herself, he should know the answer.

"She works with you," he said as he poured coffee from the glass carafe into a mug.

"Doing what?" The scent of fresh-brewed coffee wafted in her direction. It smelled pretty good, but it still didn't seem worth the trouble.

He shrugged, leaning his hip against the counter as he cradled his coffee. "Some kind of engineering-type stuff? Like you do."

She shook her head. "I'm a mechanical design engineer. Jinny's a network systems engineer."

He frowned as he blew on his coffee "What's the difference?"

"*Ask* her about it," Esther said. "Where do her parents live? What do they do for a living?"

Jonathan looked blank.

"Does she have any brothers or sisters? Where'd she go to college? Where'd she grow up?"

"I know this one," he said. "Irvine. See, I grew up in Newport Beach, which isn't that far—"

"You're talking about yourself again. We're talking about Jinny now, remember?" God, no wonder Jinny hadn't been impressed.

He pressed his lips together. "Right."

"Next time, ask her about herself and then shut up long enough to let her answer."

He walked past her, carrying his coffee into the living room, and sank down on his ugly plaid couch. "I'm not very good at this stuff."

Esther chose not to sit down. "What stuff?"

His eyes flicked up at her and then away. "Talking to women. I get nervous and can't think of anything to say. Then I end up trying to fill the dead space by rambling about something lame."

She felt a stab of sympathy. Making small talk on a date with a near stranger wasn't her favorite activity either. It was part of the reason she didn't do a lot of dating.

"That's okay," she told him. "You just need to plan ahead. Make a list of questions in advance and memorize them."

"Like what?"

She ticked them off on her fingers. "What did she want to be when she grew up? What kind of music does she like? What's her favorite book? What's her favorite movie—and whatever she says, don't argue with her or try to tell her she's wrong."

He looked up at her. "What if she is wrong though?"

"There's no such thing as a wrong answer to a question of personal preference."

His eyebrows twitched, and the corner of his mouth pulled to one side. "There kind of is though."

Esther was not going to get into a philosophical debate, even if she sort of agreed with him. "Not for the purposes of this date. Do you need to be writing all this down?"

He scowled at her over the top of his coffee mug. "No, I've got it."

"You sure?"

"I'm sure." He sipped his coffee. "Have you looked at the script yet?"

"Not yet," she lied. "It's been a really busy week."

His tongue ran over his upper lip, and Esther remembered what Jinny had said about him being a good kisser. He did have a nice mouth under that beard, now that she was studying him up close. Supple lips that were the exact right amount of full—

"So when do you think you'll have something for me? I need to have something to show my adviser in a few weeks, and also I need to know you're going to fulfill your end of the bargain if I'm going to keep going on these dates."

Esther dragged her eyes away from his mouth. "Can I have a week?"

He didn't look happy about it, but he didn't argue. "Yeah, okay."

"How about next Sunday?" She didn't want to meet with him before his next date with Jinny, because he wasn't going to like her notes, and she didn't want it affecting his attitude while he was on the date. "We'll get together to go over it, and we can post-game your second date." She pointed a finger at him. "Because you're going to call Jinny today to tell her what a nice time you had and ask her out for next weekend, right?"

Jonathan rolled his eyes like a kid who'd just been told to clean his room. "Yeah. Sheesh."

Chapter Seven

*E*very Monday night, Esther and Jinny met up with a knitting group at a coffee shop in Culver City called Antidote. When Esther got there that week, Vilma was already holding their usual table in the back corner. She was the oldest member of the group in both age and seniority, a teacher in her late forties with a husband and two teenaged sons.

As Esther walked in, Vilma looked up from the bundle of yarn in her lap and waved. Esther waved back and got in line at the counter.

One of the first things she had done two years ago, when she relocated to Los Angeles for the job at Sauer Hewson, was look for a local knitting group. She'd taken up knitting in college, when her roommate gave her a copy of *Stitch & Bitch* and a pair of Clover bamboo needles for her birthday. Esther had never considered herself a crafty or artistic person before, but she'd been pleased to discover that knitting was more like math than art. The order and repetition of it appealed to her, and since she didn't go in for the touchy-feely-ness of meditation and yoga, it was a stress reliever she could actually enjoy.

Knitting was how Esther and Jinny had first become friends.

Her second month at Sauer Hewson, Esther had been sitting by herself in the lunchroom knitting, and Jinny had sat down next to her and started asking questions about it. It turned out she'd been wanting to learn for a while, but didn't know anyone who could show her how. The next day, Esther brought an extra pair of needles and started teaching her on their lunch breaks. After Jinny had gotten the basics of casting on and the knit stitch down, Esther had introduced her to the knitting group, and she'd been a regular ever since.

Esther paid for her beer—one of the best things about Antidote was that they sold beer and wine in addition to coffee—and took it over to the low, round coffee table in the far back corner, flanked by an orange couch and a few old office armchairs.

"Congratulations on surviving another Monday," Vilma said as Esther settled into a chair across from her.

"Same to you," Esther offered, raising her beer bottle. She set her drink on the table and dug out her current knitting project. "Is that another chemo hat?" she asked Vilma.

"Mmm hmm." Vilma held up the lavender hat she was knitting. She'd been doing a lot of charity knitting since her family had informed her they already had more handmade knitwear than they could possibly wear in Southern California, and could she please find someone else to knit for. "It's a Berocco nylon and acrylic blend."

"I like it. How's it feel?"

"Very soft. You have to choose from a list of approved yarns, so it's not itchy on bald heads. I've never used this one before, but it's easy on the hands." Vilma waved as Cynthia and Olivia, two more members of the group, walked in and got in line. She raised an eyebrow at the sock Esther was working on. "Another pair of socks?"

"Yep." Esther was obsessed with self-striping sock yarn. She loved not having to make color decisions or weave in yarn ends at every color change.

Vilma pursed her lips. "You know, there is a whole wide world of things out there for you to knit that are not socks."

"I am aware. I just happen to like socks."

Esther *loved* socks. Aside from the fact that they were soft and comfy and kept your feet toasty warm, they were fast and simple to knit. She'd already knit as many scarves and hats as she could possibly wear, blankets were boring, and she could never seem to finish sweaters. But socks...socks were perfect. You could never have too many socks.

"Ladies," Cynthia greeted, setting her glass of white wine on the table and taking the seat next to Esther. She was a tall, willowy black woman who favored long skirts in bright patterns, didn't bother with makeup, and wore her hair cut short with shaved sides.

Olivia flopped down on the couch next to Vilma and dropped her messenger bag on the floor with a *thunk*. She was Cynthia's opposite in almost every way: a short, ghostly pale blonde who favored heavy black eyeliner and dark-colored lipstick and was dressed in black dress slacks and a plain gray button-down for work.

"Good evening." Vilma peered over the top of her reading glasses at the extra-large iced coffee Olivia was clutching. "No libations tonight?"

"I'm on call," Olivia said, nudging her messenger bag under the couch with her foot. She rattled the ice in her cup. "Hence the quadruple-shot of caffeine."

Olivia was a systems analyst for a power company. When she was on call, she had to be ready to log in if any of her systems went offline, or else millions of people would lose electricity—and her company would lose millions of dollars. Which meant she had to keep her laptop with her *and* she had to stay sober enough to write code at a moment's notice.

Jinny pushed through the door of the shop and waved to everyone as she got in line.

"How's the scarf coming?" Esther asked Olivia as she unpacked her knitting.

Olivia was the newest member of the group. She'd only started knitting a few months ago, in order to make herself an old school *Doctor Who* scarf.

"Slowly. I haven't even taken it out since last Monday. Work's been a real bitch and a half." She smoothed the striped scarf out across her lap. It measured about two feet already, but the Doctor's iconic scarf was twelve feet long. "I'm never going to finish this stupid thing."

"You've got until September though, right?" Cynthia leaned forward for her wine. "That's almost four months. And you'll get faster."

Olivia was a cosplayer, and every year she made herself an elaborate costume to wear to Dragon Con. The scarf was for this year's costume: a Victorian-inspired lady Fourth Doctor. She was repurposing a Victorian suit dress from a previous lady Sherlock Holmes costume, but she wanted the scarf to be authentic and of her own making, so she'd taken up knitting.

"Nothing nimbles the fingers like a hard deadline," Vilma observed.

"Am I the last one?" Jinny asked, pulling up a chair next to Esther and setting her wine glass on the table.

Vilma shook her head. "No, we're still waiting on Penny." She cocked an eyebrow at Olivia. "Assuming she's coming?" Penny was the one who'd taught Olivia to knit and introduced her to the group.

Olivia shrugged. "I assume so, but I haven't heard from her today."

"Here she comes," Cynthia said, nodding toward the door.

"Sorry, sorry, sorry!" Penny set a Tupperware container in the middle of the table. "The cookies had to cool before I could transport them."

Penny was always late, but since she usually brought home-made baked goods, nobody minded. Technically, they weren't supposed to bring food into Antidote, but the manager let it slide because their group had been coming here so long. It helped that Penny usually brought extra treats to share with the employees.

She peeled the lid off the Tupperware and frowned at the cookies. "I think some of them might still be a little smooshy."

"I love smooshy cookies." Esther leaned forward for a chocolate chip cookie. Penny always sprinkled them with sea salt, which made them extra delicious.

"Yeah, smooshy cookies are the best," Jinny agreed, taking a cookie. "Mmmm, they're still warm too. You're the best, Penny."

"Thank you!" Penny said, beaming. "Does anyone need anything while I'm up?"

Cynthia shook her head around a mouthful of cookie. "We're all set."

Penny pulled a smaller container of cookies out of her bag for the employees and got in line. A few minutes later, she came back with a fruit-flavored iced tea and a handful of napkins—which they were all desperately in need of by then—and sat down next to Cynthia.

"Oh! Is that one of your tiny sweaters?" Penny asked, pushing her bright red hair behind her ear as she leaned in for a closer look.

Cynthia nodded as she held it out. "This is sweater number two. I think I'm getting the technique down, finally." She was an artist who mostly did illustration, but she'd had an idea to illustrate a children's book with photos of miniature dioramas, so she was knitting tiny sweaters for the little clay animals to wear. Between the lace weight yarn she was working with and the size 00 needles she'd had to special order for the task, it was an awe-inspiring feat of dexterity.

"I don't know how you can work so small," Vilma said, shaking her head. "My poor old eyes hurt just thinking about it."

Esther's eyes weren't even old, and she couldn't understand

how Cynthia did it either. But that wasn't a new feeling. She couldn't understand how Cynthia did a lot of the things she was good at: drawing, painting, sculpting, photography. Esther didn't have an artistic bone in her body, and she was awed by anyone who did. She always felt a little inadequate around the other women at knitting. Everyone else in the group was way craftier than she was. Olivia sewed and did amazing things with makeup for her cosplay, Vilma made pottery and did embroidery in addition to knitting, Penny was an incredible baker who could also sew and crochet and do calligraphy, and Jinny had a terrific eye for fashion and decorating.

Knitting was the only crafty skill Esther had ever mastered, and she used self-striping sock yarn because she couldn't match colors to save her life. Her wardrobe was as drab as her apartment, she could only sew well enough to replace a button, her cooking skills were rudimentary at best, and she hadn't drawn or painted so much as a stick figure since elementary school.

Sometimes she felt like she'd missed out on some of the essentials growing up. It wasn't just arts and crafts—she'd never done any sports outside of PE class or learned a musical instrument either. Most of her childhood had been spent watching TV or reading alone in her room. Her father had been too busy to pay much attention to her even before he'd left, and her mother had been...distracted. Esther's older brother, Eric, had been the one who did most of the cooking, helped her with her homework, and taught her how to drive a car.

The Abbott household hadn't exactly been an idyllic upbringing. Still, it could have been far worse. She felt like she'd turned out pretty okay, even if she was the least talented person in her knitting group.

Cynthia's gaze slid over to Esther and she quirked an eyebrow. "More socks? Really?"

"Stop judging my socks. Socks are cool." Esther decided it was time for a change of subject. "Jinny went on a date."

Jinny looked up from the cabled hat she was working on as four sets of eyes turned toward her.

Cynthia's brow crinkled. "With Stuart?"

Jinny shook her head. "Someone new."

"I can't believe you're already dating someone else," Penny said. "It's been like five minutes since you and Stuart broke up. Teach me your mysterious ways, Obi-Wan."

Jinny shrugged. "He just asked me out, out of the blue."

Esther kept her eyes on the sock she was knitting. What Jinny didn't know wouldn't hurt her—as long as it kept her out of a toxic relationship.

"How was it?" Olivia asked.

"Do you like him?" Vilma asked.

"Is he hot?" Cynthia asked.

"Okay. I don't know. Definitely," Jinny rattled off, answering each of their questions.

"Wait..." Penny frowned, looking up from her baby hat. She was constantly knitting baby hats, because someone in her enormous extended family was always having a baby. "He's hot, but you don't know if you like him?"

"I'm not sure we had chemistry." Jinny leaned forward for her wine glass. "He kind of talked about himself a lot."

"He could have been nervous," Esther felt the need to point out again. Especially now that she knew for a fact that was the problem.

Jinny shot her a sideways look. "I don't know why you're defending him. You can't stand him."

Esther shrugged and looked back down at her knitting. "I'm just trying to be supportive."

Vilma reached for a cookie. "Esther knows him?"

"He's her neighbor," Jinny said. "And she hates him."

"Hate's a strong word," Esther said.

Jinny rolled her eyes. "A word I've heard you use about him on more than one occasion."

"I was employing hyperbole. He's not that bad."

"Why don't you like him?" Cynthia asked Esther.

She shrugged again. "He's got these wind chimes on his balcony that keep me up. Which has nothing to do with his worthiness as a boyfriend."

"And his cigarette smoke blows in your windows," Jinny added.

Penny wrinkled her nose. "He's a smoker?"

"Only occasionally," Esther said. "And he doesn't smoke inside his apartment. That's not so bad, right?" Now she was defending guys who smoked, apparently. What was happening to her?

Penny shook her head, frowning like it was still pretty bad.

"Do you hate him more or less than Stuart?" Olivia asked Esther.

"Less," Esther said. "Definitely a *lot* less."

Cynthia looked at Jinny. "But do *you* like him? That's what matters."

Jinny shrugged. "I don't know yet. I'm still trying to figure that out. He's not as hot as Stuart."

"Looks aren't everything," Vilma said.

"And Stuart cheated on you," Olivia reminded her.

"I know," Jinny sighed.

"Stuart's still begging her to take him back," Esther told them.

He was still texting her every day, although the frequency of his texts had decreased from somewhere in the dozens to only one or two daily, now that Jinny wasn't responding as much. It was progress. Esther hoped maybe in another week or two he'd give up altogether.

"Are you thinking about it?" Cynthia asked Jinny.

Jinny looked down at her lap. "I've stopped answering his texts."

Which wasn't exactly an answer. She'd been equally evasive when Esther had asked her the same question earlier that day. They weren't completely out of the woods yet.

"Tell him you're dating someone else already," Olivia suggested. "That'll send a strong back-the-fuck-off message."

Jinny put her knitting down and helped herself to a cookie. "I don't know that I'm actually *dating*. I went out on one date."

"But you're going out again this weekend," Esther pointed out. Jinny had told her Jonathan had called as promised and asked her on a second date—and she'd said yes. They were going out again Saturday night.

"That's totally dating." Olivia nodded absently as she concentrated on her *Doctor Who* scarf. "Anything more than one date totally counts as dating. Officially."

"I just don't know how I feel about this new guy yet," Jinny said around a mouthful of cookie. She finished chewing and swallowed. "I don't know that I even *want* to be dating him. I'm just keeping my options open for now."

"I'll tell you what my mother always told me," Vilma said. "Never skimp on shoes or mattresses."

Jinny's forehead wrinkled. "I don't know what that means in this context."

"Men are like shoes," Vilma explained. "The world is full of cute shoes, but not all of them are worth walking around in. If they give you blisters, it doesn't matter how much of a bargain they were."

"Or how good in bed," Esther added, to make sure that part of the analogy was clear.

Vilma nodded. "Sometimes you have to walk around in a new pair to figure out if they fit, and sometimes you have to break them in a little before they get really comfortable. But life's too short to waste on cheap shoes—or men who don't appreciate you."

Esther liked that. Maybe she'd have Vilma embroider it on a pillow to give Jinny for Christmas.

Chapter Eight

*W*hile Jinny was out on her second date with Jonathan on Saturday night, Esther forced herself to finish making notes on his script. When all was said and done, she'd filled fifteen single-spaced pages with feedback—most of it negative. It was all constructive, but it was going to be a massive ego blow for the poor guy.

Hey, he'd said he wanted her opinion, so that was what he was getting. Like it or not.

By the time Esther went to bed, sometime after midnight, Jinny still hadn't called or texted to tell her how her date with Jonathan had gone. Esther wasn't sure if that was a good sign or a bad one.

Maybe the date was so bad she didn't want to talk about it—or maybe the date wasn't over yet. She hadn't heard anything next door, but for all she knew, Jinny could be over there in Jonathan's bed right now.

Ugh. That was not an image she needed in her head. Thank god her bedroom didn't share a wall with his.

Esther fell asleep trying not to think about Jonathan and Jinny, and ended up having weird dreams all night about his stupid sci-fi script.

In the morning, when she still hadn't heard a peep from Jinny, Esther texted her.

How'd it go last night?

She was trying to play it cool and not seem overinvested in the outcome of the date, but she wanted to know what the sitch was before she saw Jonathan in a couple hours.

Going to church with my parents, Jinny texted back after a few minutes. *Call you later?*

Dammit. Jinny only drove down to Irvine to see her parents once a month, but when she did, it ate up the entire day. So much for talking to her before she had to face Jonathan.

Esther had arranged to meet with him at two o'clock. Since his place was such a dump, she had suggested they do it at her apartment.

At ten past two, he knocked on her door. "Hey," he said when she opened it, hovering uncertainly on her doorstep with his laptop.

Esther stepped back and waved him inside. "You ready to do this?"

"Yeah." He hesitated before stepping over the threshold, like maybe he wasn't all that ready after all. "You finish reading it?" he asked, setting his laptop down on her coffee table.

"Yep." She walked to the dining table and patted the printouts she'd made for him. "Got my notes right here."

He came over for a closer look, and she flipped them over so he couldn't read them. The notes could wait. She wanted to find out how his date with Jinny had gone before she crushed his ego with her script critique.

Esther placed herself between him and the table. "First, tell me —how'd it go last night?"

"Um…" He paused, scratching the back of his head. A hint of a smile tugged at the corner of his mouth. "Better, I think."

Esther's eyebrows shot up. "Yeah?"

He nodded. "Yeah. I already asked her out for next weekend."

"Nice!" That was excellent news. She was tempted to ask him what time the date had ended, but decided against it.

"Yeah." He nodded some more. "And she said yes." His smile got a little wider and...was he *blushing*?

"Wait, are you actually starting to like her?" Esther asked. "Like, *like* her, like her?"

He shrugged and looked down at his shoes, embarrassed. "I dunno. Maybe. There's potential there anyway."

Look who had mad matchmaking skills! Maybe Esther should go into business for herself. She could get her own reality show, saving women from toxic boyfriends and matching them up with slightly awkward but sweet guys.

"That's awesome!" Esther gave him a congratulatory punch in the arm. "Good job."

He was wearing a gray V-neck T-shirt that exposed his biceps, which were surprisingly attractive. As her eyes lingered on them, she wondered again if the date had gone well enough for Jinny to sleep with him.

Nope. On second thought, she didn't want to know. Definitely not.

"You want some coffee or anything before we get started?" she asked, heading into the kitchen.

"Yeah, okay," he said, following her. His lip curled into a sneer as he watched her pop a coffee pod into her Keurig machine. "Really? You've got one of *those* things?"

"I know, they're terrible for the environment, but I like the convenience." She felt guilty about it, but not guilty enough to give it up. It wasn't like she drank that much coffee anyway.

"Not only that," he said, thrusting his chin in the air, "but they make coffee so bad it shouldn't even be classified as coffee."

She rolled her eyes. "It's not that bad."

"Yeah, it is, actually."

"You're a snob, you know that?"

"I'm not a snob, I just know the difference between good coffee and bad coffee."

"You want some cream or sugar to dilute your bad coffee?" she asked when the pod had finished brewing—less than a minute later, and with no effort on her part. Beat that, fancy hipster coffeemaker.

His sneer deepened. "No."

"Your funeral." Esther pushed the mug toward him.

He sniffed it and made a disdainful face. "Awful."

"Snob."

He shrugged. "Fine, I'm a coffee snob, then. Let's see these notes." He started to make a move for them, but she snatched them off the table before he could get there.

"How about I walk you through them?" She carried them into the living room and sat at the far end of the couch. If he read them all straight through, she was afraid he'd get upset. He was probably going to get upset anyway, but she wanted to put it off for as long as possible.

"Sure, okay." Jonathan took the other end of the couch and set his coffee on the table, flipping open his MacBook and propping it on his lap. "Shoot."

"Um, let's see…" Esther flipped through the first couple pages, looking for something easy. She didn't want to dump a nuclear bomb of bad news in his lap right off the bat. "Oh, okay, here we go. Scientists use the metric system, so your asteroid wouldn't be one hundred miles across, it'd be a hundred and sixty kilometers."

His fingers flew over the keyboard as he nodded. "Convert everything to metric. Got it."

That wasn't too bad, so Esther tried another one: "On page ten, you've got a NASA scientist saying they can't predict the asteroid's trajectory because of the influence of nearby planetary bodies, which is bullshit. Predicting the orbits of asteroids is easy. The math for it has been around for hundreds of years."

He frowned, nodding as he typed another note. "Okay."

"You've also got a character on the next page claiming that lasers are less effective in space, which is backward—air absorbs the laser, making it less effective in atmosphere than it would be in space."

"This is perfect," he said, typing. "This is exactly the stuff I need."

Yeah, we'll see, Esther thought, scanning her notes. She hadn't even gotten to the big problems yet. "Okay, so, that whole part where they're talking about crashing the ship into the asteroid to set off the nuke…"

He looked up, nodding.

"Yeah, that's a no-go."

His brows drew together. "It wouldn't work?"

She shook her head. "In order to set off a nuclear chain reaction, the core needs to be compressed in a perfectly symmetrical implosion. The crash would smash the core to pieces, releasing a cloud of plutonium dust, but it wouldn't cause a full-blown nuclear explosion like you want."

He chewed on his lip. "Hmmmm."

"Also," she continued, "one warhead isn't going to do what you need it to do. The most powerful thermonuclear device ever tested was fifty megatons—but to get an object as massive as your asteroid moving off course, you'd need something like a hundred million megatons. That's just a ballpark, you understand. I haven't done the actual math."

He rubbed his knuckles over his chin, frowning. "So, you're saying my asteroid is too big?"

"Little bit. The asteroid that wiped out the dinosaurs was only ten kilometers in diameter—that's roughly the size of Mount Everest, with a mass of a trillion tons."

"Okay…" He blew out a frustrated breath and grimaced. "So, I'll make the asteroid smaller."

Esther shook her head again. "Even at ten kilometers, you're not going to be able to budge the thing out of orbit with one bomb. You'd need thousands of bombs. More than any single payload would be capable of delivering."

His shoulders sagged as he closed his eyes, rubbing his temples. "Oh."

"But there's a much bigger problem with your story," Esther said, bracing herself for the worst part.

He turned his head, giving her a wary look. "What?"

"You've basically written *Armageddon*."

"I've never seen it."

"Yeah, I can tell, because you've used the exact same premise. Piece of advice—if you're going to write a genre movie, you should probably have at least a passing familiarity with the tentpole films of the genre."

"I've seen the tentpole films of the genre," he said, sounding defensive. "*2001, Blade Runner...*"

"But you didn't write any of those movies, you wrote an asteroid movie. You need to be familiar with *Armageddon*."

"But *Armageddon* is crap. It's a stupid action movie in space."

"Yes, it is," she agreed, waiting for him to pick up on what she was saying.

She could tell the moment it sank in, because his whole face went hard. "Mine's nothing like that. It's a psychological thriller with a deep philosophical message at its core."

"Yeah, the thing is," Esther said slowly, "I'm not sure that's actually a selling point. Like, at the beginning, it feels like you're setting up a typical sci-fi disaster film—a fairly derivative one with the same premise as *Armageddon* and *Deep Impact*, by the way. But once the plot moves into space, it takes a sharp left turn into some kind of slasher flick. Then toward the end, all the action grinds to a halt, and you've got characters delivering ponderous mono-logues on the meaning of life. And that ending—what is that? I don't even understand it."

"It's *intentionally* ambiguous," he said, like that somehow made it good.

She tried to refrain from rolling her eyes, with only limited success. "It's certainly that."

"It's a commentary on post-structuralism."

"It's *unsatisfying*. The whole thing is a mess, basically."

He slammed his laptop closed. "You're saying you hated it," he said in a rigid voice, refusing to look at her.

"I'm saying it's got big problems," Esther told him bluntly, because sugar-coating it wouldn't do him any favors. Not if this was for his master's thesis. "Have you considered who your audience is for a film like this? Who are you expecting to sell tickets to? Because people who think they're signing up for *Armageddon II* aren't going to be happy when they end up watching a horror film halfway through. And people who actually want to see an ambiguous commentary on post-structuralism aren't going to buy a ticket to something that sounds like *Armageddon II*."

He nodded at the papers in her hand. "What else is written down there?"

"Ummm..." She wasn't sure if she should tell him the other stuff. It was pretty much all downhill from here, and he was already pissed.

"Go on, I can take it. Let's hear the rest."

"Okay..." She went down the page, rattling off a list of comments: "A lot of the dialogue is either meaningless word salad or lazy clichés. Characters talk at each other like robots instead of actual humans beings. Your hero is dumb as rock. Your female lead reads like the equivalent of a grown man playing with a Barbie doll. The way the mechanic character talks is definitely racist—"

"Did I do anything right?" he interrupted, staring straight ahead. His hands were knotted into fists at his side, his forearms taut.

"Well...asteroids exist," Esther said. "You got that part right."

His jaw clenched. "Great."

"Look, I'm sorry, but—"

"It's fine." He scooped up his laptop and pushed himself to his feet. "Can you just give me your notes and I'll read over them on my own?" He held his hand out without meeting her eyes.

"I didn't mean to hurt your feelings." She felt like she'd just stomped on a baby bird. A baby bird who'd *asked* her to stomp on him, but that didn't keep her from feeling like crap.

"You didn't. I asked for an honest critique and that's what you gave me. Can I have the notes?"

Esther reluctantly held them out, and he snatched them out of her hand. "Look, Jonathan—"

"Thanks for your help," he said, cutting her off as he turned to go. "I'll take your feedback under consideration."

She winced as the door slammed behind him.

Well, that went exactly as well as she'd expected.

Chapter Nine

*J*inny finally called Esther back at eight o'clock
that night.

"My mother is giving me brain cancer," she
announced.

Esther dug the television remote out from under Sally's belly
and paused *The Walking Dead* right as a zombie was about to bite
someone's throat out. "I don't think that's possible."

"Every time I see her, I get a headache. That sounds like brain
cancer to me."

"Or here's a thought," Esther said. "Maybe you just find her
aggravating, and it's a normal stress headache."

"Maybe," Jinny allowed reluctantly.

"Tell me about your date last night. How'd it go?"

Silence. "I don't know," she said after a moment. "It was fine,
I guess."

That was...not at all the reaction Esther had been expecting,
based on Jonathan's version of events. "But not great?"

"He let me talk more this time."

"That's good, right?" Nice to know he'd actually paid attention to some of Esther's coaching. But he must have done something else wrong.

"I suppose." Jinny made a dissatisfied noise. "I don't know, I'm still not feeling the fluttery thing, you know? I want him to make my heart beat faster and my toes curl. My toes did not curl, not once. Not even when we were making out."

Esther sat up straighter. "Wait, back up. You made out with him?" No wonder Jonathan had been grinning—and blushing—when he'd talked about Jinny earlier.

"Yeah. And it was nice, but not toe-curling nice."

"Maybe your expectations are too high for a second date. I mean, how many guys have actually made you feel that way so soon after meeting them?" Esther could count the number of men who'd made her feel that way on one hand. On one finger, actually.

"Stuart did."

"Okay, but—"

"I know, Stuart cheated on me. I'm not going back to him, so you can stop worrying about it."

Esther blew out a long breath. "You have no idea how glad I am to hear that." Sally rolled over, snuggling up against her thigh, and Esther scratched her neck for her.

"You were right, I needed to rebound. Now that I've put myself out there again, I have a better idea of what I want, and it's not Stuart *or* Jonathan. Like Vilma said, life's too short to waste on cheap shoes."

"You're saying Jonathan's cheap shoes?" Oof. That was rough on the poor guy. Especially when he was out there thinking the date had gone really well. Just like he'd thought his awful screenplay was some kind of cinematic masterpiece. Poor dude. It was kind of the theme of his life.

Esther could practically hear Jinny's shrug. "He's fine. He'll make a perfectly nice boyfriend for someone else. But he's not what I'm looking for. My days of settling for Payless shoes are over. I'm saving up for a pair of Manolos."

Okay, then. But... "He told me you were going out again next weekend."

"You talked to him?" Jinny sounded surprised.

"Yeah...I ran into him earlier." By appointment, but Jinny didn't need to know about that part.

"I sort of agreed to go to that new Ethiopian place with him next Friday."

"Why would you do that if you don't like him?"

Jinny huffed out an annoyed-sounding breath. "I don't know, I didn't want to hurt his feelings. He asked me right after we'd done all that making out, and it seemed unnecessarily cruel to say no at that point. And I hadn't totally made up my mind about him yet. But the more I thought about it today, the more sure I was that he's not the Manolos I'm looking for."

Esther leaned forward to snag her beer off the coffee table. "So are you still going through with the date on Friday?"

"Yeah, I guess. I don't want to break it off over the phone. I'll tell him at the end of dinner. I'll pick up the check, and then before we leave I'll tell him."

Esther shook her head, wincing. He wouldn't even see it coming. "Poor guy."

"He'll be fine. I'm pretty sure he doesn't like me that much either."

"I wouldn't be too sure of that," Esther said, biting her lip.

"Why? What'd he say?"

"Nothing. He just seemed happy to be going out with you again is all. Just...try to be gentle, okay?"

"You know me," Jinny said. "I'm always nice. It'll be as gentle a rejection as a rejection can be."

Guilt settled in the pit of Esther's stomach. First she'd gotten Jonathan to like Jinny, then she'd decimated his ego by tearing apart his script, and *now* Jinny was probably going to crush what was left of his self-esteem when she dumped him on Friday.

The guy was having a majorly bad week—and it was pretty much all thanks to Esther.

SHE DIDN'T SEE or hear from Jonathan on Monday. Or Tuesday. Every time she walked past his apartment, she slowed her steps, listening for sounds of habitation inside, but it was dark and silent. The blinds were shut tight—which wasn't unusual for him —but there were no lights on inside. She couldn't blame him for avoiding her. Maybe he'd gone out of town. Or he was staying with a friend so he didn't have to risk running into her.

She thought about texting him, just to check on him, but was afraid that might make things worse. It wasn't that she was *worried* about him, exactly, it was just that he'd looked so crushed after she'd eviscerated his script. Like a kid who'd been shoved off his bike and had his lunch money stolen. She didn't like feeling like a bully.

Apparently he wasn't used to criticism. Really though, he needed to develop a thicker skin if he was going to be a writer. Criticism was critical to improvement. You couldn't get better at anything if you weren't willing to learn from your mistakes. Wasn't the whole point of graduate school to further your education in order to master your chosen field? If his fragile ego was going to dissolve every time he got a little constructive feedback, he might as well stop wasting money on tuition and go be a barista or something.

Okay, so maybe she was a *little* worried about him. He didn't strike her as the type to do something drastic, but you never knew, right? When it came down to it, she didn't really *know* anything about him. Other than the fact that he wasn't very good at the one thing he'd apparently centered his entire identity around being.

She couldn't even be properly pleased that her master plan to keep Jinny away from Stuart had worked, because she felt too guilty about Jonathan's stupid feelings being hurt. She hated that she had to care about him at all. Things had been much easier before she'd gone and gotten herself involved in his life. Before she'd allowed herself to *care*.

Then on Wednesday night, she came home from work and found him camped outside her apartment like a homeless person.

He was sitting on the hard concrete floor of the breezeway with his back against her door and his legs stretched out in front of him. His eyes were closed, but they opened when he heard her approaching.

Esther slowed uncertainly to stop a few paces away from him. "Hey."

He looked awful. His eyes were bloodshot and shadowed, and his beard even longer and more scraggly than usual. For once, he wasn't wearing a beanie, and his hair hung down in his face like he'd been pulling at it.

He levered himself off the ground, running a hand through his hair to push it off his forehead. He was clutching a script against his chest protectively. "I read through every single word of your notes," he said without preamble. "Every. Word."

"Oh." There was that guilt again, twisting in the pit of her stomach.

He pressed his lips together into a thin line and stared at the ground. "It was a lot to digest."

"I'm sorry," Esther said, meaning it. "I wasn't trying to hurt your feelings."

He shook his head. "It doesn't matter."

It did though. That much was obvious from looking at him. "I thought you wanted honest feedback," she offered lamely.

He huffed out a bitter-sounding laugh. "I did."

"I tried to keep it constructive, but I'm not a writer. I never learned how to workshop or whatever. I probably did it wrong."

"No, you did it right." He was still staring at his shoes, like he couldn't bear to look her in the eye. "I've been thinking about everything you said and—" He shook his head, grimacing. "You were right about most of it."

That must have been painful to admit. Esther couldn't think of anything to say that wouldn't sound like some version of *I told you so*, so she didn't say anything at all.

"I haven't been…" He hesitated, his face twisting into a scowl. "I haven't been doing as well in school as…" Another pause, followed by more scowling. "I'm on the edge of getting kicked out of the program. My adviser says my work isn't graduate level. She's given me the summer to demonstrate"—he made sarcastic air quotes with his fingers—"significant improvement, or else I won't be allowed to come back for the fall quarter." He shook his head, shifting his weight from one foot to the other. When he spoke again, his voice was low and unsteady. "If I get dropped from the program, my parents will stop paying my rent, and I'll have to move back home."

That…definitely sucked.

"I'm sorry," Esther said again, even though none of it was her fault. If anything, she had *less* to feel guilty about, because she hadn't told him anything his adviser probably hadn't already said to him.

Only…she did feel guilty. She felt even *more* guilty.

Jonathan looked up, his eyes finding hers finally. "I need your help."

Oh no. "My help? What can I—"

"Read my other script. Give me notes like you did on the last one. Help me make it better."

It was the absolute last thing Esther wanted to do. Read *another* one of his scripts? The thought of it made her brain cringe in horror.

But…he looked so sad and miserable. That was a huge admission he'd just made to her. And she'd already hurt his feelings once. Plus, there was the fact that on top of everything else, Jinny was planning to dump him next weekend and he had no idea. And that part was definitely all her fault, because if she hadn't talked him into asking Jinny out, he wouldn't be getting rejected.

How could she possibly say no? She couldn't.

"Okay," she said. "I'll try."

He thrust the script he was holding at her. Reluctantly, she reached out to take it. The title on the cover page said *American Dreamers.*

"What genre is it?" she asked.

"It's a—" He stopped and shook his head. "You tell me after you've read it."

Esther nodded. "Give me a few days?"

"Yeah, sure." He ducked his head. "Thanks," he muttered as he brushed past her and disappeared into his apartment.

THE NEW SCRIPT Jonathan had given her was a love story. Only not really.

It was one of those aimless indie dramas about two people who meet by chance and change each other's lives forever blah blah blah. Like *Before Sunrise,* only more boring.

It was literally about nothing. The entire story consisted of the two main characters monologuing inanely at each other as they wandered aimlessly around Los Angeles for a night before eventually going their separate ways. Clearly, it was meant to be romantic and meaningful, but it managed to be neither.

And yet, despite the utter absence of any plot, there was something more to this one, underneath all the artifice. Esther could almost see what Jonathan was *trying* to do with it, he just wasn't getting it done.

It was definitely a more personal story than the other one had been. The main character was a blatant author insert, and she'd bet cash money the girl was based on some ex who'd broken his heart. Or maybe an unrequited love who'd gotten away.

She was going to have to be even more careful how she couched her feedback this time. She'd already brutalized him once, and Jinny was about to do it again. Plus, she couldn't dump all over an autobiographical story without dumping on him personally. It needed to be handled delicately.

But how?

Fuck, how did she get herself into this situation?

Did you read it yet? Jonathan texted on Friday afternoon.

Yes, Esther texted back.

When do you want to talk about it?

Sunday?

He was going on his last date with Jinny tonight. If Esther put him off until Sunday, maybe his wounds would have time to scab over from being dumped. You know, before she ripped them off again.

OK, he replied. *Same time & place?*

Esther texted him back a thumbs up emoji.

Man, this was going to suck.

"I did it," Jinny announced when Esther answered the phone later that night. It was only nine o'clock. She must have come straight home after dumping Jonathan at dinner.

"How'd it go?" Esther asked.

"Really, really well. Best breakup I've ever had."

That was... *Huh*. She'd anticipated more drama. Crying, maybe. Jonathan seemed like he might be a crier.

Esther set her laptop aside. She'd been working on her notes for Jonathan all night. Trying to make them sound nicer, which didn't come naturally to her. It was an uphill struggle. "He really took it okay?"

"Yeah, we were both very mature about it. I told him I didn't feel like we were right for each other. And he said if that's how I felt, then we should just be friends."

"Wow." Okay. Esther had not expected him to be so mature about it. Given his emotional state earlier in the week, she thought he'd take it harder than that. She was glad though. Hopefully, it boded well for their next critique session. Or as well as possible, anyway.

"The friends thing is total bullshit, obviously. It's not like we're going to be hanging out platonically after this. I'll probably never see him again except when I bump into him at your place."

"That's going to be awkward." They might need to stop hanging out at the pool. At least for a while.

"I don't think it'll be too bad. It's not like we slept together or anything."

"Sure," Esther said. "Yeah." *Thank god.*

"I'm kind of wishing I had now though."

"Uh—why?"

"Curiosity. I still want to know what he's like in the sack."

"It's probably just as well you didn't. If you didn't like him, I mean."

"I guess. I mean I *liked* him, I just couldn't see us getting serious. To be honest, he reminded me too much of Stuart."

"How?" Esther couldn't think of a single thing Jonathan had in common with Stuart other than superficial stuff like his beard and his beanie habit.

"He just seemed...I don't know. Distracted? Like he was going through the motions. Like he wasn't invested. I didn't want to do that again. I deserve someone who's all in."

"You definitely do," Esther agreed. That was what she'd been trying to tell Jinny for months.

"Although..."

"What?"

"He was different tonight."

"Different how?"

"More subdued, I guess? Sweeter. It almost felt like the guy from the first two dates was an act and I was finally starting to get a glimpse of the real Jonathan underneath."

"Huh." Esther stared at his script, lying open on the couch next to her, and felt like shit all over again.

"Honestly, I almost changed my mind about dumping him at the last second."

Esther squeezed the phone. "Really?"

"Yeah, but then I thought, this is what I always do. I make excuses for them. I tell myself they're going to change, and things will get better. But they never do, do they?"

"Not usually, no."

"I'm done waiting for guys to change. If they aren't treating me the way I deserve to be treated, then I'm out."

Esther reached over and flipped Jonathan's script closed. "Good for you."

"I'm turning over a new leaf. Go me!" At least Jinny sounded happy. Esther hadn't ruined Jonathan's week for nothing. That was something.

"So you're really okay with the Jonathan situation?" Esther asked, riffling the edges of the script pages with her thumb. "And with Stuart?"

"Yeah, totally. I'm *way* over Stuart. Going out with Jonathan was clarifying. I know what I want now. No more Payless shoes for me."

"That's great." All Esther wanted was for Jinny to be happy. To understand her own worth. To not settle for some shithead who treated her like crap.

"Yeah, so, I was gonna suggest a pool hang tomorrow to celebrate, but it'd probably be cruel to lurk outside Jonathan's apartment right after dumping him, huh?"

"Probably. We could meet for brunch though. Let someone else make the mimosas for a change."

"You're on."

After they hung up, Esther went back to working on her script notes for Jonathan. She really wanted to do a good job with them. He had a lot riding on it, and she felt like she had to do right by him.

She owed him that much, at least.

Chapter Ten

"You brought your weird coffeemaker," Esther said when she opened the door for Jonathan on Sunday.

"Chemex." He strode past her, carrying it into the kitchen. It was already ready to go with a filter and coffee grounds. "Do you have a kettle?" he asked, setting it on the counter. He was back to his signature plaid shirt and beanie look today. There was a pack of cigarettes tucked into his front shirt pocket and a brown canvas messenger bag slung across his chest. "If not, I can go back for mine."

"Next to the fridge," Esther said.

He filled it up with water from the tap. "I'm going to show you how much better this coffee is than that sludge you're used to drinking. You'll never look at coffee pods the same way again."

"Sure, whatever," she said, chewing on her thumbnail.

He seemed oddly perky for a guy who'd just been dumped. A little too perky, maybe. Almost manic, like he was working extra hard to pretend everything was great.

"Mugs?" he asked over his shoulder as he started the kettle.

Esther got out two mismatched mugs and set them in front of him.

His fingers drummed impatiently on the edge of the counter while he waited for the kettle to boil. "Thank you for doing this," he said without looking at her.

"Getting out coffee mugs?"

He shook his head, frowning. "Helping me with my scripts."

"You might want to hold your thanks until you hear what I have to say."

A muscle twitched in his jaw. "That bad, huh?"

She'd considered just telling him what he wanted to hear—that this screenplay was great and only needed a few minor tweaks. But if she did that, he'd probably fail his class, get kicked out of grad school, and have to move back home with his parents. In order to actually help him, she had to be honest—as kindly as she could possibly manage.

"I liked it better than the last one," she offered.

He turned away, lifting his messenger bag over his head as he went into the living room. "I guess that's something."

"It's got potential," she said, following him.

He dropped his messenger bag onto the couch and pulled out his laptop. "Great." He hadn't actually looked her in the eye since he'd walked in.

"Look, if you don't want to do this—"

"I do," he said, still looking down. "I need this. It's just not very much fun."

"Okay. As long as you're not going to hate me."

"No promises." He looked at her, finally, mustering a thin smile. "But I'll try."

The electric kettle clicked off. "Water's done," Esther said.

He went back into the kitchen and started the insanely tedious process of pouring water over the grounds. Seriously, if they'd used Esther's coffee pods, they'd both already be drinking their coffee by now.

When he was *finally* done brewing his special fancy coffee, he divided it up between the two mugs and pushed one toward her. "Try it."

"I don't like black coffee," she said, wrinkling her nose.

"You have to drink it black to appreciate the complexity of the flavor. Diluting it with sweeteners and additives is like putting fruit juice into wine."

"You mean like sangria and mimosas and a hundred other popular cocktails?"

"Those were all invented as a way to make bad wine drinkable. You don't use Dom Pérignon to make mimosas. This isn't shitty donut shop coffee, it's artisan-roasted beans. You want to be able to taste it."

Esther rolled her eyes at him as she picked up the mug and blew across the top. It did smell amazing. She took a tentative sip and made a face. "I don't like black coffee. I'm putting cream in this."

"Barbarian," Jonathan said as she poured half-and-half into her mug.

"Snob," she shot back.

"Not sugar too," he said when she reached for the sugar bowl.

She smirked at him as she dumped a teaspoon of sugar into her coffee.

"You're hurting my soul."

"Get over yourself. It's just coffee." She took another sip. Wow. Okay, as much as she was loath to admit it, his stupid fancy coffee was genuinely incredible.

It was Jonathan's turn to smirk. "It's great, isn't it?"

She shrugged. "It's okay."

His smirk got wider. "It's better than okay. It's the best coffee you've ever tasted."

"Maybe," she admitted. "It's still just coffee though."

Still looking pleased with himself, he went into the living room and dropped onto the couch, setting his coffee mug on the table.

Esther took the opposite end of the couch. "Are you sure

you're ready for this?" she asked, cradling her coffee in her lap. He hadn't said anything about Jinny yet, and she was afraid to ask. No point in poking a sore tooth.

He clenched his jaw and nodded. "I can take it."

She wasn't entirely sure that was true, but she leaned over for the notes she'd left on the coffee table.

Sally had worked up the courage to venture out of the bedroom, and she wandered over to the couch, jumping up between them.

Jonathan startled at her sudden appearance beside him. "I didn't know you had a cat."

"That's Sally," Esther said. "As in Sally Ride."

"Like the Clapton song?"

"Like the *astronaut*. The first American woman in space?"

"Right." He nodded, watching warily as Sally stepped onto his leg, purring at him.

"She likes you." Esther was surprised. It had taken six months of concerted coaxing before Sally would come near Jinny, and she still wasn't exactly friendly to her. Jonathan had only been here twice, and Sally was already investigating his lap. "She doesn't usually like new people."

"Does she have to do that?" he asked as Sally started to knead his thigh.

"Are you allergic?"

"No, I just don't like cats. Or cat hair all over my clothes."

"How can you not like cats?" Esther leaned over to stroke Sally's back. "Cats are great."

"Cats are assholes." He held a hand out tentatively, and Sally smushed her face into his palm. Like a real asshole, clearly.

"They're not assholes." Esther leaned back against the armrest as Jonathan scratched Sally's head. "They're just not servile like dogs."

"I happen to like my animal companions servile."

She rolled her eyes. "Of course you do."

He cocked an eyebrow at her. "What? You don't like dogs?"

"Dogs are great." She shrugged as she sipped her coffee. "I love dogs. I just like cats better. When a cat shows you affection it means something, because they don't do it for everyone. They're selective."

"I guess." He picked up his laptop and gently displaced Sally from his lap. She turned around twice and then flomped down with her back pressed against his thigh, rolling her head to gaze at him through half-lidded eyes.

Jesus, was he wearing some kind of cat pheromone or something? She'd never seen Sally like this with anyone but her. It was like being cheated on right in front of her face.

"Let's get this over with," Jonathan said, blowing out a long breath.

Right. The script notes. The whole reason he was here.

Esther stared at the pages in her hand, gritting her teeth. There was no way out but through.

"Okay." She pulled her feet up under her. "I really liked the scene where the two main characters first meet, when he offers to buy her a coffee. It was charming." It had taken her forever to think of something she liked about the script. But she figured she ought to start off with something positive to ease him into it.

He nodded warily. "That's good to hear."

Unfortunately, that one observation had pretty much exhausted all of Esther's positive feedback. Time to rip off the Band-Aid. "I guess, overall...the biggest problem I had with it is that it's not really about anything."

"Yes it is," he said. "It's about love."

Esther shook her head. "That's what the characters *talk* about. It's not what *happens*. Nothing happens."

"Things happen." They'd barely even started and he was already bristling. This was going to go great.

"I'm not trying to be mean," she said. "I'm just giving you my impression. That's what you asked for, right?"

He shook his head, clenching his jaw again. "Yes, I'm sorry. I'm just—go on. I'm listening."

Esther flipped through the first few pages of the script. "She loses her wallet, and he offers to buy her coffee—so far so good. But then they just wander around the city talking. There's no action."

"There's the encounter with the homeless vet."

"Yeah, but it doesn't have any consequences. It doesn't change either of them. In fact, neither of the characters change at all over the course of the story. By the end, when he puts her in the Uber and they go their separate ways, they're both the exact same people they were when they first met."

"That's not true." Jonathan shook his head. "She has a profound effect on him. He never forgets her."

"That may have been what you were trying to convey, but it's not on the page."

He scowled and leaned his head back against the couch.

"Maybe if the characters had a little more depth, it'd be easier to show how they change each other?"

He rotated his head in her direction. "You're saying my characters have no depth?"

"Not *no* depth," she tried to explain. "Just...they could use a little more, maybe. They're both a walking grab bag of quirky stereotypes and personality tics, but I don't feel like I *know* either of them. They don't feel real."

"Great. That was the one thing I thought I did right." He shoved his laptop aside and leaned forward, resting his elbows on his knees as he rubbed the sides of his head.

"Your male lead is a busker in a train station," Esther said. "That's not real life, that's a cliché."

"Buskers actually exist." He pushed up his glasses so he could rub his eyes. "Just like asteroids," he added, throwing a bitter glance her way.

"Okay, but do you actually know anyone who's a busker? Have

you spent time talking to one of them about what it's really like? I think you might be over-romanticizing it."

Sally bumped her forehead against Jonathan's arm, but he ignored her in favor of rubbing his temples some more. "Fine, what else?" His entire body was taut, like he was bracing for an attack. Like every word Esther said was hurting him.

She set her script notes down on the couch between them. "Maybe we should stop. I don't think I'm helping you."

"No, please." He dropped his hands, turning his head to give her a beseeching look. "This is exactly what I need to hear."

"Are you sure? Because I feel like a real shitnugget here." It was like kicking a puppy. Over and over again. Esther had never considered herself a particularly nice person, but she wasn't a puppy-kicker either.

He dragged his beanie off and tossed it on the table, running a hand through his hair. "I'm sorry. You really are helping, it's just hard to hear." He stretched his arm across the couch so his finger-tips brushed against her leg. "I promise I won't hate you."

She looked down at his hand, nodding. "Okay."

He retracted his arm and sat back on the couch again. "What about Emily, the female lead? Did you like her?"

Esther winced. "Well…"

Jonathan groaned. "What's wrong with her?"

"She's a Manic Pixie Dream Girl—you know what that is, right?"

"I'm in film school," he said with a scowl. "Of course I know what it is, and Emily's not a Manic Pixie Dream Girl. She's real."

Esther shifted on the couch so she was facing him more. "You mean she's based on a real person, right? Someone you cared about?"

He looked down at his hands, which were clenched in his lap. "Sort of."

Esther tilted her head to catch his eye. "Tell me about her. The real Emily. What made her special? What did you like about her?"

His fingers drummed on the cushion next to his thigh, and Sally took the opportunity to smush her face against them. "I don't know," he said, idly scratching her head. "I guess...she's funny."

"Okay, that's a start," Esther said. "Funny's good. The script could use a little more humor. Make her funny."

He gave her a weary look. "I thought I had."

She pressed her lips together to suppress the urge to smile. It wasn't funny, but in a way it kind of was. Darkly funny. "You've got to actually write her *being* funny, not just say she's funny in the character description." Esther tipped her head to one side, peering at him. "Can you write jokes?"

He let out a long-suffering sigh. "Apparently not."

"We'll put a pin in funny for now. What else do you like about her?"

"She's smart, I guess."

Esther shook her head. "Smart's hard too. Give me something more concrete. Like, a specific moment when she did something small and seemingly insignificant that made you feel something about her."

She propped her elbow on the couch, watching him while he thought about it. He was chewing on his lower lip, with his face all scrunched up in a frown. He was more than cute; he was actively attractive. Why hadn't she seen it before? Her hate goggles had blinded her to the fact that there was a hot guy underneath that beanie.

After a moment he sat up, shifting to face her. "This is kind of lame, but...there was this one time, we were at the beach, and she spent like an hour building this really elaborate sandcastle with a bunch of kids we didn't even know."

"That's perfect." Esther said. "That's *real*. Put that in there."

His brow furrowed. "How am I going to get a sandcastle into the script if they don't go to the beach?"

"It doesn't have to be a sandcastle. Make it sidewalk chalk or

Legos or something. Whatever. It can be anything. But that tells me something about who she is. It makes me like her."

"Yeah," he said, reaching for his laptop. "Okay." He was almost sort of smiling, for the first time since he'd showed up at the door. His hair was sticking up, and it made Esther want to smooth it down for him.

She cleared her throat. "Am I allowed to ask who Emily was?"

His smile faded. "Just some girl I knew."

"She seems like more than that."

He stopped typing and stroked his hand down Sally's back. "She was my first girlfriend. My only really serious girlfriend."

"What happened?"

"She dumped me for someone else."

"I'm sorry."

"It happens, right?" He shrugged and looked up at Esther. "Have you ever been cheated on?"

She shook her head. It would be nice to be able to say it was because she'd never dated anyone who would cheat on her, but the actual reason was that she'd never dated anyone long enough to get cheated on. She had a history of breaking things off before anyone got around to thinking about cheating.

"Have you ever cheated on anyone?"

"No," Esther answered truthfully. Again, that itchy breakup trigger had prevented her from ever dealing with the temptation. If the thought so much as entered her head that she might want to sleep with someone else, she was out the door—usually she was out the door way before that, actually. She couldn't understand why anyone would ever cheat, when breaking up was such an easy alternative.

"Well, you're a rarity," Jonathan said, digging his fingers into Sally's ruff as she lolled beside him purring. "Everyone else I know has either cheated or been cheated on at one time or another. Or both."

Esther sipped her coffee. "That explains the hostility, I guess."

The corners of his mouth drew down. "What hostility?"

"In your script. I thought it was misogyny, but it's more personal than that."

He stopped petting Sally and looked up. "You thought I was a misogynist?"

Esther shrugged. "That whole daddy issues thing is pretty distasteful. Not to mention the part where you compare her to the White Witch, and the way you have her using her sexuality to get strangers to do things for her."

He looked away.

"You haven't forgiven her for breaking your heart. You're still hung up on her."

"It was three years ago. I'm over her." His voice sounded rough, like it had been scraped over sandpaper.

"You wrote an entire screenplay about her," Esther said, trying to sound gentle.

He shook his head, but his eyes stayed fixed on a spot on the opposite wall. "I wrote a story about love, and she's the only woman I've ever been in love with. She's all I had to go on."

"Well, it feels like you don't like her character very much, so when I read it, *I* didn't like her very much."

His expression shifted into another scowl. "She broke my heart. I *don't* like her."

Esther felt for him, but sympathy wasn't going to fix his problems. "You've got to find a way to get over that if you want this story to work. Or else find a different muse. Because right now, the way you feel about her is hurting your script."

"I need some air." He pushed off the couch and went out onto her balcony, sliding the door closed behind him as he reached into his pocket for his cigarettes.

Esther stayed on the couch petting Sally for a couple minutes to give him a chance to cool off before she got up and followed him.

"You shouldn't smoke," she said when she joined him outside.

He was hunched over, leaning forward with his forearms resting on the railing.

The balconies were small, only barely deep enough for a chair, and hers overlooked the alley and the apartment complex next door. It wasn't exactly picturesque. Esther didn't spend much time out here, and it was dusty and covered with seedpods from a nearby tree.

"I only do it when I'm stressed," he said without looking at her.

If that was true, she felt even sorrier for him, because it seemed like he smoked a lot. She leaned against the railing beside him and bumped her arm against his. "I'm sorry I'm making you stressed."

He picked at the filter of his cigarette with his thumbnail. "It's not you." He didn't look stressed anymore, he looked sad. She didn't like seeing him sad—not that she liked seeing him stressed either. But it was better than this sad, dejected person who made her want to gather him up and give him a hug.

"Is it talking about her?" Esther asked. "Real Emily. The girl who broke your heart."

He took a long drag on his cigarette and turned his head to blow the smoke away from her. "It's not just that, it's all of it. Her, my adviser, the fact that I'm failing at the one thing I ever wanted to do." His eyes flicked her way. "Then there's Jinny."

Esther winced. "Oh."

His mouth flattened out. "You didn't ask how it went Friday, so I assume you already know she told me she didn't want to see me anymore."

"I'm sorry," Esther said, feeling like a shitnugget again. "I really thought you guys might be good together."

Shrugging, he took another drag on his cigarette. "It's whatever. It's one more in a long list of things I suck at."

He was *too* sad. She wanted to make him feel better, but she didn't know how. So she did the only thing she could think of, which was to confess something embarrassing about herself: "The reason I've never been cheated on is that I've never been in a serious relationship."

He looked over at her, eyebrows raised. "Really?" He sounded as surprised as if she'd told him she'd never tasted ice cream.

"I've had sex," she said, so there wasn't any misunderstanding. "Plenty of times. I'm not a—"

He put his hands up in a warding gesture. "I wasn't asking."

Esther looked down at the sidewalk. If the wind was just right, she could probably spit on her car from here. Or Jonathan's. "I don't think I'm built for commitment," she said. "Some people just aren't, right?"

"Why do you think that?"

She shrugged. "I've never liked anyone long enough to keep them around."

"You've never been in love?" There he went again, sounding shocked.

"Nope."

It wasn't a big deal. Plenty of people had never been in love. The world was full of people still waiting to find their soul mate— not that Esther believed in soul mates. She was better off than most of the rest of them, because she didn't need to be in love. She wasn't waiting for a man to come along and complete her. She was perfectly happy on her own. *Most of the time.*

He flicked ash over the railing. "That's sad."

She swiveled her head to glare at him. "Thanks."

He didn't look as sad anymore—probably because he was too busy thinking about how sad she was. She'd successfully distracted him with her own patheticness.

He shrugged, smiling at her. "Well, it is."

"It's not like I haven't been attracted to people. I've had crushes. But after the initial excitement wears off I always end up feeling meh."

He looked thoughtful. "Maybe you're gay."

"I'm not gay."

"How do you know?"

"Because I want to sleep with guys and I don't want to sleep with girls. That's pretty much the textbook definition of not-gay."

Not that she hadn't considered it. She'd even tried to date a girl once—in college, which was such a cliché—but that had been a big nope. Girls were definitely not for her. She liked men, and she liked sex with men. She liked it a *lot*. She just didn't like the men hanging around afterward. Esther was the opposite of Jinny. Instead of keeping men around past their expiration date, she tossed them out as soon as the freshness had started to wear off.

She looked down at her hands. "I just think all that sappy, hand-holding, love song stuff isn't for me."

Jonathan shook his head, gazing across the alley at the building next door. "That stuff's all performative. That's not love. Love is madness. It's a compulsion. It's passion and torment and exhilaration and fear."

"You make it sound awful," Esther said, shuddering. "Like skydiving or something."

"It is. But it's also incredible."

"If you say so. Seems like more trouble than it's worth." Look at him—he'd only been in love once and he was still fucked up from it. If that was what was in store for her, she didn't mind taking a pass.

He took another drag on his cigarette. "You only say that because you've never experienced it. Most of art and literature was inspired by love."

Esther rolled her eyes. "A lot of it was inspired by religion, but I'm not inviting missionaries into my house to proselytize me."

He looked over at her. "So you've just given up on ever falling in love?"

Maybe. It was easier than being disappointed over and over again. Or wondering whether there was something wrong with her. Plenty of men preferred casual sex over relationships, and no one ever blinked an eye at them. Esther was only doing what they did. That didn't make her broken.

She shrugged. "It's not like love's even real."

"Sure it is."

"No, gravity's real. The laws of thermodynamics are real. You know how I know? Because I can measure them. I can make reliable predictions about how objects will behave under their influence. You can't do that with love. It's just a feeling. A temporary delusion caused by rising cortisol levels and depleted serotonin."

"You say that like feelings don't matter."

"Maybe they shouldn't matter as much as they do."

"Now you're talking crazy."

"I just think maybe I was meant to be alone." She stared down at the sidewalk. "I'd rather be by myself or with my friends than with any guy I've ever dated, so why bother dating?"

Jonathan stubbed out his cigarette and flicked the butt over onto to his balcony. "Maybe the problem isn't you, it's the kind of men you date."

She looked at him sharply. "What's *that* supposed to mean?"

He shrugged. "I just think you shouldn't be dating anyone you don't want to be friends with. If you're looking for a real partner, there's got to be more than just sexual attraction there. You should be looking for someone you actually enjoy spending time with. Ideally, you're looking for a best friend. That's the goal, isn't it? To marry your best friend."

"Wow," she said.

He glanced her way. "What?"

"That is shockingly sentimental, coming from the guy who wrote a love story where two people totally fail to fall in love."

His mouth twitched, but he looked more amused than irritated. "Thanks a lot."

"Come on." She tugged at his sleeve. "Smoke break's over. Let's go channel some of that squishy romantic center you've been hiding into that script of yours."

He followed her back inside, and they worked for another few hours, going over the rest of Esther's notes and talking them through. By the time he finally packed up and went home, Esther had convinced him to make some major overhauls. He took it pretty well, considering how much work it was going to take to implement the changes. Instead of being pissed or disheartened, he seemed downright cheerful.

On his way out the door, he paused on the threshold, clutching his laptop and the copy of her notes she'd given him. "Thank you." He met her eyes and smiled. Not the half-assed mouth twitch that usually passed for a smile either, but a real smile. Soft and genuine and a little shy. "It sounds hyperbolic, but I think you may have saved my life."

Esther felt her cheeks warm as she smiled back at him. "You're welcome."

Maybe she wasn't so bad at this critiquing stuff after all.

Chapter Eleven

"*D*o you think I have bad taste in men?" Esther asked Jinny at lunch on Monday. It was taco salad day, and the cafeteria was more crowded than usual. Everybody liked taco salad day, and unlike lasagna, they never seemed to run out.

Jinny's eyes narrowed over her tostada bowl. "Is this a trick question? It feels like a trick."

"It's not a trick. It's a regular question."

It was just the two of them today, because Yemi was on a conference call. Esther had promised to bring him back a taco salad.

Jinny was still suspicious. "Why don't you tell me what you want to hear, and then I'll decide if I agree or not."

"I'm not looking for validation," Esther told her. "I want to know what you really think." She hadn't been able to stop thinking about what Jonathan had said. About how her problem was the kind of men she dated.

Jinny pursed her lips. They were a matte pinkish orange today. Esther couldn't think of a single other person who'd look good in that particular color, but on Jinny it was perfect. "I think…" She paused, carefully considering her words. "I think you gravitate toward men you're in no in danger of getting serious about."

"That's not true!"

"I knew it was a trick." Jinny shook her head as she stabbed a chunk of chicken fajita with her fork.

"Sorry," Esther said. "Tell me why you think that. I'm listening." She made a zipping motion across her lips.

"Fine," Jinny said. "You haven't been in a single serious relationship since I've known you. Your M.O. is to meet a guy, sleep with him once or twice, and then get bored."

She wasn't wrong, but Esther still felt the need to defend herself. "Sometimes they're the ones who get bored."

"Because you always pick guys who clearly aren't looking for anything more than a casual hookup."

"Not always." Just *mostly*.

"Leo didn't get bored," Jinny said. "He would have happily boned you for the rest of his life if you'd let him."

Leo was a vendor who worked with Jinny. Esther had gone home with him after Jinny's New Year's Eve party last year. And then she'd lost interest. Fast. She wrinkled her nose. "Leo was obsessed with anime figures."

"So what? You've got some Funkos on your desk."

"No, I mean he was *obsessed*. He had an entire room of his house devoted to them. Have you ever seen a entire room full of nothing but shelf upon shelf of anime figures? *Super* creepy. You wouldn't have wanted to go back to that house either." Esther shuddered. The memory of all those unnaturally wide, vacant eyes staring back at her still haunted her.

"I'm just saying, you could have given him more of a chance. He might have eased up on the doll obsession a little once he had a real girl to care about."

Esther shook her head as she reached for her iced tea. "No, see, that's your M.O. You're always thinking you can change the guys you date, remember?"

Jinny pointed her fork at Esther. "Nice try, but we're not talking about my hang-ups right now, we're talking about yours."

"I liked Diego." Esther set her tea back down. "It's not my fault he moved to Texas."

Jinny rolled her eyes. "Please. Diego was already halfway out the door when you slept with him. You worked with him for a year and didn't show the slightest interest until he took that job at NASA." She reached for a packet of hot sauce and tore it open with her teeth. "This is what you do," she said, squeezing hot sauce onto her taco salad. "You either pick a guy you don't actually like, or you pick someone who's 'safe' because he's physically or emotionally unavailable. And if one of the unavailable guys starts showing signs of wanting to hang around—god forbid—you immediately stop liking him and run for the hills."

"When have I done that?" Esther asked.

Jinny fixed her with a pointed look. "Arun. You crushed on him *hard* for like three straight months, and as soon as he started showing actual interest in you, you immediately stopped liking him."

"That's because I found out he was vegan! I can't date a vegan. I like cheese way too much."

"There's always a reason if you invent one," Jinny said, shaking her head.

"I don't have to invent reasons. The reasons are just there." It was called having standards, and there was nothing wrong with it. Esther refused to feel bad about it.

"You picked *cheese* over an attractive man who liked you."

Esther broke off a piece of tostada chip and scooped up a big pile of cheese and sour cream. "My relationship with dairy is deeply fulfilling. You're lactose intolerant. You can't possibly understand." She shoved the chip in her mouth and smiled happily.

"I'm not lactose intolerant, I just refuse to put up with lactose's shit." Jinny picked an olive out of her salad and popped it into her mouth. "When's the last time you were in a relationship that lasted longer than a month?"

Esther swallowed. "High school."

Jinny's eyes widened. "Are you kidding?"

"There was a guy in college, but it was more like a friends with benefits arrangement." She shrugged. "He wasn't interested in being serious."

"How long did it last?"

"Two semesters, give or take."

"How'd it end?"

"He met a girl. They started dating." It was the last time she'd actually felt invested in a relationship, and the memory of it was still a little tender. That was what trying to date a friend had gotten her.

Jinny leaned forward. "How did that make you feel?"

Esther scowled. "What are you, my therapist?"

"Answer the question, or I'll be forced to treat the witness as hostile."

"You watch too many *Law and Order* reruns."

"Come on, fess up."

"It hurt," Esther admitted, casting her eyes down. "It wasn't that he didn't want to be in a relationship. He just didn't want to be in one with me." She squirmed in her seat, regretting that she'd started this conversation.

Jinny's expression softened. "You really liked him, didn't you?"

There was still a box of memorabilia devoted to him on the top shelf of Esther's closet. Ticket stubs, Post-It notes, a paperback book he'd lent her. So yes, she'd really liked him.

She shrugged like it wasn't that big a deal. "He was the only guy I've ever been friends with that I actually wanted to sleep with."

"Did you ever tell him how you felt?"

No. That would have given him a chance to reject me.

"I didn't want to scare him off," Esther said, reaching for her iced tea. "We had a good thing going." She'd been afraid to change the status quo. Part of her had always wondered whether they would have stayed together if she'd done things differently. Maybe he wouldn't have moved on—or maybe he'd have broken things off even sooner. She'd never know.

"Until he found someone else."

Esther swallowed a mouthful of tea. "Yeah."

"That sucks. I'm sorry." Jinny reached across the table and squeezed her hand. "Now I've made you all sad."

Esther shook her head. "It was four years ago. It's not like I'm still hung up on him."

"I'll buy you a cupcake at knitting tonight to cheer you up."

"Okay, but don't say anything to the rest of them about any of this. I don't want my love life dissected by the whole group." Talking about it with Jinny had already exceeded her quota of sharing for the entire month.

"You know, talking about things can actually make you feel better sometimes."

Esther broke off another piece of chip. "I talk about things. We're talking right now."

Jinny leaned forward, frowning slightly. "Do *you* think you have bad taste in men? Since you're the one who asked the question in the first place."

"I don't know," Esther said. "I never thought about it before."

"What made you bring it up?"

She didn't want to tell Jinny that she and Jonathan had been having a heart-to-heart about their love lives. Not after they'd just broken up. It felt disloyal. Esther reached for her iced tea again to cover her floundering. "Because of what you said about Stuart and Jonathan, I guess. It got me thinking about...things."

Jinny nodded, stabbing at her taco salad. "You've met plenty of men—you've slept with even more than I have. But none of them are ever good enough to do more than just sleep with them. Why do *you* think that is?"

"I don't know," Esther said.

Maybe she *was* broken inside. Maybe she just couldn't love the way other people did.

Or maybe Jinny was right, and she was sabotaging herself. Because she was afraid. If you never let yourself care about people, it didn't hurt as much when they didn't care back.

It was easier to not want things, because then you couldn't be disappointed when you didn't get them.

WHEN ESTHER GOT home from knitting that night, Jonathan was sitting outside her door, smoking a cigarette. She waved her hand to break up the cloud of smoke as she stepped over his legs.

He pushed himself to his feet and waved a handful of wrinkled papers at her. "I made some changes to the script and I want to know what you think."

"Hello to you too," Esther said as she shoved her key in the lock.

He dropped his cigarette and ground it out with his shoe. "I need to know if I'm on the right track before I do anything else."

Esther glared at the cigarette butt. "You're not going to leave that there, are you?"

He picked it up and gave her an imploring look. "Please?"

"Fine." She held out her hand, and he passed her the script pages.

"Thank you."

Instead of going away, he continued to stand there crowding her doorway as if he expected to follow her inside. He was so tall, her eyes only came up to his collarbone.

"You want me to read it right now?" she asked his collarbone.

He nodded. "If you have time."

"Were you expecting to come in and watch me?"

"It's only a few pages."

"I can't focus with you staring at me and being all twitchy."

"I can go on the balcony." His shoulders sagged. "Or wait out here, I guess."

It was impossible to say no to him when he was being this pitiful. Esther sighed and let herself into her apartment, leaving the door open behind her. She wasn't nearly as annoyed as she ought to be. Maybe he was growing on her.

He followed her inside and went into the kitchen to throw his cigarette butt away. Esther dropped her purse and knitting bag on the dining table, then gestured to the couch with the script pages she was holding. "Sit. I'll go read it in the bedroom." She arched a warning eyebrow at him. "Don't touch anything while I'm gone."

He gave her a military salute and a lopsided grin.

She went into the bedroom, shut the door, and flopped onto the bed. There were only a few pages, so it didn't take her long to read them.

Shockingly, they were actually...almost good. It was only the first five pages, but it was already a huge improvement. He'd ditched the female lead's purple hair and dumb vintage Volkswagen, and moved their encounter from the train station to the airport. The whole thing felt a lot more grounded in reality and less clichéd. There was still a long way to go, but it was definitely progress.

When she came back out of the bedroom, Sally was sitting in Jonathan's lap getting scratched under the chin.

"I told you not to touch anything, and here you are caressing my cat."

"It's not my fault," he said, still scratching Sally. "She put herself here and started head-butting my hand until I petted her." He nodded at the pages she was holding, eyebrows raised. "Well?"

Esther smiled. "It's good. I like it."

He stopped petting Sally, looking surprised and also skeptical. "You do?" Sally head-butted him, but he ignored her.

"I think you're on the right track," Esther said.

"Yeah?" His mouth curved into a tentative smile.

"Yeah," she said. "Only..."

His face fell. "What?"

"That joke you added at the top of page two?"

He nodded. "You said it needed more humor."

"Yeah, it still does."

"You didn't like it? I thought it was pretty good."

"It's bad," Esther said. "Really terrible."

He ran his hand over the back of his neck. "Oh."

"Overly complicated, difficult to parse, flaccid—"

"Okay." He got to his feet, smiling as he snatched the pages out of her hand. "I get the picture. The joke is bad. Ditch the joke."

"Weak," she continued, having too much fun teasing him to stop. "Flabby, limp. Really not getting the job done at all."

"But you liked the rest?"

"The rest is great. Really." It felt good to be able to say something complimentary about his writing and actually mean it.

His whole face lit up, like she'd just told him he'd won the lottery, and something fluttered in Esther's stomach. He was shockingly handsome when he smiled like that. Too bad he didn't do it more often.

"All right," he said, waving the script pages at her as he headed for the door. "Thanks."

"You keep working on those jokes, friend. One day you'll be funny."

He raised his middle finger at her, grinning as he let himself out.

"I believe in you!" she shouted as the door slammed behind him.

Chapter Twelve

*T*hursday was Esther's performance review at work—her first review with her new manager, Diane.

Esther wasn't worried about it. She was good at her job. She always got her work done under deadline and made fewer errors than most of the other design engineers.

"Have a seat," Diane said when Esther showed up at her appointed time. Diane had an office to herself, because her job involved interviewing new hires and doing performance and disciplinary reviews. Also firing people. It didn't seem like a fun job, even if she did get her own office with a door and a window.

"How's your week been going?" Diane asked, lacing her fingers together on top of her desk and smiling. She was in her forties, but she looked much older. Everything about her was dowdy: her hair, her clothes, her glasses, even her smile. She reminded Esther of her fourth-grade teacher, Mrs. Kopecki, who had been in her seventies.

"Good." Esther shifted in her seat and tugged her skirt down over her knees. Even though she wasn't worried about her review, it felt a little like being called to the principal's office.

"Glad to hear it." Diane's smile got wider. "Shall we get this over with?"

Esther nodded. "Sure."

Diane looked down at her desk and shuffled some papers. When she looked up again, she wasn't smiling as much. "I'd like you to know you're one of the most promising engineers we have. You're technically brilliant, and your ability to quickly find innovative, efficient solutions to engineering problems is second to none."

So far, it was all good. But something about the way she said it made Esther feel like there was a "but" hanging out there.

"However…"

And there it was.

"At times you can come on a little too strong, or give the impression that you're impatient or disdainful of your peers and their abilities."

Esther's mouth opened, but all that came out was, "Oh."

Diane paused, tilting her head to meet Esther's eye. "You're one of the best engineers on your team, Esther. Which means that most of your coworkers won't be as good as you at what they do. But everyone here has a contribution to make, and you need to be able to work cooperatively—with everyone."

Esther nodded, feeling numb. This wasn't at all how she'd thought this would go. Her last review had been stellar. Her old manager hadn't had any criticism for her at all. They'd spent the whole time talking about what kind of project she'd like to move to next, and the path to becoming a subject matter expert, and what kind of technical areas she might be interested pursuing.

It hadn't gone anything like this.

"It might be helpful to remember this is a team," Diane continued, "and not a collection of individual heroes. In order for your own work to be effective, you'll need to be able to work with your peers and superiors in a smooth, efficient manner."

The urge to argue was almost overwhelming, but Esther knew

arguing in your performance review wasn't a good look. She clamped down on her tongue and nodded again.

Diane leaned back in her chair. Her lipstick was uneven, and Esther couldn't stop staring at it. "Perhaps once you've amassed more capital in terms of seniority and successful projects delivered, you'll be able to push everyone else harder, and they'll feel bound to keep up. But for now, you need to adjust your approach." Diane smiled at her. "Think of it as another engineering problem to solve."

"Do people not like me?" Esther asked. Because that's what it sounded like she was saying.

"I wouldn't say that at all. Some of them just find you a little...aggressive."

"Aggressive?" Esther repeated. She couldn't believe she'd just been called "aggressive" in a performance review. By a woman, no less. Was Angelica Sauer too aggressive? Wasn't that how she'd succeeded in business? By suffering no fools and taking no shit? Esther wondered what their CEO would do anyone who dared to complain she was too aggressive.

"Perhaps aggressive isn't the best word," Diane said, backtracking. "Let's just say you can be a little too blunt sometimes."

"You mean *honest*?"

Diane's smile tightened. "No one likes to be told they're wrong. If you're trying to win someone over to your point of view, it can be more helpful to take a diplomatic tack. Soften the blow a little."

Esther stared down at her hands, which were clenched in her lap. "I see," she said, choking back the urge to defend herself. To point out how sexist it was to criticize her for being too aggressive when she knew damn well a man would be praised and rewarded for the exact same behavior. But all that would do was prove Diane's point, that Esther was too *aggressive*.

"Esther, you're someone who has a lot to offer," Diane said kindly, "not just the company, but also your peers, as a mentor and example of what a good engineer looks like. If you can moderate your approach to your coworkers, I think you'll find they begin taking your advice more and coming to you for guidance, which is how you advance from baby engineer to senior engineer —maybe even an SME one day."

Maybe she'd get to be a subject matter expert? Her last manager had acted like it was a given. He'd told her to keep doing what she was doing and she would be able to choose her own path. Now Diane was making it sound like she needed to shape up and fly right or she wouldn't advance at all.

Esther ground her teeth, smiling and nodding her way through the rest of the conversation, trying to be pleasant and act like she was taking the feedback to heart. But she left Diane's office fuming.

Aggressive. She'd actually had the nerve to call Esther aggressive. Would a man ever be called aggressive? No, because in men it was seen as a desirable trait. A man would be told he was assertive, that he'd displayed leadership skills. Only in a woman would it be considered a negative. Because women were expected to be meek and subservient. Passive. Agreeable.

Fuck that.

Fuck that and fuck Diane. And fuck everyone who'd told Diane that Esther was too blunt. She didn't need to soften her approach, they needed to do their damn jobs better. She refused to adapt to incompetence because some men might get their fee-fees hurt.

Fuck all of them. And fuck this place.

"How'd it go?" Yemi asked when Esther got back to her desk.

"Piece of cake," she told him, forcing a smile. She didn't want to talk about it. If she talked about it, she'd get even more angry than she already was.

She sat down in front of her computer, put her headphones on, and kept them on for the rest of the day.

ESTHER WAS STILL in a royally crappy mood when she got into her car to drive home at five o'clock. Then she remembered she had to go the grocery store, and her mood got even worse.

She hated grocery shopping, but she hated doing it after work worst of all. Everyone else in LA was at the grocery store after work too. Which meant the parking lot was a madhouse, the aisles were crowded with tired, cranky people, and the checkout lines were interminable. There were never enough checkers, and she always ended up trapped in the self-checkout lane behind the person who had to turn every single item over four times before they found the bar code, and then had to pass it over the scanner three times before it registered.

It was almost seven o'clock by the time Esther pulled into her parking space at home, still fuming about the inefficiency of the modern grocery store. She turned off the engine, shoved open her door, and almost had a heart attack when Jonathan popped up in front of the car.

"*Jesus.*" She laid her hand on her chest. "Are you stalking me now?"

"No, I was in the courtyard and I heard you pull in."

She slammed her car door and went around to the back to get her groceries. When she opened the hatchback, he leaned in and grabbed half her grocery bags for her.

"Thanks," Esther muttered as she locked the car.

He tipped his head, smiling. "I aim to serve."

As she followed him up the stairs, she noticed a roll of papers stuck into the back pocket of his jeans that looked suspiciously like script pages. That explained his sudden appearance. He'd been waiting in the courtyard for her to get home. The floor outside her door must have gotten uncomfortable.

He waited for her to unlock her apartment and followed her inside, setting his grocery bags on the counter next to hers.

"You know, you could just text me," she said as she jerked open the fridge. "To find out when I'm going to be home."

He grinned as he handed her a carton of milk. "Noted." He fished the cold stuff out of the bags and passed it to her to put in the fridge. She didn't love the fact that he was poking through her groceries, but she didn't quite hate it enough to turn down the help.

"Is that grocery store sushi?" His lip curled into a sneer as he held it out. "Please tell me that's for your cat, not you."

"I didn't feel like cooking tonight," she said, snatching it out of his hand.

"It's your funeral."

"Yeah, it is."

He frowned. "You okay?"

"I'm fine."

"You don't seem fine. You seem..."

She turned to glare at him. "What?"

His eyebrows lifted. "More annoyed than usual."

"I had my performance review at work today." She grabbed a handful of yogurt cups and shoved them in the fridge.

"Ah," he said. "Didn't go well?"

She glared at him again. "I'm fucking great at my job, okay? I'm the best design engineer on that team."

He nodded. "Is that what your boss said in your review?"

"Yes, actually. But she also said I didn't play well with others. She called me aggressive. Can you believe it?"

He tilted his head. "Wellllll..."

Esther's eyes narrowed dangerously. "What?"

"You can be a little...prickly."

"*Prickly?*"

"Judgmental?"

"It's called having high standards."

He held his hands up in surrender. "Okay."

She unpacked the rest of her yogurt and stacked it in the fridge. They'd been out of her favorite flavor, so she'd had to settle for fucking blueberry. It was just one more way this day had disappointed her.

She heard Jonathan shuffle his feet behind her. "It's just—"

Esther slammed the fridge and wheeled on him. *"What?"*

He flinched. "Nothing."

"No, come on, you were going to say something. I want to hear it." She probably didn't, but she couldn't let it go now.

"Fine," he said shrugging. "When you first started helping me with my writing, you came off a little..."

"What?" she prompted when he hesitated.

"Mean?"

She folded her arms across her chest. "Is that so?"

His eyebrows lifted again. "Yeah. Nothing at all like the warm, cuddly teddy bear you're being right now."

"You said you wanted honest feedback."

"I did, it's just—there's honest and then there's honest."

"I don't know what that means."

Sally wandered over to Jonathan and started winding between his legs, purring. *Traitor.*

"You were pretty blunt about it that first time," he said, "and I didn't exactly take it well, if you'll remember."

Blunt. That was exactly what Diane had said. She was too blunt. That's why people didn't like her, apparently.

"Don't get me wrong," Jonathan said, "I needed to hear it, and I'm grateful you said what you said. But it wasn't exactly pleasant." He reached down to scratch Sally on the head, and she purred even louder. "The second time, you were more diplomatic about it though. Kinder, I guess. You said nice stuff to cushion the blow before you delivered the bad news. In my writing group we call it a feedback sandwich."

That was what Diane had done to her, Esther realized. She'd started out the review by complimenting her before she dropped the hammer. She'd ended on a positive note too, like a consolation prize. A feedback sandwich.

"Did you want to show me something?" Esther asked irritably. She didn't want to talk about this anymore, especially not with Jonathan. She didn't even want to *think* about it anymore.

He looked up from petting her cat. "What?"

"Your script?" He'd rolled the pages up into a tube, and was clutching them in the hand that wasn't petting Sally. "I assume that's why you were lurking around my parking space."

He straightened, tapping the roll of papers against his palm. "I wasn't lurking, I was having a smoke in the courtyard and heard your car pull in."

"While carrying around script pages?"

He shrugged.

She held out her hand. "Lemme see."

He shoved the rolled-up pages behind his back. "Don't worry about it."

"Come on." She wiggled her fingers impatiently.

He shook his head, backing toward the door. "Nope. It can wait until you're in a better mood. I don't want you taking your bad performance review out on my writing."

"Chickenshit."

His mouth curved into a lopsided smile. "You know it."

"Fine," Esther said. "Come back tomorrow, then."

He pulled the door open, pausing on the threshold. "I'll bring pizza to properly butter you up. What kind do you like?"

"Hawaiian," she said, just to be contrary, because most people hated Hawaiian pizza.

He grinned, unfazed. "You got it."

When he was gone, Sally came over and bonked her head against Esther's leg. Esther scooped her up and buried her face in the cat's fuzzy mane. "You don't think I'm mean, do you?"

She took Sally's purr as confirmation of the affirmative.

Chapter Thirteen

The first Friday of the month was goulash day at the Sauer Hewson cafeteria.

Esther always made a point to bring her lunch every first Friday of the month. Beyond the special of the day, the other choices on the menu were pretty dire: a selection of sad, soggy, plastic-wrapped sandwiches that had been sitting around for god only knew how many days, and a pitiful salad bar with wilted lettuce and no sneeze guard. Someone had once found a dead garter snake in the salad bar, so Esther would rather starve than eat anything out of it.

She'd forgotten she needed to pack her lunch until the last minute this morning though, so all she had was a hastily prepared peanut butter and jelly sandwich. It was a pretty sad lunch, but it was still better than the cafeteria's goulash. She'd console herself later with some Oreos from the vending machine.

Yemi sat down in the chair across from her and sighed at the steaming pile of goulash on his tray. "I forgot my lunch today," he said glumly. "I have to eat the goulash."

It looked like someone had eaten dog food and vomited it onto a plate. It smelled kind of like it too.

"Here, have half my sandwich," Esther said, pushing the other half of her peanut butter and jelly toward him.

He reached for it gratefully. "You're very kind. You're welcome to have half my goulash if you want."

"Pass," Esther said. "But thanks."

"I'll bring you some of my mother's yam pottage on Monday."

"What's that?"

"It's a stew made with yams, tomatoes, dried fish, and ground crayfish."

Esther wrinkled her nose. "No disrespect to your mother's cooking, but that sounds terrible."

Yemi shrugged. "You don't have to eat it if you don't like it. But you'll like it."

She nodded, frowning at her peanut butter and jelly sandwich. "Do you think I'm too honest?"

"No. I like that you're honest."

"Thank you." At least someone she worked with liked her.

"You're welcome," he said. "I'm probably the wrong person to ask though. People complain I'm too honest all the time."

Esther wondered if Yemi had ever been told he was too aggressive in a performance review. Probably not. He was so soft-spoken and polite, it was hard to imagine him being described as aggressive, even when he was being blunt. Also, he was a man, so he had that going for him. Although, he was a black man, which added a whole other layer to the issue. Maybe that was *why* Yemi was so polite and soft-spoken. So he wouldn't be seen as aggressive or threatening.

"It smells like a squirrel crawled up someone's ass and died in here," Jinny said, sitting down next to Esther. She'd brought her lunch today too: some kind of healthy-looking quinoa salad.

"Yemi forgot his lunch," Esther said.

"Here, you can have some of my salad." Jinny pushed the Tupperware into the middle of the table. "I've got orange slices too." She set out a Ziploc bag of orange segments.

Yemi helped himself to an orange slice, but didn't make a move on the quinoa salad. "Thank you."

"Do you think I'm too honest?" Esther asked Jinny.

"I'm gonna need more context," Jinny said, taking back her quinoa salad.

"At work. Am I overly blunt and aggressive?"

Jinny frowned. "Is this about your review?"

Esther nodded.

Jinny's eyebrows lifted. "She actually used the word aggressive?"

"I know, right? She might as well have said abrasive."

"And we all know what that means." Jinny shook her head as she stabbed at her salad. "Sexism blows."

"You told me your review went fine," Yemi said.

"It did," Esther said, avoiding his eyes. "Except for the part where apparently I'm aggressive and no one like me."

"Don't be stupid," Jinny said. "Everyone likes you." She looked to Yemi for confirmation. "Right?"

"I like you," he told Esther. "Otherwise I wouldn't eat lunch with you so often."

"See? People like you," Jinny said. "Don't let one mediocre review get under your skin."

Esther nodded as she reached for her iced tea. "It's just... someone else recently told me I can be mean sometimes."

"Well..." Jinny tilted her head to one side. "That's not *entirely* inaccurate."

Esther stared at her. "Seriously?"

"You're only mean to people who deserve it."

"Great, thanks."

"You have a low tolerance for incompetence," Jinny said as she stirred her quinoa salad with her fork. It had cherry tomatoes and bell peppers and something else slimy and unidentifiable in it— squash, maybe. It looked almost as dire as the goulash. "But when it's someone you like, you're *extremely* patient and supportive. Like when you taught me how to knit."

"That's true, I guess," Esther said, feeling a little better.

"It's just when you're dealing with someone you don't like that you can maybe be a little brusque," Jinny added. "You're very binary about people. You either like them or you hate them. There's no in between with you."

Yeah, okay. Jinny might have a point. Esther had never been much of a people person. She liked her friends and was willing to do almost anything for them, but she didn't have an abundance of patience for everyone else in the world. Most people were an inconvenience she'd just as soon not have to deal with. She supposed it was possible she let that show a little too much in her attitude at work.

She sighed as she helped herself to one of Jinny's orange slices. "Maybe Diane's right. Maybe I am too blunt sometimes."

"Look," Jinny said, "it was unfair and sexist of her to call you aggressive—"

"Yeah, it was," Esther grumbled.

"But I think I get what she was trying to say. Just because it's a double standard doesn't mean you don't still have to figure out how to navigate it. The world's an unfair place and sexism isn't going away anytime soon. She should have chosen a different word, but I think you should consider that she was trying to help you."

"So, what? I'm supposed to censor myself? Play along to get along?" The idea of sucking up to less competent male engineers to bolster their fragile egos left a bad taste in Esther's mouth. She looked over at Yemi. "You've been awfully quiet. What do you think?"

He looked up from his peanut butter sandwich, blinking like a possum caught in the headlights. "This situation is outside my experience. I don't feel qualified to have an opinion."

"Cop-out," Jinny said.

"Yeah," Esther said. "Come on, you have to weigh in on behalf of your gender."

He frowned and pushed his glasses up. "Speaking only for myself, I think it's possible for something to be two things at once. I think you can be angry that it's sexist, but also try to learn something from it that will help you advance in your career."

Leave it to Yemi to be pragmatic when Esther wanted to rage against the machine. She knew he was right though. You did have to play along to get along, even when it was unfair.

"Who called you mean, anyway?" Jinny asked, frowning.

"No one important," Esther said with a shrug. "It doesn't matter."

"Well, just say the word and I will happily kick the ass of anyone who says anything bad about you."

"You're going to kick my manager's ass?" Esther asked, quirking an eyebrow.

Jinny shrugged. "Maybe not kick her ass literally, but I'll totally key her car for you if you want."

"Let's put a pin in that for now," Esther said. "But thanks."

"Anytime," Jinny said, smiling.

JONATHAN SHOWED up at Esther's apartment with Hawaiian pizza that night, just as promised. He even texted her first, to ask when he should come over, instead of camping outside her door or ambushing her by her car. Progress.

"It's too early in the summer to be this hot," Esther complained, switching on the fan in her living room while Jonathan set the pizza box on the coffee table. She'd opened all the windows as soon as she got home, but it hadn't helped much. "I passed this cyclist on my way home today and I was like, 'Dude, it's hotter than the surface of the sun out here, what are you doing? How are your tires not melting into the asphalt?'"

Jonathan dished a slice of pizza onto a plate and passed it to

Esther. "The wasps have started swarming around the palms in the courtyard already. They nearly got me when I came home from class today."

That was the one downside of the courtyard—in July the trees filled up with wasps, and every time you walked past them, you risked reenacting that scene in *My Girl* where Macaulay Culkin gets murdered by bees.

"Well, of course," Esther said, sinking down onto the couch. "Ninety fuckillion degrees is the devil's perfect temperature."

Jonathan pulled a battered Moleskine notebook out of his back pocket, grabbed the pen tucked behind his ear, and started scribbling.

"What are you doing?" she asked, frowning at him around a bite of pizza.

"I'm writing down what you just said."

"Why?"

"Because it's funny. I might use it in a script."

"Don't do that."

He shut the notebook with a snap. "Too late."

"I hate that."

He grinned wide enough to show off his teeth. "Too bad."

He never used to smile this much. She'd thought he was so arrogant and humorless before she got to know him. He was always walking around with his nose in the air, scowling at everyone. She'd hated his mouth and that smug expression it always had. She never knew it could look this playful and warm.

Esther wasn't sure when her feelings had changed, but he didn't annoy her at all anymore. Jonathan Brinkerhoff wasn't so bad, as it turned out. You just had to get to know him to figure that out.

She shook her head at him, smiling as she rolled her eyes. "What did you want to show me?"

"It's an outline." He pulled a battered roll of papers out of his back pocket. "I've been reworking the sci-fi script. I want to know what you think before I actually start writing it."

"Give it here." She waved her hand at him. "I'll read it while I eat."

He handed it to her, then turned his back and bent down for a piece of pizza, gracing her with an eyeful of his backside. His Levi's were just the right amount of tight in all the right places and—what was she doing? *Stop staring at his butt.*

Esther looked down at the papers in her hand. It was about five pages of notes. She scanned the first page while Jonathan settled onto the other end of the couch. "This is totally different," she said, looking up at him after a moment.

"I was thinking over what you said about genre-hopping, so I decided to ditch the action-disaster movie stuff at the beginning and make it a more deliberate crossover between two genres I actually like to watch: hard sci-fi and horror."

"You wrote a horror movie set in space?"

"Well, I haven't written it yet, but that's the idea. What do you think?"

"I love it." Those were Esther's two favorite genres of movies. She watched horror movie marathons whenever she needed cheering up. Nothing pulled her out of a funk like twenty-four straight hours of *Friday the 13th* movies, or the entire *Evil Dead* series.

Jonathan's face split into a grin. "Yeah?"

"Are you kidding? I *love* horror movies, and obviously I love space movies. It's a perfect mashup, because space is already so scary, what with the no-air thing and the claustrophobia—"

"And the existential dread of a cold, dark vacuum stretching out to infinity," Jonathan added.

"Not to mention the high potential for catastrophic failure."

"Exactly," he said, looking pleased with himself.

"Plus, there haven't been all that many good ones—the *Alien* movies, obviously, being the exception."

"And *Moon*."

"Oh, yeah, *Moon* was great!"

"There've been a couple set on Mars—"

"Both of them awful," she pointed out.

"And *Apollo 18*—"

"Don't even talk to me about that movie. It made me so mad." There were enough loony conspiracy theories out there about the Apollo program. The last thing anyone needed was some crap horror movie fueling the fire. "Have you seen *Europa Report* though?"

Jonathan shook his head.

"That one was pretty good. Documentary-style alternative history. You should check it out."

He shoved his pizza between his teeth, pulled out his note-book, and made a note. When he was done, he pulled the pizza out of his mouth. "There was *Event Horizon* too."

Esther's nose wrinkled. "A truly, truly terrible film. I will not allow you to commit such a travesty."

He grinned at her. "See, this is exactly why I need you."

She felt her cheeks warm and looked back down at the pages in her lap. "All right, shut up and let me read the rest of this."

It was actually good. At least, it had the *potential* to be good. He'd chucked most of the plot from the other script. A lot of the main characters were more or less the same, but the structure of the story was totally different. The whole film took place in space now, with no scenes on earth. And it was set in a near-future world, so the technology was slightly advanced.

"You know what it reminds me of?" Esther said when she'd finished reading it. "That *Firefly* episode—"

"'Bushwhacked'?" he said around a mouthful of pizza.

"Yes! The one about the Reavers! So great!"

"That's exactly what I was going for." He swallowed, wiping his mouth with the back of his hand. "I mean, that was kind of what I was going for before, but now instead of switching genres midstream, I'm establishing it right up front. At least, that's the idea. We'll see how I do with the execution." His blue eyes twinkled behind his glasses. He was so excited, he was smiling with his whole face, from the bottom of his beanie to his bearded chin.

Esther couldn't help smiling back at him. "Jonathan Brinkerhoff, I think there may just be hope for you yet."

Chapter Fourteen

"Talk to me about explosions in space," Jonathan said as he strode into Esther's apartment a few weeks later.

"What about them?" Esther asked, closing the door.

He'd been coming over two or three times a week to ask her science questions or show her the latest pages of his script. Or sometimes for no reason at all. Weirdly, she didn't mind having him around so much. She'd even started to enjoy it.

After two years of having only a passing acquaintance with her neighbors, it was nice to be friends with one of them. To have someone to hang out with who was living right next door. Someone she could see without making plans in advance or having to fight LA traffic. It was like living in a sitcom—she was Monica with the nicer apartment, and he was Chandler, dropping by all the time just because.

Esther never knew when Jonathan was going to turn up. Sometimes he'd text in advance to ask if she was going to be around, but sometimes he'd drop by with no warning. Because he was bored, she supposed—or lonely, maybe. When he wasn't in class, he spent most of his time alone, writing. It seemed to leave him craving human company some days.

Instead of being annoyed by his unexpected visits, Esther had begun to look forward to them. They broke up the monotony of her routine—and okay, maybe she was a little lonely too. She liked having someone she could talk about her day with when she got home from work. It was better than spending every night alone with her cat.

Jonathan went straight to her fridge and helped himself to a beer. She didn't mind that either, because they were beers he'd brought over last week. He was always bringing her things: takeout, beer, coffee, even ice cream one time.

"Would you be able to hear an explosion in space?" he asked as he dug her bottle opener out of the drawer by the fridge.

"Depends."

"On what?"

She sat down at her usual end of the couch. "If you were in a vacuum yourself. Sound is a pressure wave that requires matter to propagate."

"Matter like the atmosphere in a pressurized spaceship?" He flopped down beside her with his beer.

"Exactly," Esther said. "But it wouldn't sound like a regular explosion. If you were close enough, you'd hear the expanding cloud of gases slamming against the vehicle, which could be pretty violent. Farther away, you might just hear projectiles and debris from the explosion colliding with the hull. Which again, could be highly dangerous, because with no gravity or air drag to slow them down, they'd travel outward virtually forever, with the same kinetic energy they had right next to the blast."

"Yikes, okay."

"That answer your question?"

"Yep." He nodded and took a swig of beer. He'd brought his laptop, but he hadn't gotten it out, and he didn't bother writing down what she'd told him.

"You wanna watch a movie tonight?" Esther asked. "We could watch *Europa Report*."

Jonathan swiveled his head in her direction, eyebrows arching. "It's nine o'clock. I don't want to keep you up past your bedtime." Usually, she shooed him out of her apartment by ten on weeknights. He kept a student's hours, which meant staying up later and sleeping in later than she had the luxury of doing with her office job.

She shrugged. "I made the mistake of stopping for Starbucks on the way home tonight and they put an extra shot in my iced coffee. I'm pretty sure I can see through the fabric of time, so there's no way I'm getting to sleep at a decent hour tonight."

He grinned at her. "Yeah, okay."

She leaned forward to grab the TV remote out of the basket on the coffee table. "That reminds me, there was a woman at Starbucks who looked like Lady Gaga. But she was wearing pajama jeans, so I'm pretty sure it wasn't her."

"I passed a guy on campus yesterday who looked like Channing Tatum."

"Was it Channing Tatum?" Esther asked as she navigated through the Netflix menus.

"No. But I followed him for like five minutes before I figured that out."

She shot him a glance, quirking an eyebrow. "You followed some random strange dude around campus for five minutes?"

Jonathan shrugged and stretched his arm out along the back of the couch. "Look, I'm pretty squarely on the hetero end of the Kinsey scale, but Channing Tatum is my Get Out of Straight Free card. I had to know if it was him."

Her mouth curved into a smirk. "Channing Tatum? Seriously?"

"What's wrong with Channing Tatum?"

"Nothing. He just never struck me as a universal sexual donor." She went back to typing the movie title into the search bar. "Now if it was Idris Elba..."

"I've got nothing against Idris Elba, but Channing's more my speed."

"What is it about him, exactly, that appeals to you?"

"I don't know. He seems like he would be a gentle, caring lover. Like, he'd tell you what a great job you were doing, and then put in some quality spooning time afterward."

Esther snorted. "See? I knew you could be funny."

"I'm writing that down," Jonathan said, pulling his Moleskine out of his pocket.

"The spooning thing or that I said you were funny?"

He smiled at the page as he scribbled on it. "Both."

He'd let her look inside his notebook once. It was filled with doodles, random words and phrases that appealed to him, and snippets of half-formed ideas for his scripts. He never went anywhere without it and one of his favorite pens. He had strong opinions about pens, she'd learned, and never used anything but black Pilot G2 Ultra Fines. His fingers and his face were usually dotted and smudged with black ink stains. There was a smudge on his face right now, on his cheekbone, just below his glasses.

Esther waited for him to put his notebook down before starting the movie. It had been a few years since she'd seen this one, and she worried it wouldn't hold up—or that he wouldn't like it as much as she did.

A few minutes into the movie, Jonathan shifted on the couch, pulling his feet up and stretching his long legs out beside her. He'd walked the few feet between their apartments barefoot, and his toes were propped against her thigh. When she looked over at him, he grinned like he was daring her to object.

Esther shook her head and turned back to the TV screen. Jonathan's toes stayed where they were for the next hour.

The movie held up pretty well, but Esther was yawning by the time it was over.

Jonathan sat up when the credits started to roll, stretching his arms overhead. "That was good."

"Yeah, I like that one," she said, pleased he'd enjoyed it too. She covered her mouth as another yawn slipped out.

Taking a cue, he heaved himself off the couch and grabbed his laptop. "We should do that again."

"Sure."

"How about Saturday?" he proposed, backing toward the door. "I'll even let you pick the movie again."

"Um…" Watching a movie on a Saturday sounded like a vaguely date-ish activity. So far they'd confined almost all their hanging out to Sundays and weeknights. But she didn't have any plans for Saturday, so why not? "Yeah, okay. How do you feel about zombie movies?"

He pulled the door open and gave her a lopsided grin. "I *love* zombie movies."

"Is that the biggest sock I've ever seen or are you knitting a *hat?*" Olivia asked when Esther got out her knitting Monday night.

Vilma looked up from her needles. "Someone go outside and make sure the sky isn't boiling. If Esther's knitting something other than socks, it must surely be the End Times."

"Hilarious," Esther said as she spaced her stitches out along her circular needles.

"What's the occasion?" Cynthia asked, lifting an eyebrow.

"No occasion," Esther said. "Just stash busting. I had this skein hanging around, and it's too thick for socks, so I figured I'd use it up on a hat."

"Who's it for?" Jinny asked. "You never wear hats."

Esther didn't like wearing hats with her heavy bangs. She either had to pin them back, or they got all smushed against her forehead and it looked weird.

"Is it for a boy?" Penny leaned forward for a better look. "It looks like a man's hat."

"It could just as easily be a woman's hat," Olivia said with a disapproving frown. "It doesn't have to be gendered."

"I'll probably just give it to my brother," Esther lied.

She was thinking of giving it to Jonathan. Might as well give the thing to someone who would get some use out of it, and the guy wore knit hats almost every day. Besides, this gunmetal gray yarn would look nice with his blue eyes—not that she'd been thinking about his eyes or anything.

She didn't want to say who it was really for though. Jinny thought she still hated Jonathan. She didn't know how much they'd been hanging out—or that they'd been hanging out at all.

He'd come over Saturday night to watch *28 Days Later*, and wound up staying until one a.m. so they could watch the sequel too. When Jinny came over the next morning, Esther had cleaned up all evidence of his presence. Which felt a little underhanded. She didn't like lying to Jinny, even by omission. It was just that she felt weird about being friends with someone Jinny had dated. The fact that Esther had started hanging out with him right around the same time he'd asked Jinny out didn't help either. Not to mention the fact that he'd asked Jinny out at Esther's urging. It was all a big mess, basically.

She wasn't planning to keep it from Jinny forever. She'd tell her eventually. Just…after some time had passed. When it wouldn't seem so weird anymore.

"I feel like my world's been thrown out of kilter," Cynthia said, shaking her head. "Esther knitting socks on Mondays was the one constant in my life."

"I know, right?" Olivia said.

Jinny turned to Esther and waggled her eyebrows. "Next thing you know, she'll turn up with a steady boyfriend."

"Ha ha," Esther said, keeping her eyes fixed on her knitting.

Chapter Fifteen

---

*I*t was Saturday, and Jonathan was parked on Esther's couch with his laptop again. He liked to work at her place, he said, because he could ask her questions on the fly. Also something about the change of scenery bringing out his muse. Whatever.

Esther was making chili for the two of them tonight. She didn't do much in the way of cooking, but she made a mean pot of chili.

She could hear Jonathan tapping away on his laptop in the next room, his fingers flying over the keys like Mozart at his piano. The sound was oddly soothing, like having a tennis match on the TV in the background. Esther's dad had watched a lot of tennis when she was little, and the sound of televised tennis always reminded her of lazy weekend afternoons when her dad was still living at home. When her family had still felt like a family.

The typing stopped, and she peered through the pass-through into the living room. Jonathan frowned at his screen, shoulders hunched, chewing on his bottom lip. He was working on his sci-fi script still, but he was close to being done. He'd showed her bits and pieces along the way. There were only a couple more scenes left, and then he'd let her read it all the way through.

As if he could feel her watching him, he looked up from his computer and broke into a smile as his eyes found hers.

"Whatever happened to your other screenplay?" Esther asked, turning back to the stove to dump a can of diced tomatoes into the pot. "The love story. You haven't mentioned it in a while."

"I'm still working on it."

She poured a bottle of beer into the chili and stirred it together with the tomatoes, meat, and onions. "Are you going to let me read it?"

"When it's done."

She glanced back at him. "Not before?"

He looked down at his computer, shaking his head. "Nope."

"Why not?"

He gave a one-shouldered shrug without looking at her. "It's not ready to share yet. I don't want you to see version 2.0 before it's fully taken shape."

"Whatever, Picasso." She opened the spice cabinet and got out the paprika, cumin, and cayenne.

"I'm focusing on this one first, since it's the one I need your help with the most." When she snuck a look over her shoulder at him, he was drumming his fingers on the side of his leg. He levered himself off the couch, patting the pocket where he kept his cigarettes and lighter. "I'll be right back."

She made a face. "I hate that you smoke."

He halted his pilgrimage to the balcony, tilting his head to peer at her through the pass-through. "You do?"

"It stinks."

"I always go outside."

"It blows in through the windows. And you smell like an ashtray." She wrinkled her nose. "I can smell it on you right now."

"You can?" He sniffed his shirt.

"Yes."

He went back to the couch and sat down. "Then I won't smoke anymore."

"You're going to quit smoking? Just like that?"

"Just like that." He shrugged. "Who wants to smell like an ashtray?"

Esther's phone rang. It was on the coffee table by Jonathan, and he leaned over to read the screen. "It's your mom."

"Ignore it," she said, turning back to the chili.

"Letting your mom go to voicemail. Cold."

"You don't know my mom. I'll deal with it later."

Her mother only called when she had a problem she wanted Esther to fix for her. Which would be fine, except her mother had a lot of problems, mostly of her own making. Esther had forcibly distanced herself from her mother's constant drama for the sake of her own mental health. It was why she'd left Seattle after college and taken a job out of state.

Whatever her mom was calling about, it was better to wait and talk to her after she'd cooled off a little.

Esther went back to measuring out spices for the chili, and Jonathan went back to working on his script.

A few minutes later, Esther's phone rang again.

"It's someone named Eric this time," Jonathan said, lifting one eyebrow.

"Shit." Esther put down the cumin and went into the living room. She grabbed the phone off the table. "Hey bro, what's up?"

"Don't give Mom any more money this month," her brother said.

Esther sent her mother five hundred dollars out of her paycheck every month. That, combined with whatever her mother made temping part time and selling essential oils and wellness products through one of those multilevel marketing schemes, was all she had to live off. In other words, not much.

"Why?" Esther asked.

"Did she already ask you for it?"

"She tried to call a few minutes ago, but I haven't listened to the voicemail yet."

"She's going to ask for more money. Don't give it to her."

"What happened?"

Jonathan looked up and gestured at the door, offering to leave. Esther waved for him to stay and wandered into the kitchen.

"The usual," Eric said. "This time it was Fiestaware on eBay."

Their mom was a shopping addict. Nothing as extreme as the people on *My Strange Addiction*, but she did have a tendency to impulse buy more than her monthly budget allowed. She'd grown up with money and married money, but two divorces later, she was living on a limited budget without the skills to cope. She kept trying to live like she was still married to a successful orthodontist, even though that hadn't been her life for fifteen years.

"How bad is it?" Esther asked, stirring the cumin into the chili.

"Two hundred dollars and change."

"Fuck."

"She's gonna tell you she needs the money for utilities or groceries or something. But it's really for the Fiestaware."

"Okay, but *can* she pay her utilities? We can't just let her starve or whatever."

"She's not going to starve. What she's gonna have to do is return the fucking plates. Don't give in to her sob story, sis. It just enables her."

Eric was Esther's older brother. He and his wife, Heather, lived in Seattle with their two-year-old son, Gabriel. Eric sold medical equipment to hospitals and doctors' offices, and Heather was a preschool teacher. They couldn't afford to support Esther's mother on top of all their own bills, but Eric made up for it by taking point on all her crises. It was part of the bargain Esther and Eric had made: he provided physical and emotional support to their mother locally, and Esther provided financial support long distance.

"Fine," Esther said. She peeked into the living room at Jonathan. He was typing on his laptop, politely pretending not to listen.

"It's the right thing to do," Eric said.

"I know." She *hated* having to say no to her mother. She hated even more that her mother was constantly putting her in the position of *having* to say no. "How's my nephew?" she asked, changing the subject.

"Mouthy, like his aunt."

Esther smiled. "Good."

"I gotta go get his dinner ready. Mom's gonna be fine. Don't give in."

"Okay. Give Gabe a kiss for me."

"Will do."

Esther ended the call and deleted the voicemail from her mom unheard. She'd call her back tomorrow, after she'd properly girded herself for it. Something like this came up every few weeks. It was practically the only conversation she ever had with her mother.

"Sorry, that was my brother," she said, going back into the living room.

Jonathan looked up. "I gathered. Everything okay?"

She flopped onto the couch next to him. "No worse than usual."

"Want to talk about it?"

"Nope."

His eyes traveled over her face, like he was evaluating her for signs of damage. "Okay," he said after a moment, and turned back to his computer.

"It's my mom," Esther said. Maybe she wanted to talk after all. "She's not very good at being a grown-up sometimes."

Jonathan set his laptop aside and turned toward her, resting his elbow on the back of the couch. "You and your brother look out for her?"

"Mostly Eric does. He lives near her in Seattle. I just send money. I've got the easy job."

"Doesn't sound easy to me."

Esther looked down at her lap and shrugged. "Mom's okay. She's just not very responsible with her money."

"What about your dad?"

"Divorced. Remarried." *Disinterested. Emotionally unavailable.* He'd paid for Eric and Esther to go to college, but after that he'd considered his obligation to them discharged. They only saw him once a year now, on the day after Christmas. They didn't even rate time on the actual holiday.

Jonathan's forehead had furrowed in concern. She wanted to reach up and smooth away the crease between his eyes. "Are your parents still together?" she asked him.

He snorted. "Sure, if by together you mean sleeping in separate bedrooms and barely speaking. They both work crazy hours— Mom's a surgeon and Dad's a partner in a law firm—so they hardly ever see each other. It's more like a business arrangement than a marriage."

"Are you an only child?"

"No, I'm the baby." He shifted on the couch, propping his feet up on the coffee table, and slouched down next to her. "I've got two older sisters, both of them type A's like my parents. One's an investment banker and the other's in med school at Stanford." His mouth twisted. "I come from a whole family of overachievers."

"And you're the sensitive artist?"

He rubbed his thumb over his palm, staring down at his hands. They were sitting close enough that their shoulders were touching. "Or the prodigal disappointment, if you're my parents."

"They don't think that," Esther said, enjoying the warmth seeping into her arm from his.

"Yeah, they do. They tell me all the time. My dad literally used those words once."

She'd never seen Jonathan's face look so hard before. Esther's parents might have their issues, but they'd never said anything actively hurtful to her like that. "I'm sorry," she said. "That sucks. At least they're supporting you through school though."

"Only grudgingly. They'll probably be relieved if I get kicked out of the program. Once they get over the embarrassment of having a failure for a son."

"Hey." She bumped his leg with her knee. "You're not a failure, and you're not going to get kicked out."

He nodded without meeting her eye.

"If your professor doesn't give you an A after all this work you've put into these scripts, I'll go down there and kick her ass myself."

He bumped her leg back and smiled. "Thanks."

"What are you going to do after you finish your degree though? I mean, screenwriting's not exactly the kind of job you can just walk right into."

His shoulders dipped. "I'll get a job and write in my spare time until I sell a script."

"Have you ever had a job?"

He shot a defensive sideways look her way. "I have a job *now*. I'm a TA for one of the professors in the department."

"Okay, but you can't keep doing that after you graduate next year."

"No, but I might be able to get an adjunct teaching position. There's a lot of competition for those though. I might try background work—you know, being one of the extras walking around in the background on movies and television shows. If you get a regular spot on a TV show, it's pretty steady work."

"Really?" She'd never thought about it before. She'd just assumed all those people were actors too. Or wannabe actors.

"Yeah, I've got a buddy who does it on a cop show. He might

be able to get me in. And if not, there's always temping. I'll figure something out."

"Okay."

He looked over at her, and the crease between his eyes made a reappearance. She used to hate that crease, but she couldn't remember why anymore. Now she found it endearing. It was his worry crease. The one he got when he was feeling sad or anxious. It made her want to gather him up and hug him until it went away.

"I can support myself," he said. "I've had jobs before, you know."

"Like?" She couldn't picture him working for a living or doing anything other than writing. In her imagination, he was forever hunched over his laptop. As far as she was concerned, he'd been hunched over a laptop since the day he was born and would be until the day he died—most likely from a caffeine overdose.

"I worked at a Trader Joe's for a while—that's a pretty good gig. I could go back to that. I was a barista briefly—wasn't so good at that."

Esther tried to imagine him restocking organic produce or whipping up Unicorn Frappuccinos. It was like picturing a cat fetching a Frisbee.

"And then there was one particularly excruciating summer I spent grading standardized tests."

"That doesn't sound so bad." It was easier to picture him doing something like that than working a retail service job. Grading was part of what he did as TA in grad school.

He snorted. "That's what I thought, until I started the job. We worked out of an old supermarket that had gone out of business, filled with rows of tables and cheap laptops. They made us sit on folding chairs and work in complete silence all day. No talking to the people around you, no headphones, no nothing. You even had to ask permission to use the bathroom. I spent eight hours a day, every day, reading high school essays about conservation and trying not to lose consciousness. I lasted six whole weeks before quitting, and spent my last day on the job giving every test I graded a perfect score."

"You didn't," Esther said, grinning.

He nodded, smiling a little. "I did."

"Nice. Way to fight the system."

He laughed. "Yeah." His knee fell against hers again, heavy and warm. "Is everything going to be okay with your mom?"

"Yeah, we'll figure it out. We always do." One way or another—usually after a lot of stress and anxiety on Esther's part. She sighed and let her head fall onto Jonathan's shoulder. His body radiated a reassuring warmth that made her want to snuggle into him.

Esther didn't get a lot of physical human contact outside of her occasional sexual hookups. She wasn't much of a hugger or a toucher with her friends. But it was surprisingly easy being close to Jonathan. Comfortable.

More comfortable than it should be. Guilt twinged in the pit of her stomach, and she lifted her head off his shoulder. He was Jinny's Jonathan, not hers. Esther had seen to that by fixing them up. It didn't matter that Jinny didn't want him anymore, he was still off-limits. You don't date your BFF's ex. It was one of the cardinal rules of friendship. Inviolable.

She should move. She shouldn't be sitting this close to him.

The thing was, though...she didn't want to.

One of his hands was resting on his thigh, and she imagined taking it in hers, interlacing her fingers with his. She wanted to know what his skin felt like. If it was rough or soft. If his hands were as warm as the rest of him.

"Let's watch something fun tonight," he said. "No horror movies."

"Horror movies are fun." She was still staring at his hand. She couldn't take her eyes off it. He had beautiful hands under all the ink stains. Long, slender fingers and neatly trimmed nails with matching half-moons at each cuticle. He could be a hand model. The things he could probably do to a woman with fingers like that...

He nudged her shoulder with his. "I need a laugh tonight. And so do you."

"*Cabin in the Woods?*" she suggested, tearing her eyes away from his hands.

"I meant a comedy."

"That's a comedy."

"Satire isn't the same thing as comedy. And the ending is a total downer."

"Fine, what do you want to watch?"

"*Raising Arizona?*"

"Okay." She didn't care what they watched, as long as they did it together. She would have agreed to watch *The Three Stooges* if that was what it took to keep him there.

He leaned across her for the remote. As his body pressed against hers, she closed her eyes and breathed him in. The cigarette smell didn't bother her as much as it should. For the first time in her life, she actually found it kind of sexy.

Uh oh.

"How long before the chili's ready?" he asked, turning on the TV and settling back into the couch. He was sitting even closer now, slouched down so that his elbow was resting on her thigh. Warmth from his body seeped into hers like warm butter.

"Another couple hours, probably." She'd forgotten about the chili. She couldn't even remember if she'd finished adding in all the spices. Probably. Hopefully. She certainly wasn't getting up to do it now.

"Tell me you've seen this before," he said as the movie started.

"Yeah, it's great." She'd seen it dozens of times. She could practically recite the whole thing from memory.

"It's my third-favorite Coen brothers film."

He obviously wanted her to ask what the first two were, so she did.

"*Blood Simple* and *Miller's Crossing*," he answered with a self-satisfied smirk.

When had his smugness become so adorable? *What is happening to me?* Had she completely lost her grip on her sanity?

Jonathan settled in to watch the movie, and Esther watched him watch the movie.

After a while, he tilted his head and rested it on her shoulder. "Is this okay?"

"Yeah, it's fine."

Her pulse pounded in her ears. She tried to ignore it and concentrate on the movie. His hair was tickling her neck, and all she could think about was how badly she wanted to run her fingers through it. How easy it would be to just reach up—

"Did you know Joel Coen was an assistant editor on *The Evil Dead?*" Jonathan asked.

"Oh yeah?" she said, trying to sound interested. Her entire consciousness was focused on the places where his body touched hers. There wasn't room for anything else.

"The push in on Florence Arizona in this scene was a direct homage."

"Cool." Her skin felt raw and hypersensitive, like a sunburn. Every little move he made, every place his body came into contact with hers, caused her nerve endings to shriek like a tornado klaxon. *Proximity alert! Proximity alert!*

She passed the entire movie that way. It was almost a relief when the credits rolled and Jonathan shifted away from her.

"That movie always makes me feel better," he said.

"Me too."

He stretched his arms overhead, causing his T-shirt to ride up. Esther glimpsed a tantalizing sliver of abdomen and a faint dark trail disappearing into the waistband of his jeans. "How about that chili?" he said.

She pushed herself to her feet. "Right. Chili. I better go check on it." It should be ready by now. She went into the kitchen to dish it up.

They ate out of bowls in front the TV while they argued about what movie to watch next. When they were finished eating, Jonathan carried their dishes to the sink and rinsed them. They wound up watching *What We Do in the Shadows*, which immediately led into a *Flight of the Conchords* marathon. She kept to her own end of the couch this time, maintaining a safe distance between them.

Two episodes into *Conchords*, Jonathan fell asleep. He was slumped down on the couch with his legs stretched out in front of him and his head lolling to one side.

Esther's eyes took a walking tour of his body as he slept, consuming every detail. The cords in his wrists. The tendons snaking up forearms that were as long as her shin. The smooth curve of his biceps. How would it feel to be wrapped up in those arms?

She usually preferred thick, muscular guys. Lumberjack types. She wasn't exactly petite herself, and she liked men who looked like they could carry her out of a burning building without throwing out their backs. But maybe she was changing her tune. Starting to appreciate the virtues of tall, lanky men.

Yeah, okay, she needed to stop this. Drooling over him while he slept, like a creepy creeper.

She reached over and nudged his shoulder. "Hey, Sleeping Beauty, wake up."

His eyes snapped open. "Hmmm?"

She smiled at his adorable sleepy-face. "You fell asleep."

"Oh." He sat up and stretched. When his T-shirt rode up this time, Esther made herself look away. "What time is it?"

"Almost midnight." Jinny was coming over tomorrow morning, and Esther would need to clean up before she got there. If there were too many beer bottles in the trash or dishes sitting out, she might ask who Esther had been entertaining.

"Better take myself off to bed before my chariot turns back into a pumpkin."

"That's Cinderella."

"Whatever." He got to his feet, shouldered the messenger bag containing his laptop, and extended a hand to Esther. "Walk me out?"

Against her better judgment, she let him pull her off the couch. He held on to her hand, tugging her along with him to the door. When they got there, he stopped and faced her. "Tonight was fun." He held fast to her hand, rubbing his thumb over her knuckles.

"Yeah. It was." What she saw in his eyes made her chest felt tight, like she couldn't get enough air.

A soft smile stole over his face. The way he was looking at her…it was like he wanted something but was afraid to ask. No, not something. Her. He was looking at her like he wanted *her*.

He leaned closer, and Esther tensed. Flinched, really. Oops.

He halted, his blue eyes locked on hers. Studying her. She couldn't seem to look away, even when she felt a flush creep up her throat and spread out over her face. His body loomed over hers, as close as they could be without actually touching. Breathing each other's air. His heat warming the surface of her skin like sunshine.

The silence stretched out between them. She felt like she should say something, but the power of speech had abandoned her.

His hand squeezed hers. Then he bent his head, twisting it to the side, and kissed her cheek. Her eyes fluttered closed as his lips lingered on her skin.

When he straightened, his eyes searched hers again. Evaluating her reaction.

She wondered what he was seeing. Her emotions were a messy, churning stew of relief, disappointment, hope, lust, guilt, and embarrassment. God only knew what that looked like on her face.

A crooked grin spread over his face. "I'll see you around," he said, and let himself out.

When Esther got into bed that night, her face was still tingling where his lips had touched her. If she closed her eyes, she could feel the rasp of his beard on her cheek. His breath hot and sultry on her skin.

Sleep was a long time coming.

Chapter Sixteen

Okay, so maybe Esther wanted to sleep with Jonathan. She was a grown woman, in charge of her own libido. Just because she wanted something didn't mean she was going to do it. It wasn't like he was irresistible.

Only, he kind of was. Every time she thought about his stupid cute face with his stupid kind eyes and stupid sexy mouth, her insides started to feel all soft and squishy, like she was full of marshmallows. Then she got distracted imagining what it would be like to kiss that mouth. And after that she started imagining doing *other* things to him—

Nope. Bad idea. *Such* a bad idea.

In addition to the Jinny of it all, he was a nice guy. Sweet, thoughtful, sensitive. He deserved someone as nice as he was. Someone who could actually care about him.

Esther didn't do nice, and she didn't do relationships. She was both unwilling and incapable. If they slept together, she'd only end up hurting him, which she did not want to do. She liked being friends with him. Throwing that away for one night of sex would be stupid. Even if it was very, *very* good sex—at least the way she imagined it.

Jonathan was off-limits. No matter how hot he was, Esther needed to keep her libido in check.

"Have you ever been measured for a bra?" Jinny asked. The heat wave had broken, so they were down at the pool for the first time in weeks.

"Why are you asking me that?" Esther peered down at her cleavage and frowned. "Is there something wrong with the bra I'm wearing?"

Jinny licked her thumb and flipped to the next page in her *People* magazine. "My sister says most women are walking around in an improperly fitted bra, and everyone should get professionally measured at a lingerie boutique. She went and did it last week and says her new bras are so comfortable they cleared her skin and watered her crops."

"Your sister doesn't have crops."

"I think we should do it. I'm going to make us an appointment."

One of the apartment doors slammed overhead and Esther tensed, but it was only stoner Brent.

This was the first time they'd hung out by the pool since Jinny had dumped Jonathan. Every time Esther heard a door, she was afraid it might be him. Jinny still had no idea that Esther and Jonathan were friends—because Esther was a coward who hadn't worked up the nerve to tell her—and she didn't want her finding out because of a chance encounter in the courtyard.

She should just come right out with it and tell her now. It didn't have to be a big deal. Except...Jinny would ask a bunch of questions. She'd want to know how it had started, and what had possessed Esther to start spending time with a guy she supposedly couldn't stand. Why she had agreed to help him with his script in the first place. And there wasn't a good explanation for that, unless she also told Jinny about the bargain she'd made with him and how she'd coerced him into asking her out. That was the part that was really bad. Because if Jinny found out—

"Hey, so lemme ask you something," Jinny said, tossing aside her magazine. "What do you think about Yemi?"

Esther leaned over to dig another beer out of the cooler she'd brought down. "I love Yemi. You know that."

"No, but...what do you think about him as, like, a *man*?"

"Yemi?" Esther swiveled to look at Jinny. "Wait, do you like Yemi? Like, *like* like him?"

Jinny's lips pursed and twisted to the side. "Maybe?"

"Since when?"

"I don't know. I never really thought about him like that until..." She trailed off, biting her lip.

"Until what?"

"Remember when I was trying on that new dress at work? And he said I looked beautiful?"

"Yeah." That was over two months ago. Had she been harboring a crush on Yemi all this time and was only just now getting around to saying something?

Jinny ducked her head, picking at the lavender polish on her thumbnail. "It was the way he looked at me. Like I was something rare and special. Like he was looking at the Hope Diamond or a new *Star Wars* movie."

Esther thought about the way Jonathan had looked at her before he'd left her apartment last night. It would be easy to get used to being looked at like that.

"And then the other day, he was wearing that pink shirt, remember?"

Esther didn't, but she nodded anyway, taking a swig of her beer. "Uh huh."

"And I thought to myself, 'That shirt looks really good on him.' And then I noticed he had muscles that you could see through the shirt, and I realized—Yemi's cute."

"He is," Esther agreed.

Jinny shook her head. "No, he's like *hot* cute. He's got this nerdy Chadwick Boseman thing going on that I never noticed before but…" She broke into a slow smile. "I think I like it."

Esther smacked her on the arm, grinning. "You like Yemi!"

"I don't know." A blush spread across Jinny's cheeks. "Maybe. Do you think he likes me?"

"I know he likes you, but I don't know if he likes you like *that*. He can be a little hard to read."

"Right? He's always so polite, it's hard to know what he really thinks of you."

"But he's also very forthright. He doesn't do pretense. If you ask him straight out, he'll give you an honest answer."

Jinny's mouth pulled into a frown. "You think he would have told me if he liked me?"

"Not necessarily. Not if he thought it might be impolite or inappropriate. Or unwelcome."

"Hmmm," Jinny said.

"Do you want me to ask him?"

"No!" Jinny shook her head violently. "Don't you dare."

"He'd probably appreciate the directness."

"My reproductive organs are not goods to be bartered via mediator. I'll manage my own love life, thank you very much."

Esther stared at the surface of the pool, wincing internally. If Jinny ever found out she'd been behind Jonathan asking her out, she would be super pissed. "Why don't you just ask Yemi out yourself?"

"I think he might be a little old-fashioned. He might not like it."

"I don't know. Sure, he goes to church with his parents every Sunday, but he's never struck me as chauvinistic or narrow-minded. He might be relieved you'd made the first move."

"Maybe." Jinny picked up her *People* magazine again.

Now that Esther thought about it, they'd make a great couple. They were both Catholic, both close to their families, and both ridiculously smart. Plus, Yemi was a good guy who seemed like he'd be a terrific boyfriend. Considerate, attentive, loyal. Much better stock than most of the men Jinny had dated. And the two of them seemed to get along really well.

Esther didn't push it though. She'd said what she had to say, and now the ball was in Jinny's court. Her matchmaking days were over. Even though she'd accomplished her goal of keeping Jinny and Stuart apart, it wasn't worth the guilt and secrecy.

Another door slammed overhead, and Esther saw Jonathan head for the stairwell.

Shit.

Maybe he'd walk around the outside of the building to his car without cutting through the courtyard. He must have seen that Jinny was out here with her. Hopefully he'd want to avoid an uncomfortable encounter.

"Hey," Jonathan said, striding toward them.

Shit.

Jinny looked up from her magazine and smiled warmly. "Hey!" Only someone who knew her as well as Esther did would be able to detect the edge under her cheerful exterior.

Esther nodded a greeting and took a swig of beer to disguise her discomfort.

Jonathan's eyes lingered on her for a moment before moving back to Jinny. "How've you been?" His keys were in his hand, and they jingled as he flipped them around his index finger.

"Good," Jinny said without letting her smile slip. "I'm good. How about you?"

Jonathan's eyes flicked over to Esther again, then back to Jinny. "I'm good. Great, actually." He flipped his keys again. Once. Twice. Three times. "Well, I've gotta…" He tilted his head toward his car, already backing away.

"Sure," Jinny said, still smiling at him.

"I'll see you," he said, looking at Esther again.

"Yep." She raised her bottle and took another drink.

"Bye!" Jinny called out. Her smile faded as soon as his back was turned. "Geez, that was mega awkward," she said when he was out of earshot.

"Yeah," Esther agreed and guzzled the rest of her beer.

THE FOLLOWING WEEK, Esther started paying more attention to Yemi at work.

She watched him closely every time Jinny came up in conversation, and even more closely whenever the three of them were together. After four straight days of observation and data collection, her results were still inclusive.

Yemi was too difficult to read. He was reserved, even-keeled, and unfailingly polite to everyone he talked to—even the people Esther knew for a fact he disliked. If he was secretly harboring an attraction to Jinny, she could detect no obvious signs of it.

At least her scrutiny of Yemi's behavior gave her something to think about other than Jonathan. She'd only seen him once since Saturday. On Wednesday night, he'd stopped by to show her a few more script pages. He hadn't stayed long, and there'd been no repeat of that weird moment from Saturday night, which was good. Hopefully they'd moved past it and Esther could forget it had ever happened.

Friends didn't have weird moments like that. And she wanted to be Jonathan's friend. She *liked* being his friend. She didn't want to screw that up.

On Friday morning, something else cropped up to distract Esther from lusting after Jonathan. "Hamburger Helper is at it again," Yemi told her when she got into work.

She groaned as she sank into her chair. "What did he do now?"

Hamburger Helper was their nickname for Dan, one of the design engineers on the payload team. Esther was on the power team, and Dan's components were forever getting in the way of hers. They called him Hamburger Helper because he always pretended he was being helpful, when really he was trying to get everyone to do things his way. Also, his face sort of looked like a hamburger: round and flat and slightly bumpy.

"Open your email. He stopped by already to make sure you saw it."

"Of course he did. I'll bet he sent it after work last night, to make himself look busier."

She started up her computer and clicked over to her email inbox. As she'd suspected, Dan had sent the email at seven thirty last night, and copied both team leads to make sure everyone knew he was working late. She groaned again as she scanned the text of the email. "Is he serious with this shit?"

"Isn't he always?" Yemi said.

It was a request for Esther to make modifications to one of her components in order to accommodate his. Which would be fine, except her power converter had been on the live model for a few weeks already, and this was the first he was bringing it up. Because he hadn't bothered to tell everyone before now that his antenna pointing mechanism conflicted with the placement of her part.

"No way," Esther muttered. "No fucking way."

She got up and walked over to her team lead's desk. "Hey, Bhavin, did you happen to see this email from Dan?" She tried to keep her voice mild and even-toned. *Don't be too aggressive,* she reminded herself bitterly.

Bhavin was a small-framed Indian man who wore a lot of hair product and owned a different pair of Air Jordans for every day of the week. Today's were navy blue with bright yellow trim. He nodded distractedly without looking up from the spreadsheet on his computer screen. "Yeah. You can do it, right? I already told Dmitri you could."

"I can," Esther said to the back of Bhavin's coiffed head. "But I shouldn't have to. He's the one who failed to check the model before diving into a design."

Bhavin's thumb tapped a high frequency drumbeat on the

desk. He was always tapping his fingers or jiggling his leg, like he'd had too much caffeine. "Okay, but it's less work for you to make the small change to one part that he's asking for than for him to redesign the entire sub-assembly."

"It's not less work for me."

He turned around to face her, frowning. "It's less work for the *project*. His stuff's on the critical path right now and yours isn't. We're all part of a team, remember?"

She could feel her blood pressure rising as her hands clenched into fists at her sides. "I'm not the one who designed an entire sub-assembly without consulting the other members of the team."

"Is this going to be a problem? I told Dmitri you'd be happy to do it." Dmitri was Dan's team lead, and he and Bhavin were buddies. They were in the same fantasy football league and played Magic: the Gathering on the weekends.

"It's not a problem," Esther said, forcing herself to smile. "I'm just pointing out this is an issue that could have easily been avoided. And it's not like this is the first time he's done something like this either."

Bhavin's head bobbed in a rapid-fire succession of nods. "I'll bring it up with Dmitri, all right? But in the meantime, I need you to go ahead and make the changes."

"Okay," Esther said. "Thank you."

She went back to her desk, knowing nothing would come of Bhavin's conversation with Dmitri. The payload team had more clout than the power team, because their system served the mission—even though you couldn't *do* the mission without power. And Dan was chummy with his team lead, Dmitri, who in turn was chummy with Bhavin, which meant they'd invariably take Dan's side. She knew this, because it was what had happened *every single time* she'd tried to object to something he'd done. Magically, the modifications that Dan wanted were always deemed the simplest solution to a problem that Dan himself had created. The guy was made of Teflon. She'd bet cash money he'd never been called "aggressive" in a performance review either.

"Any luck?" Yemi asked when she got to her desk.

"What do you think?"

"At least you tried."

"I don't know why I bother." They never took her side, and now she was the one who looked like she wasn't a team player.

It wasn't even nine a.m. and today already sucked.

ESTHER WAS STUCK in Friday evening traffic on Overland, still fuming about fucking Dan getting his way that morning, when her brother called. She hit the Bluetooth button on her steering wheel as the car ahead of her lurched to another stop.

"We have a problem," Eric said.

Awesome. Exactly what she needed right now. She hadn't talked to their mom since she'd had to refuse to give her money for the eBay Fiestaware. Esther couldn't wait to hear what her mother wanted now. "What is it?"

"Mom's losing her apartment."

"*What?*" Esther's fists tightened on the steering wheel.

"I told you not to freak out."

She let her foot off the brake as the car in front of her started creeping forward. "How? What happened? What'd she do?"

"It's not her fault this time. Her landlord decided to cash out and sell the building. She's got to be out by the end of next month when her lease is up."

"We're never going to find another place she can afford in that neighborhood." Her mother had been living in the same duplex apartment building in Lake City for six years. Rents in the whole area had skyrocketed as a lot of the older buildings were torn down in favor of new construction, or renovated so they could command the same outrageous prices as the rest of Seattle.

"I know," Eric said. He sounded exhausted.

Esther could only imagine how the conversation had gone when their mother had told him the news. Once again, she was grateful she'd removed herself to another state—and even more grateful Eric was in Seattle to handle things there.

Their mom was going to have to move farther north, probably. Maybe out to Lynwood or Everett, even. Which would make it more difficult for Eric to get to and from her place, making his life more difficult. Plus, she wasn't going to want to do it. She'd put up a fight, drag her feet, complain that it was too far out, that everything in her price range was a dump. She'd do everything in her power to make this as difficult as possible, refusing to accept the reality of her situation, because that's what she always did.

Esther could feel an anxiety stomachache ramping up already. "What are we going to do?"

"We'll figure something out. We always do. I'll help her start looking for a new place."

She hit the brakes as a BMW swerved into her lane. "She's not going to want to—"

"I know," Eric said irritably.

Esther bit down on her thumbnail. "I could send more money."

"No. Don't you dare tell her that."

"Why not? I can make it work if I have to." She could cut back on luxuries like cable TV and the satellite radio in her car if she needed to. Start packing her lunch more often instead of eating in the cafeteria every day.

"She's got to start taking responsibility for herself, not mooching more off you."

They had this same fight a lot. Esther was always tempted to give in to her mother's demands, just to get her off her back. But Eric insisted that if they gave in, it would only encourage her to keep doing it. And since he was the one who had to deal with their mother in person, he usually got the final say.

"Promise me you won't offer her more money."

"Fine," Esther agreed. Reluctantly.

"It'll work out," Eric said. "I just wanted to give you a heads-up before Mom called you."

"Yeah. Thanks." She ground her teeth as the car in front of her dawdled just long enough for the light to turn red before Esther got through the intersection.

"Don't stress about it."

"Sure." Like that was possible.

"I'm serious. Go do something fun tonight and forget about Mom. Go out with some friends or something."

It wasn't a bad idea. She could definitely use some company tonight. She always could call Jinny, but it was Friday, and Jinny would almost certainly want to go out. Which would involve makeup and dressing up and more traffic—none of which Esther felt like dealing with.

Alternatively...she could see if Jonathan was around tonight. They could stay in, order pizza, and watch movies again. The prospect was more appealing than going to a crowded bar with Jinny.

She'd knock on his door when she got home, she decided as the light turned green and she finally made it through the intersection. See if he wanted to hang out tonight.

She'd be the one to drop in on him for a change.

Chapter Seventeen

---

*E*sther didn't get to knock on Jonathan's door after all, because he was down in the courtyard when she finally made it home. He was camped in one of the lounge chairs with his legs splayed out in front of him and his laptop balanced on one thigh. It was the first time she'd ever seen him in shorts. His legs were long, covered in dark hair, and strikingly muscular.

"Hey," he said, looking up from his computer as she walked up.

Esther sank down in the chair next to him with a loud, dramatic sigh.

"Good day at work, I take it?"

"Everyone sucks today."

He lifted an eyebrow.

"Present company excepted."

He picked up the beer sitting on the ground next to him and passed it to her. She took a big swig, letting the alcohol relax some of the tension in her shoulders. It wasn't enough to wash her bad mood away, but it was start.

"Keep it," he said when she tried to hand it back. "You obviously need it more than me."

"Thanks." She took another swallow, and her eyes drifted back to his legs. She'd never seen so much of his skin before. It had a golden, sun-kissed glow to it. Was he a runner? She'd never seen him leave his apartment in anything resembling exercise clothes. But now she was imagining what he'd look like shirtless and in jogging shorts, all sweaty and glistening with his hair drenched and dripping—

"Did something happen at work?"

She made herself stop staring at his legs. "Sexism happened."

"Can you be more specific? It's my understanding sexism happens every day."

Esther sighed again, scraping at the beer label with her thumb. "This guy at work fucked something up, but because he's bros with the team leads, I'm the one who has to redo a bunch of stuff to fix it."

"You're right, that does suck."

"But when I try to point out his bullshit, I'm the one who's not a team player."

Jonathan shut his laptop and set it on the table next to him. "So, some other guy screwed up, but you're the one who looks bad for calling him out?"

Something was different about him today, other than the shorts. She couldn't put her finger on it.

"Pretty much, yeah." Her eyes went to his legs again. What was with her? Drooling over a glimpse of calf like a sex-starved Victorian duke in a romance novel.

He shook his head in commiseration. "That is totally sexist."

"Thank you."

He wasn't smoking—that was what was different. There was no cigarette smell hovering around him, and no butts lying nearby. Had he really quit because she'd told him she didn't like it?

She looked away, watching a wasp hover over the surface of the pool. "That's not even the worst thing that happened today. My brother called. Our mom's losing her apartment."

"Shit."

"Yeah." She took another swallow of beer. "Her landlord's selling the building. Seattle's so expensive, I don't know how we're going to find anything in her budget." She could feel the grinding edge of anxiety building already, and tried to push it out of her mind. This was why she needed company tonight. To distract her from tormenting herself over something she couldn't control.

"What are you going to do?"

She shrugged. "Sulk. Stress. Drink." *With you, hopefully.*

She was about to ask if he wanted to join her when he said, "You should come out with me tonight."

She looked over at him, startled. "What?" It sounded like he was asking her out on a date.

"Some friends of mine are having a party tonight. You should come."

Oh. Not a date, then. He already had plans.

She rolled her eyes to disguise how disappointed she was. "Pass."

"It'll cheer you up. Come on."

She took another swig of beer to soothe the tightness in her throat. "I don't think hanging out with a bunch of writers is going to cheer me up. No offense."

"They're not all writers. These are my undergrad friends. They're cool. You'll like them."

She seriously doubted that. Even if they were the coolest of the cool, Esther plus party rarely equaled a good time. She wasn't into making small talk with people she didn't know unless there was a likelihood of sex in it for her at the end of the night. Even then, it was an ordeal. A gauntlet she had to run to claim the prize. She wasn't in the mood for gauntlets tonight.

"Come on, what else are you going to do tonight? Sit around your apartment alone feeling sorry for yourself?"

That was *exactly* what she was going to do. "Did you not hear my sulking and drinking plan?"

His face crinkled with concerned disapproval. "Don't do that. Come out with me and drink around other people. It'll be more fun." He leaned over and nudged her arm. "You know you don't want to be alone."

She didn't. But she had no desire to go to a party either. She wanted to have him all to herself.

But she couldn't very well ask him not to go. If she wanted to spend time with him, it would have to be on his terms.

She blew out a breath through her front teeth. "Fine."

ESTHER COULDN'T BELIEVE she was putting on more godforsaken makeup. Fresh foundation and blush and an extra coat of mascara. A darker lipstick than the tinted balm she wore to work. She'd even let her hair down and taken a curling iron to the ends. And changed into a pair of skinny jeans and a low-cut top with a coordinating scarf.

She'd wound up going to more trouble than she would have if she'd gone out with Jinny tonight.

Her carefully laid plan to spend the night snuggling on the couch with Jonathan had fallen to shambles. Not that she'd necessarily *planned* on snuggling with him. It was just that his limbs were long and her couch was only so big. Some physical contact was inevitable.

Well, she didn't have to worry about that now. She'd be spending her evening trying to think of interesting things to say to strangers. *Joy.*

The way Jonathan's eyes bulged when Esther opened the door made the effort she'd put into her appearance worth it. His gaze dropped furtively to her chest then quickly away again, giving her a sharp thrill of satisfaction.

He'd dressed up too. "I almost didn't recognize you without a hat on," she said, smirking at him. In addition to losing the beanie, he'd changed into a dark blue denim button down and black pants with ankle boots. Esther was getting to see Date Jonathan tonight.

He ran his hand through his hair. "Funny."

"Don't do that." She reached up to smooth his hair back down. "I like your hair. You should show it off more often." It was thick and silky soft, and it made her want to bury her fingers in it.

His mouth dimpled in surprise. "Really?"

She forced herself to stop petting his hair and dropped her hand to her side. "Yeah, really."

His eyes slid up and down the length of her body, lingering on her cleavage again before skimming away. He cleared his throat, blushing a little. "You look very nice."

My god, he was adorable. He smelled nice too. Clean and masculine, like some kind of piney soap, with no trace of cigarette smoke on him. She could get used to Date Jonathan.

She stepped outside and locked her apartment. "I can't believe I let you talk me into this." As much as she appreciated Date Jonathan, the prospect of this stupid party filled her with dread. The only upside to the ordeal was that she'd be there with him.

"Don't be negative," he said. "You're going to have fun." He waited for her to stuff her keys in her pocket before presenting his arm like they were attending a cotillion. "I promise."

She took his arm and let him lead her away. Like a lamb to the slaughter.

Chapter Eighteen

The sun was a blinding orange blaze in the rearview mirror as Jonathan drove toward downtown. The farther east they got, the more nervous Esther got. She sank into a moody silence and turned her face to the window, watching the palm trees and shiny glass buildings glide by in the coppery light.

By the time they found a parking space on the crowded Echo Park street where the party was being held, it was full dark and growing slightly chilly. A brisk wind blew in, smelling faintly of tar, and Esther wished she'd brought a sweater.

"Who are these people again?" she asked as they walked the three blocks up the street to the party.

Jonathan cut a sideways look at her and reached for her hand. Warmth seeped into her skin from his palm, bolstering her courage a little. "This is Kelsey and her girlfriend Devika's place."

Esther leaned into him, angling to absorb more of his warmth. "Kelsey and Devika," she repeated, trying to memorize the names. Why had she let him talk her into this? She was terrible at parties; she didn't even like them when she was in a *good* mood. She hated trying to get people to like her. They were probably going to hate her anyway, and Jonathan would abandon her in favor of his friends, and she'd end up standing awkwardly by the food all night.

She should have stayed home with her cat. Sally liked her without expecting her to be friendly and interesting.

Jonathan glanced at her again and put his arm around her shoulders, gathering her to his side. He smelled like warm cotton and whatever woodsy soap he used. She nestled into him shamelessly, craving the contact even though it wasn't that cold.

"The party's for my friend Lacey." His fingers smoothed down the inside of her arm as he led her around the side of a beige stucco building. "She just got accepted into the LAPD training academy."

Esther nodded. "Lacey, police academy."

He dropped his arm and took her hand again as they ascended a flight of rusty metal stairs. "Lacey's girlfriend, who's also hosting the party, is named Tessa."

"Tessa. Got it." She glanced at him. "How do you know so many lesbians anyway?"

His mouth dimpled. "I've known Kelsey and Lacey since my freshman year at UCLA, and they're not lesbians, they're bisexual. Lacey just came out a few months ago, so be cool."

"I'm cool," Esther said as they stopped in front of a green door. There was music coming from inside, and voices and laughter. "Kelsey and Devika. Lacey and Tessa." She should probably be writing all this down. She was bad with names. If she didn't learn them in advance, she'd never be able to remember them.

Jonathan gave her hand a squeeze. "It's going to be fine. They're going to love you and you're going to have a great time tonight. Trust me."

She pressed her lips together and nodded, unconvinced.

He squeezed her hand once more before knocking.

The door was thrown open by a woman who looked like she should be painted on the side of a WWII fighter plane. "Johnny!" she shouted, and threw her arms around Jonathan's neck.

Johnny. Esther had never thought of him as a Johnny before.

His hand fell away from Esther's to return the woman's hug, and he wrapped his long arms around her waist. "Hey, Kels." He was smiling when he let go of her.

Esther had shrunk back, but he snaked his arm around her shoulders again, drawing her forward. "This is Esther. Esther, Kelsey."

Kelsey's eyebrows lifted and she beamed a perfect red-lipsticked smile at Esther. "Esther! What a fantastic name!"

"Thanks." *Kelsey,* Esther repeated in her head. *Kelsey the pin-up girl.*

Kelsey stepped back, gesturing them inside. "Drinks are over there." She waved toward the small kitchen, which was packed with people jostling for access to the fridge. "Food's on the dining table, and the guest of honor's in the living room, last I saw."

"Come on," Jonathan said, steering Esther into the crowd. "Let's say hi to Lacey."

People were jammed in like sardines near the door, and Esther pressed her body against his as they squeezed through a narrow gap.

"Johnny?" she said, arching an eyebrow at him once they had a little more breathing room.

He gave her a sheepish shrug. "It was freshman year."

It was less crowded in the living rom. Just a few smaller groups talking over the indie music being played on a speaker hooked up to someone's phone.

"Lacey!" Jonathan called out, waving to someone on the couch.

An intimidatingly fit Latina woman jumped up to greet them. "You made it!"

Jonathan let go of Esther and gave Lacey a hug vigorous enough to lift her off the floor. "Of course I made it! I'm so proud of you!"

"Who's your friend?" Lacey asked, eying Esther when he set her down.

Jonathan made the introductions, and Lacey smiled as she stuck out her hand. "It's nice to meet you."

"Congratulations," Esther said. "The police academy, that's really cool."

Lacey shrugged. "My dad's a cop, so I'm a legacy."

"Don't listen to her," Jonathan told Esther. "Lacey's a total badass. She could probably kill me with one of her thumbs."

"I'd need both of them to do a really good job," Lacey said wryly.

"Yeah, well, study hard," he said. "I'm going to be using you as a source from now on whenever I need to write about police procedure."

"Oh god." Lacey groaned as she turned to Esther. "Has he roped you into helping him with one of his scripts yet?"

"Actually, yes," Esther replied, feeling herself smile.

"It never stops." Lacey waved to someone on the other side of the room. "Tessa! Come meet Johnny!"

Esther smirked at Jonathan and he rolled his eyes.

"Hello," said the slender blonde who joined them, slipping her arm around Lacey.

"This is my friend Johnny," Lacey said to Tessa. "We went to college together."

"Jonathan," he corrected, shaking Tessa's hand. "No one calls me Johnny anymore."

Lacey punched him in the arm. "*I* call you Johnny. And so does Kelsey."

He rubbed his arm, wincing. "You're the only ones besides my sisters."

"This is Johnny's friend Esther," Lacey told Tessa.

"Hello," Tessa said warmly. She had a surprisingly strong grip for her size.

"Lacey says you're a yoga instructor?" Jonathan said to her.

Tessa nodded. "And a massage therapist." That explained the iron grip, then.

"I should book an appointment with you," Jonathan said. "I get this crick in my neck sometimes from hunching over the keyboard."

"Get my number from Lacey. I'd be happy to work on you." Tessa smiled at Esther. "What about you, Esther, what do you do?"

"She's a rocket scientist," Jonathan said before she could answer. He was beaming like a proud parent.

"No shit?" Lacey said, eyes widening.

"Aerospace engineer," Esther said. "But yeah, kind of."

"That's so cool!"

"I'm gonna go get us some drinks," Jonathan said. "Who needs a refill?" Lacey and Tessa both shook their heads. "Beer?" he asked Esther.

She nodded. "Yeah, thanks." *Shit.* He was already leaving her on her own.

"I've got a friend who works for an aerospace company," Lacey said. "Two friends, actually. They're supposed to be here."

"How long have you and Jonathan been together?" Tessa asked.

Esther felt her face redden. "Oh, we're not—we're just friends. Actually, we're neighbors."

Tessa smiled. "Right."

"How about you two?" Esther asked, shifting the subject off her and Jonathan.

Lacey laughed. "That's a complicated question."

"Sorry." Great. Here five minutes and she'd already put her foot in it.

"It's fine," Tessa said, laying her hand on Esther's arm. "We started seeing each other before Lacey came out, is all. So officially, it's only been a few months, but really more like a year."

"Wow," Esther said. "A year, that's a long time."

Jonathan had gotten sucked into a conversation with someone

in the kitchen. Esther could see him in there, holding two drinks and chatting happily away.

"Hey, Devika!" Lacey called out. "Come meet Johnny's friend Esther. She's a rocket scientist."

"No shit?" said a tall black woman with copper braids.

"Devika? This is your place, right?" Esther said, proud of herself for remembering.

"Yeah, me and Kelsey. Did you meet Kelsey yet?"

Esther nodded. "She let us in."

"Devika's a pediatric nurse," Tessa said.

"That's really cool," Esther said, and Devika shrugged.

She could already feel the conversation petering out. Lacey's attention was on something across the room, and the other two wore the sort of bland smiles you offered to someone you'd rather not be talking to. Any second now, they'd wander off and she'd be left by herself.

Jonathan had made it halfway back from the kitchen, but he was talking to someone else now. He seemed to know everyone here. Unlike Esther, who knew no one.

Lacey excused herself to go greet some other party guests, but Devika and Tessa stayed with Esther. Devika mentioned that Kelsey was an actor. She'd played a dead body on a network procedural, which was pretty cool. Chris O'Donnell had knelt over her and talked about blood spatter. Then she and Tessa started talking about someone else at the party. Someone Esther didn't know. But at least they hadn't abandoned her. After a minute, Tessa smiled at her as if she'd noticed she was feeling left out, and complimented her scarf.

Esther had made it herself. They seemed excited to discover she could knit. Tessa said she'd always wanted to learn. Devika said her mother had tried to teach her, but she didn't have the patience for it—or maybe it was her mother she hadn't had the patience for. They all laughed.

The conversation stayed on knitting until Jonathan finally

made his way back and slipped a beer bottle into Esther's hand. After that, things were a little easier.

They talked about movies for a while, and it turned out Tessa and Devika shared a lot of Esther's opinions. Jonathan tried to make a case for some turgid Australian art film being the best thing he'd seen this year, but the three women united against him in favor of the latest Marvel movie.

"Oh, hey, there's Melody," Tessa said after a while, tugging Devika away. "Let's go say hi."

"Shit." Jonathan muttered, sidling around so his back was to the door. "I didn't know she'd be here." He took a swig of beer.

"Who?" Esther craned her neck for a better look at the person who'd just come in.

"Melody. Lacey set me up on a blind date with her a few months ago."

Oooh, interesting. She was cute. With the glasses and the long hair, she looked a little like Supergirl's alter ego Kara Danvers.

"I'm guessing it didn't work out," Esther said, based on the way he seemed to be trying to fade into the ficus.

"Not so much, no."

"Who's she with? Is that her boyfriend?" Melody's date looked vaguely familiar, but Esther couldn't place him. Maybe he was an actor? He was good-looking enough to be on TV.

"I don't know." Jonathan didn't turn around to look.

"Holy shit," Esther said when she realized where she recognized the guy from. There was a photo of him in the lobby at work, along with his parents and his sister. These must be the friends Lacey was talking about who worked for an aerospace company. Only, the guy didn't so much *work* for the company as own it. Or his family did, anyway.

"What?" Jonathan said.

"Her date is Jeremy Sauer."

Jonathan frowned and glanced behind him. "That's Lacey's ex."

Esther's eyes widened. Lacey's ex currently had his hand on this Melody chick's ass. "Lacey dated Jeremy Sauer?"

Jonathan turned back to Esther, still frowning. "How do *you* know him?"

"The company I work for? Sauer Hewson? He's one of those Sauers."

"Fantastic." Jonathan took another swig of beer.

"Hey, if you're going to be passed over, at least it was for a gorgeous billionaire, right?"

He gave her a sour look. "Is that supposed to make me feel better?"

"Yes. He was on some list of the country's most eligible bachelors. Who can compete with that?"

Jonathan's scowl deepened. "Clearly not me."

Esther hooked her arm through his. "Hey, you're a pretty good catch too."

She meant it. He was excellent boyfriend material—insomuch as she was qualified to determine such things. Considerate, easy to talk to, sweet. Some woman was going to be lucky to have him.

The thought made her sad. One day he'd find a girlfriend who appreciated him, and he wouldn't need her. He wouldn't drop by her apartment to hang out anymore, because you couldn't do that sort of thing when you had a girlfriend. They'd go back to being just neighbors who said hello when they saw each other in the laundry room. She already missed him just thinking about it. She didn't want to lose him.

Her eyes found his, and her stomach did a little drop. She let go of his arm. "Maybe not Jeremy Sauer good," she said, trying to sound light.

Jonathan didn't smile. "Awesome." He took another swig of beer.

Esther felt out of her depth. Like she was doing everything wrong. "Do you want to leave?"

His gaze dropped to his shoes, and he shook his head. "It was one date. It doesn't matter."

It seemed like it did though. "You sure?"

"Yeah, it's fine." He forced a smile.

She'd made the offer and he'd rejected it. Unless she wanted to drag him out of here against his will, she'd have to take him at his word. "Good," she said, "because I'm having a good time." It surprised her how much she meant it.

"Are you?"

She shrugged. "You have cool friends. Who'd have thought?"

His mouth curved a little. "I *told* you."

"You did."

His smile made it all the way to his eyes. "I'm glad you came."

She smiled back at him. "I'm glad you asked me."

Something shifted in his expression and the moment stretched out, growing heavy. It made Esther feel unstable. Her hand twitched at her side, looking for something to grab onto for support, but there was nothing within reach except Jonathan. She couldn't grab onto him, because he was the one upsetting her equilibrium.

"I need another beer," he said, looking away. "You need anything?"

"I'll come with you," she said and followed him into the kitchen.

JONATHAN WAS AN EXCELLENT DATE. He stuck close by Esther the whole night, introducing her to people, including her in conversations, fetching her drinks. Showing her off. He loved to tell people she was a rocket scientist. It was one of the first things out of his mouth when he introduced her to someone new.

She'd never seen him around his friends before. He smiled a lot more and seemed easier in his own skin. It was as if he'd reverted to a younger version of himself that was more carefree. Less self-conscious.

Until Lacey towed Jeremy Sauer and his girlfriend over to meet them.

"Johnny's friend Esther works for your company," Lacey said to Jeremy. "Small world, huh?"

"Hi, Jonathan," Melody said, her eyes flicking to his face with the barest trace of unease. "How've you been?"

He nodded a greeting without quite meeting her gaze. "I've been good. Great, actually."

Esther recognized the same flat affect he had used with Jinny at the pool last weekend. Relaxed, smiley Jonathan had disappeared, replaced by the Jonathan she remembered from before she got to know him. The one who looked disapproving and grimaced instead of smiled.

All that time she'd spent thinking he was an arrogant ass, when he was just suffering from insecurity and social anxiety. The realization made her feel protective. She wanted to wrap him up and whisk him away somewhere he could be himself. Somewhere he'd smile again.

"I forgot, I fixed you guys up on that date!" Lacey said, grinning with delight. "Funny."

Esther couldn't decide whether she'd actually forgotten or was messing with them. She seemed to be enjoying herself an awful lot.

"Yeah," Jonathan agreed, giving Lacey a wry look. "Funny."

Jeremy Sauer's eyebrows lifted slightly, and Melody glanced down at her shoes.

"Welp, I've got some more guests to greet," Lacey announced, leaving them to fend for themselves.

Definitely messing with them, Esther decided.

Jeremy turned to her, beaming a smile dazzling enough to melt permafrost. "Nice to meet you. I'm Jeremy, and this is Melody."

Esther met his smile with one of her own, determined to

ignore the fissures of tension around them. Jonathan had dutifully propped her up all evening. Now it was her turn to step up and repay the favor.

"Lacey says you're an aerospace engineer," Melody said, throwing her hat in the *this is fine* ring.

Esther nodded. "I work at the El Segundo campus."

Jeremy asked which project she worked on, and was familiar enough with it to identify the telecom customer they were developing it for. Esther learned that he and Melody both worked at corporate in Glendale. Melody was a software developer, and Jeremy worked under the CFO—the same CFO who had recently married his mother. The Sauers really did like to keep the business in the family.

As they talked, Esther could feel Jonathan shrinking beside her. He'd shuffled back a half step and retreated into a glum silence.

"Did you guys meet at work?" Esther asked, trying to keep the conversation going.

Melody and Jeremy regaled them with an overly-detailed story about hooking up four years ago and then reconnecting when she came to work at Sauer Hewson, doing that nauseating couple thing where they finished each other's sentences. The longer it went on, the more Jonathan edged behind Esther, pressing his body against hers like he was seeking shelter. As Melody and Jeremy smiled blissfully into one another's eyes over a shared joke, Esther reached behind her back for Jonathan's hand and tangled their fingers together. He clutched it gratefully, shifting toward her a little more.

"How about you two?" Melody asked when they'd concluded the narrative of their lengthy courtship. "How long have you been together?"

Esther felt Jonathan go rigid, and he dropped her hand like it was on fire.

"Actually—" he started.

"Only a few weeks," Esther finished for him. She wrapped her arms around his waist, snuggling into his side like an affectionate girlfriend.

Jonathan looked down at her in surprise, and she lifted her eyebrows, daring him to contradict her.

"Um, yeah." He turned back to Melody and Jeremy, hugging Esther's shoulder with his arm. "We're neighbors. She lives in the apartment next door."

"That's so cute!" Melody said. "It's like a movie."

"It is," Esther agreed, giving Jonathan a little squeeze. His scent filled her senses, making her feel lightheaded. "Just like a movie."

"How's your writing going?" Melody asked Jonathan.

He cleared his throat. "It's going okay, I guess." His hand spread out across Esther's shoulder blade, his fingertips stroking bare skin on the back of her neck.

"He's being modest," Esther said, trying not to shiver. She launched into an enthusiastic description of his sci-fi screenplay, waiting for him to pipe up and take the baton from her. Instead, he just watched her, listening with a bemused look on his face.

After a few more minutes of polite chat, during which Jonathan barely spoke or took his eyes off Esther, Jeremy and Melody excused themselves to greet a newly-arrived friend.

"Thank you," Jonathan said into Esther's ear as they moved off. "You didn't have to do that."

She gazed up at him, feeling that swell of protectiveness again. His hair had gotten fluffy on top, and she reached up to smooth it down. "That's what friends are for."

He blinked at her, something uncertain stirring in his eyes. He opened his mouth to speak, but before he could they were interrupted.

"Jonathan!" a guy in a green baseball cap said, clapping him on the back. "How's it going, man?"

Jonathan pivoted to greet him, leaving Esther to wonder what he'd been about to say.

Two hours later, Esther was deep in a conversation with one of Kelsey's actor friends. He'd done small parts in a few movies she'd seen, and a short arc on a network drama series. He had a lot of good Hollywood gossip to share: which actors were assholes, who was sleeping with who, that sort of thing.

The guy seemed nice, but she wished she was talking to Jonathan instead. They'd only split up when she'd ventured off on her own to check out the food spread, and gotten sucked into conversation with the actor over the crudités.

Jonathan was on the other side of the room talking to some college friends. But while he was talking to his friends, he was watching Esther. Checking on her. Every time she looked over at him, his eyes were on her. It made her feel nervous, but in a good way. A fluttery, excited, breathless kind of way.

"Do you need a drink?" the actor asked her. She couldn't remember his name. Something with a B, maybe.

"No, I'm good." She felt the exact right amount of relaxed. One more drink and she'd start to feel too loopy. Out of control. She didn't like feeling out of control.

The actor—Bryan? Brandon?—started telling her about a famous movie star he'd worked with who had a drug problem. He didn't want to say the guy's name. He wanted her to guess. Esther didn't feel like guessing, but she played along.

Jonathan was watching her again. When he caught her eye this time he lifted his chin, and her stomach did an unexpected barrel roll.

"Excuse me," she said to the actor. "I've got to go talk to my friend." She made her way over to Jonathan. "Hey."

He turned his back on the people he'd been talking to. "Hey." His eyes had gone dark beneath his heavy lashes.

Something fluttered in her chest. "I didn't mean to interrupt your conversation."

"You didn't."

"Okay." They were standing close. It had gotten crowded in the living room, and they were practically chest to chest.

He leaned even closer to speak into her ear. "Are you still having a good time?" The warmth of his breath on her cheek sent goose bumps down her arms.

"I am." Her heart felt like a balloon that had been filled beyond capacity. In danger of popping at any second. "Are you?"

He shrugged.

The nearness of him was fogging her brain. He hadn't smoked all night, and he still had that intoxicating piney smell. Maybe it wasn't pine, maybe it was cedar. Whatever it was, she liked it. Had he always smelled this good beneath the cigarette smoke?

Heat prickled at the back of her neck. The room was starting to feel claustrophobic. "Do you want to get out of here?" she asked, hoping he'd say yes.

Jonathan gazed at her, taking his time before he answered. The space between them seemed to crackle with potential energy. "Do *you* want to get out of here?"

"Yes." She swallowed. Her mouth had gone dry. "I do."

A slow smile spread across his face, and he reached for her hand. "Come on."

Chapter Nineteen

_T_hey lapsed into silence on the drive home. The air in the car felt like it was full of static, like it would shock her if she breached the invisible barrier between them.

She kept casting furtive looks at him. He was kicked way back in his seat to make space for his long arms and legs, with his right hand resting on top of the steering wheel. Every once in a while he'd glance over at her, and the way his eyes glittered made her stomach feel tight.

His car smelled like coffee. It was newish. A luxury sedan with a sunroof and leather seats. She assumed his parents had given it to him—one of their hand-me-downs, maybe. The back seat was littered with discarded cardboard coffee cups from a cafe in Westwood where he went to write during the day when he wasn't in class.

Esther had the urge to open his glove box, just to see what was in there. Moleskine notebooks and Pilot pens, probably. She wanted to dig one of his notebooks out of the glove box and flip through the pages, soaking up all his stray thoughts and absent-minded doodles. She wanted to peel away his layers like an onion, digging deep into the substratum to the foundation underneath.

She wanted a peek at his most secret, innermost desires. The ones he kept locked away in his heart.

Instead of indulging her desire to snoop, she kept her hands folded primly in her lap and crossed her legs at the ankles to stop them from jiggling. Why was she so nervous? She wasn't sure what she thought was going to happen. She wasn't even sure what she *wanted* to happen. The warmth pooling in the pit of her stomach wanted one thing, but her brain was telling her something else.

This *shouldn't* happen. She had a clear sense of the right and wrong of the situation. Seducing your best friend's ex was wrong. End of story.

Esther uncrossed her legs and turned her face to the side window for the rest of the drive home.

Ten minutes later, he pulled into his assigned parking space between her Prius and a white metal pole covered with scuff marks. He came around to open her door for her and followed her upstairs with his hands in his pockets, jingling his keys as he walked.

They slowed to a stop in front of his apartment door, and she shifted nervously as he turned to face her. She wasn't ready for the evening to end yet, but she was scared of what might happen next.

"Thank you for tonight," she said to fill the loaded silence. She was having trouble meeting his eyes. Now that they'd been freed from the confines of the car, she'd lost the urge to peer into his psyche. She was too afraid of what she might find there. Afraid she might not be able to resist it.

He shifted closer. "Did you really have fun?" He was looming over her, crowding her a little. She shouldn't like it, but she did.

Instead of moving away, she moved closer. She couldn't help herself. He was warm, and he smelled nice. The scent reminded her of a library in an old house. Not like a real library—those smelled like paper dust. He smelled the way she'd imagined old libraries should smell when she was kid. Full of secrets and magic, like the wardrobe in *The Lion, the Witch and the Wardrobe*. She wanted to bury her face in his scent. Crawl inside the wardrobe and see what adventures lay ahead.

"I did." She let herself look into his eyes. They were bright and inviting. Brimming with promise. "I really did."

"You sound surprised."

"I am. I didn't think I could have fun at a party where I didn't know anyone."

"You know *me*."

"That's true," she said, still gazing into his eyes. "I do know you." He had amazing eyelashes. Long and thick. Any woman would sell her soul for eyelashes like that.

"Do you want to come inside?" he asked.

Yes. She wanted that. She wanted *him*. Every atom in her body was vibrating with it.

"What's inside?" she asked, trying to play coy. Stalling for time. Her brain was fizzing in her ears, like her head was full of Pop Rocks.

"Me." He wasn't playing coy. He was staring at her mouth.

She stared back. She couldn't tear her eyes away. His mouth moved closer.

When their lips met, the fizzing in her brain got even louder. He tasted malty, like the beer he'd been drinking. His beard felt rough, but his lips were velvety soft. Gentle as a whisper.

She wasn't prepared for it to feel so good. Usually, when she kissed someone it was fine. Not unpleasant, but not all that exciting either. Usually, it was easy for her to stop kissing someone.

Kissing Jonathan wasn't like that. It was magnetic. Addictive. It made her want to kiss him even more. It made her want to kiss him a *lot* more, like a junkie itching for another hit.

Her hands curled into the front of his shirt as his palms spread out over the small of her back. His fingers were so long, they almost spanned her whole waist.

She pressed her mouth against his harder, aching for more. Nipping at his lower lip. Chasing his tongue with hers. His arms tightened around her, pulling her flush against his hips, and she moaned with pleasure. One of his hands curled into her hair, holding the back of her neck, sending shivers skittering down her spine.

Pornographic images flashed through her mind. Her mouth on his skin: teasing, taunting, tasting. His long fingers sliding into her. Sweaty, trembling limbs and labored breaths.

Her hands found their way to his hair. She relished the sensation as her fingers sank into the silky locks. It felt even better than she'd imagined. Everything felt better than she'd imagined.

He pressed his forehead against hers, still holding her flush against him. They were sharing the same air. Their bodies touching from tip to toe. She could feel how badly he wanted her, and she wanted him just as much. Maybe more.

He fished his keys out of his pocket and let go of her long enough to unlock the door. She followed willingly when he tugged her inside, his eyes locked on hers. They were alone. In the privacy of his apartment. The knowledge that his bedroom was just a few feet away burned in the pit of her stomach.

It was dark, but he didn't bother switching on a light. Enough light from the courtyard slanted in through the blinds to see by. With slow, deliberate movements, he unwrapped her scarf from around her neck. It was all she could do to hold herself still when his fingers grazed her skin.

He tossed the scarf onto the couch. His hands settled on her hips, his fingers digging softly into her flesh as he urged her closer. She eased into his warmth and let his scent enfold her.

It would be so easy to lose herself in his comforting bubble. To melt right into him and never look back.

He reached up to stroke a single, trembling finger along her jaw. When she leaned into his touch, his mouth curved into a smile.

He bent his head toward her, and she rose up on her toes to meet him halfway. As their mouths crashed together, a tiny voice in the back of her head whispered that this was a bad idea. That it was going to end in disaster, probably. But she didn't want to stop. It felt too good.

He wanted her, and she needed this. She needed to feel wanted and appreciated for once. She needed something good to happen to her.

Jonathan liked her. She just wanted to feel liked. Didn't she deserve that? For once?

His hands went to her hips again, and he pushed her up against the door. He was crowding her again, his belt buckle pressing into her stomach as his hips pinned her in place.

She liked feeling his weight against her. She liked the taste of his tongue in her mouth, and the rasp of his beard on her lips. She liked the way he smelled, and the way his hands felt as they roamed over her body.

She liked *him*.

It had been a long time since she'd liked anyone this much. She'd almost forgotten the feeling. The exhilaration. The light-headedness. The lust.

His hands smoothed up her bare arms, then moved to her hair, tilting her head back to deepen the kiss. She scrabbled at the front of his shirt, her fingers fighting with the buttons.

The yellow light leaking in cast a golden glow over his exposed torso. His chest was smooth except for a small patch of dark hair in the middle that trailed down his stomach and disappeared below the waist of his pants. He groaned as her fingers traced it, ghosting over his bare skin.

Their mouths came together again, messy and fierce. Teeth clashing. Needy. When his glasses bumped her nose he yanked them off and tossed them onto the couch with her scarf.

He looked different without his glasses. Younger. More vulnerable. She reached up to stroke his jaw, and felt his pulse jump under her fingertips.

He kissed her forehead, then her temple. "I want you," he murmured into her hair. "I've always wanted you, from the first moment I saw you."

The tiny voice in Esther's head started to whisper its warning again. But then Jonathan's mouth was on hers again, and the last remnants of her reluctance melted away on his tongue like sugar.

His fingers dipped into the waistband of her jeans, and he stumbled backward, pulling her along with him through the apartment. To the bedroom. To his bed.

It was darker in there. She couldn't see his face anymore. He kissed her again, softer than silk, light as air. She didn't want soft and light though. She wanted rough and fierce. She wanted to devour him.

Arching against him, she dragged his mouth down her hers. Her teeth caught his lip and he let out a rough breath, digging his fingers into her skin. Desperate. Just like she was.

They groped for each other in the darkness, clumsily exploring with their hands as they undressed each other. The surface of Esther's skin felt like it was rimed with ice, but Jonathan's touch was warm and soothing. She wanted him everywhere, all at once, warming her from the inside out.

They fell onto the bed and he moved over her body, leaving a trail of soft kisses on her skin. Her hands glided up his arms and over his shoulders. He was so solid. So heavy. His muscles taut under her fingers.

His mouth found hers again, and she closed her eyes as they came together. Skin to skin. When he moved inside her, her fingernails curled into his back, leaving marks, probably. Pulling him deeper and deeper.

Never wanting to let go.

ESTHER WOKE WITH A START, her heart pounding in her chest. She was too warm, and there was something heavy draped over her waist, trapping her.

It was Jonathan's arm.

She was in Jonathan's bed. *With Jonathan.*

She'd *slept* with Jonathan.

The room glowed with lazy morning light. His bedspread was plaid, she could see now. Across the room, his closet door was open, exposing hanger after hanger of even more plaid.

He stirred behind her, and his arm tightened around her waist, pulling her closer. Yep, he was naked. They were both naked. Because they'd had sex last night. Great sex. Mind-blowing, off-the-charts sex. The kind of sex that made you fantasize about quitting your job so you could do nothing but have sex all day long.

"Hey," he murmured into her hair.

"Hey yourself." Her voice came out rough and scratchy.

His lips found her shoulder, mouthing a wet trail over her skin.

She closed her eyes, trying to enjoy it, but couldn't help flinching as he moved up her neck.

He stopped kissing her. "What's wrong?"

"Your beard tickles."

"Oh yeah?" He rubbed his beard against her neck and she twisted away, turning onto her back. Even though it felt like it was a hundred degrees in the room, she pulled the bedspread up, covering her breasts. As if he hadn't seen them last night. As if he hadn't had his mouth on them only a few hours ago.

Jonathan propped himself up on one elbow above her. "You look beautiful." His hair was all fluffy and mussed. Sex hair. She probably had it too. It was unfair how attractive his was.

She could feel last night's eye makeup caked around her lashes. "I'm pretty sure I look like Alice Cooper."

He leaned in and kissed her, smiling against her lips.

For a fleeting moment, she relaxed, sinking into the sensation. Something fluttered in her chest, making her feel light and floaty.

He pulled away. "You're always beautiful."

The floaty sensation evaporated, and she came thudding back to earth.

His blue eyes were brimming with affection. *Too much* affection. It was painful to look at. Like stepping out of a dark building into blinding sunlight.

Her chest prickled uncomfortably and she kicked her feet out from under the covers. Why was it so dammed hot in here? She felt like she was getting a heat rash.

His hand came up to caress her cheek, tilting her face back toward him. He was frowning slightly. "You sure you're okay?"

She tried to smile. "Yeah, I'm fine."

She wasn't fine. There was no air in the room. It was suffocating her.

His frown deepened as his fingers trailed down her throat. "You're all tense."

"It's too hot in here." Throwing back the covers, she sat up on the edge of the bed, keeping her back to him. She grabbed a piece of clothing off the floor to cover herself up.

It was one of Jonathan's shirts. She dropped it like it was covered in acid.

There. *That* was her shirt. She snatched it off the floor and pulled it over her head.

"Hey," Jonathan said behind her.

She twisted around. She wasn't wearing a bra, so she crossed her arms over her chest.

His worry crease was as deep as she'd ever seen it. "Tell me what's wrong."

"Nothing."

He could definitely tell she was lying.

"Jinny's coming over soon," she said. "I have to get back to my apartment." That much was the truth, at least. She turned her back on him and his unfairly attractive sex hair and grabbed her underwear off the floor.

"Oh." She could hear the disappointment in his voice. The hurt. It made her glad she wasn't looking at him. "Can I see you later?"

"Um." Her jeans were wadded up at the foot of the bed, and she snatched them off the floor. "I don't know how long she'll be here." She nearly fell over trying to struggle into her pants. Stupid skinny jeans that made her ass look hot. She never should have worn them. She shouldn't have worn the low-cut top either. It was like she'd wanted this to happen.

Because she had.

Admit it, you've been lusting after him for weeks.

"Oh," he said again.

She kicked his pants aside, searching for her shoes. Refusing to look at him. "I'll text you," she said, hating the sound of the words as they came out of her mouth.

"Okay."

She got down on her hands and knees and peered under the bed. *Aha!* She retrieved her shoes and stood up, still avoiding his eyes. An edge of familiar blue lace caught her eye, peeking out from under Jonathan's boxer briefs. Great. She plucked her bra off the floor and shoved it in her back pocket before turning to face him, finally.

He looked confused, and more than a little hurt.

Her cheeks burned with shame, but she forced herself to look him in the eye. Swallowing, she tried to soften her voice. "Last night was fun."

"Right." His mouth had compressed into a hard, thin line. It was the same expression he got when he was talking about his parents, and she hated herself for making him look that way. For making him feel that way.

"I'm sorry," she said, even though she wasn't sure exactly what she was apologizing for.

He looked away.

She stood uncertainly in the doorway, clutching her shoes as she hugged her arms across her chest. "I'm just— I'm gonna go."

He nodded, still refusing to look at her.

Esther let herself out.

Chapter Twenty

*W*hen Esther got back to her apartment, she took a shower and stood under the hot water for forty-five minutes, trying to wash away the feeling of regret.

It didn't work.

She still felt just as awful when she got out of the shower.

The look on Jonathan's face when she'd left haunted her. She never should have let things go this far.

He wanted more from her than she could give. She could see it in his eyes. He was looking for a relationship. A girlfriend.

That wasn't her. She wasn't the girlfriend type. He *knew* that. And even if she was interested in being in a relationship—which she wasn't—it could never happen with him.

He'd dated her best friend. You weren't supposed to sleep with guys your best friend dated. Even if it was only three dates, and even if she'd broken up with him. He was a guy Jinny had liked. According to the Friend Code, he was officially off-limits.

This was a disaster. Esther had fucked up. She'd let herself get swept up in the moment. Because she was selfish.

Last night shouldn't have happened. And it could definitely never happen again.

She fastened her wet hair into a bun and sank onto the couch. Sally jumped up beside her and started purring. She didn't like it when Esther spent the night away.

"I did something bad," she said, scratching Sally under her chin. "Your human is a real shithead."

Sally smushed her face into Esther's palm, unconcerned with the romantic affairs of humans. Lucky cat.

"Us Weekly IS SAYING Ben and Jen are back together *and* Brad and Angelina are back together," Jinny announced as she breezed into Esther's apartment an hour later. "It's like 2005 all over again, and I love it."

Esther smiled weakly, feeling sick to her stomach.

Jinny went into the kitchen and pulled open the fridge. "I'm taking a water bottle. And one of your yogurts."

Guilt burned in the back of Esther's throat. She needed to confess. She'd been keeping too many secrets from Jinny. It was time to come clean.

"Wait," Esther said. "Before we go, I have to tell you something."

Jinny set the yogurt and water down. "This sounds serious."

Esther looked at her feet. Best to just get it out, rather than try to sugarcoat it. Rip off the Band-Aid. She looked up at Jinny and took a deep breath. "I slept with Jonathan."

Jinny went still, her eyes widening. "*My* Jonathan?"

Esther swallowed. Nodded. "The Jonathan who lives next door, yeah."

"But—but how? *Why?* You don't even like him."

"I didn't mean to. It was an accident."

"An accident?" Jinny's forehead scrunched. "How does that work, exactly? Did you trip and fall onto his dick?"

"No, he invited me to this party Friday and—"

Jinny's mouth fell open. "Like a *date?*"

"No, definitely not like that. Just as friends."

"Friends who sleep together?"

"That's the part that was accidental." Esther could feel herself getting defensive and tried to squash it. There was no defense. She couldn't even claim she was drunk. She'd done it because she'd wanted to.

Jinny looked confused. "Since when are you two friends at all? I thought you couldn't stand him."

Esther's cheeks heated and she looked down at the floor, shoulders hunching in shame. "We've been sort of...hanging out."

"For how long?"

"A couple months, I guess."

"A couple of *months*?"

Esther cringed, lifting her eyes. Jinny looked shocked. Rightfully so. They'd always told each other everything.

She hadn't meant to keep her friendship with Jonathan a secret. She just hadn't known how to bring it up without raising other questions. It had seemed safer not to mention it at all.

That ship had sailed now, though. It was time to fess up. To all of it.

"It was—it was around the same time you started dating him," Esther said. "He asked me for help with one of his screenplays."

The look on Jinny's face sank straight into the pit of Esther's stomach. "Let me get this straight—you started hanging out with him at the same time he started dating me, and didn't think to mention that before now?"

Esther winced. "It wasn't like that."

"What was it like, then?"

"He was writing this sci-fi script, and he knew I worked in aerospace, and he needed help with the science. It was no big deal."

"If it was no big deal, why didn't you tell me? I don't understand why you'd keep it a secret that you were hanging out with him. For *months*."

Esther chewed on her lower lip. "There's something else I haven't told you."

Jinny crossed her arms, bracing herself. "What?"

"Jonathan asked me to help him with his screenplay before he asked you out. I told him—I told him I'd only do it if he went out with you."

"What?"

Esther cringed, wishing she could sink into the floor. "I know."

"How could you do that?" Jinny's voice had gone icy.

"I was afraid you were going to get back together with Stuart." It sounded so pathetic now. So flimsy.

"Why *the fuck* is that any of your business?" she demanded, eyes blazing.

"He was an asshole, Jinny, and you were about to go right back to him. I didn't want you to get hurt. I thought if you went out with someone else, like a rebound guy, you'd get over Stuart. And you thought Jonathan was cute, so…" Esther had been so proud of herself. She'd thought she'd come up with the perfect plan. That she was helping Jinny. What an idiot she was.

"So you pimped me out."

"No! I pimped myself out to get a cute guy you liked to ask you on a date."

Jinny shook her head. "You pimped *him* out. *On me.* He never even liked me, did he? It was all a lie."

"That's not true! He thought you were cute! You thought he was cute. It seemed like a perfect match." It had. Her intentions had been good. As if that counted for anything.

"I can't believe you. That's exactly the kind of shit my parents pull on me, trying to make me date the men *they* want me to date. And you *know* how I feel about it, but you did it anyway."

Esther's stomach dropped into her shoes. "You're totally right, and I'm sorry."

Jinny paced from the kitchen to the front door and back again.

"Oh my god, I can't believe I went on three dates with that guy. I *made out* with him. And it was all just a scam."

"It wasn't a scam. He really did like you." Which didn't exactly make the fact that Esther had jumped into bed with him any better.

Jinny shook her head, her lip curling in disgust. "Thank *god* I didn't sleep with him. Can you even imagine?"

"I'm *really* sorry. I didn't think it through. I thought I was helping." A lump tried to squeeze Esther's throat closed, making her voice tremble.

"By lying to me? Going against my explicit wishes? And then turning around and sleeping with the guy you'd tricked into pity-dating me?" There was no forgiveness to be found in Jinny's face.

"That's not—it wasn't like that." The words sounded hollow as Esther spoke them. Because it was like that. It was exactly like that.

"I can't believe you would do that to me." The coldness in Jinny's expression couldn't mask the hurt underneath.

Esther's eyes burned, and she blinked. "Jinny, I—"

"You know what? I can't even look at you right now. I have to go." She gathered up her things, moving toward the door.

Esther couldn't let her leave yet. Not until they'd worked this out. She had to make her understand. She had to *fix* this. "Jinny, wait. Please, I—"

She didn't wait. When the door slammed behind her, it felt like all the air had been sucked out of the room.

Esther sank down on the couch and pressed her palms against her forehead.

Fuck. Everything was a disaster.

What was she going to do? She had to find a way to make this better. To make Jinny forgive her. But she didn't know how. She didn't even know where to start. She'd betrayed her best friend's trust, and she didn't know how to get it back.

There was a knock on the door.

Esther leapt off the couch and threw it open, hoping Jinny had come back and she'd have another chance to explain.

Except it wasn't Jinny. It was Jonathan.

"What?" The word came out harsher than she intended.

He flinched. "I, um…heard you and Jinny fighting."

"Oh." Esther went back to the couch and sank down on it again, leaving the door open.

He followed her inside and stood at one end of the couch, shifting his weight. "Are you okay?"

She looked away, swallowing. Unable to stand the pity in his eyes. "Not really."

"Is Jinny okay?"

"*No*, she's not okay. She's pissed at me. And she has every right to be."

"Did you tell her about—"

"I told her *everything*."

"Oh."

Esther leaned forward and cradled her head in her hands. "Fuck."

He shuffled closer, hovering over her uncertainly. "Is there anything I can do?" He sounded so kind. So concerned about her. He had no idea she was about to break his heart. She squeezed her eyes shut so he wouldn't see that they were full of tears.

"Esther?" He moved even nearer.

She exhaled a long, ragged breath and looked up at him. "Last night was a mistake. It can't happen ever again."

He took a stuttering step back. "What?"

"You dated my best friend."

His eyebrows drew together. "It's not like I really dated her though."

"Yeah, it is."

"Wait," he said, looking confused. "You mean because I fake-dated Jinny—"

"It wasn't fake dating. It was real dating. You liked her, and she liked you."

His expression hardened. "Not enough to keep dating me."

"It doesn't matter. You can't sleep with a guy your best friend dated. That's Friend Code 101. She gets forever dibs. I never should have let it happen."

"Don't I get a say in who has dibs on me?"

"No."

"Are you serious right now?" He looked pissed.

"Look, I'm sorry, okay. None of this is fair to you, I realize that." He hadn't done anything wrong. He'd just been in the wrong place at the wrong time. Collateral damage.

"So that's it?" The bitterness in his voice made her stomach churn painfully.

She looked down at the floor and swallowed. "We can still be friends." She hated herself for saying it, because it was so obviously a lie. They'd never be able to go back to the way things were.

"Wow. Really?"

She glanced up at him and immediately regretted it. He looked like she'd just kicked him in the stomach. "I don't have a choice." She wished she could go back in time and erase the last twenty-four hours. Back to when she and Jonathan were just friends, and Jinny was still speaking to her. She'd ruined *everything* by sleeping with him.

His eyes narrowed with contempt. "Of course you do."

"I don't! Because of Jinny, you and I—"

"That's bullshit. Jinny doesn't give a crap about me. She never did."

"She cares that I lied to her about you."

He shook his head. "That doesn't have anything to do with *us*. It's just an excuse. What's really going on is that you have feelings for me and you're scared."

Esther thrust her jaw out. "That's not it."

"Of course it is. You're fucking terrified of letting yourself care about someone."

A memory of the night before forced its way into her consciousness—the way his hand had trembled when he'd touched her face—and she looked away, unable to meet his eye. "You don't understand."

"I think I understand better than you do."

She couldn't keep debating this with him. He was never going to see her side of it or be okay with her decision. Talking it through more wasn't going to make either of them feel any better.

"I'm sorry," she said again, feeling miserable. "But if I have to make a choice between you and Jinny, then I pick Jinny. Every time. She's my best friend."

He didn't say anything.

Esther's stomach did another twist, wringing itself out like a wet washcloth. "Do you understand? Please tell me you understand."

His gaze locked on the floor, like he couldn't even look her. Just like Jinny hadn't been able to look at her. "I do," he said. "I get it."

"I don't blame you for hating me." She already hated herself. He was entitled to get in on the hating train.

He pressed his lips together and shook his head. "I don't hate you. That's the problem." His voice was so quiet it was almost a whisper. When his eyes found hers, what she saw in them cut her to the bone. "I feel sorry for you."

When the door banged shut behind him, Esther let out a choking sob. She hugged her knees to her chest, and the tears she'd been holding back burst through the floodgate.

See? She knew it would end in disaster.

Chapter Twenty-One

*E*sther stared at her computer screen. The 3-D render of the part she was supposed to be designing looked like one of those Escher paintings that seemed to have an extra dimension.

It wasn't a complicated part, she was just having trouble concentrating today. Every time she tried, the lines on the screen would drift in and out of focus until it looked like a bunch of gobbledygook instead of a simple wireframe drawing.

Jinny hadn't returned any of the approximately eleventy-hundred texts and voicemails Esther had left since yesterday. Esther had considered seeking her out this morning when she got to the office, but decided work wasn't the best place to hash out their friendship drama. If Jinny didn't want to talk her, forcing a confrontation in front of her coworkers wasn't likely to win Esther any brownie points.

On top of that, she couldn't stop thinking about Jonathan. She honestly wasn't sure which she felt worse about—hurting Jinny or hurting Jonathan.

So here she sat, feeling helpless and miserable as she tried fruitlessly to concentrate on work. All she had to do was make two small adjustments to the design. It was a simple fix. It should only take ten minutes.

She'd been staring at it for an hour, and hadn't gotten anywhere yet.

Yemi kicked her chair. "What are you doing?"

Esther didn't turn around. "Working on my battery charger."

"No, you're not. You're staring into space and sighing a lot."

"Am I?" She hadn't realized she'd been sighing. "Sorry, I'll try to sigh more quietly."

"Why are you sighing at all?"

"I didn't sleep well last night." Like, pretty much not at all. She'd tossed and turned with anxiety the whole night, and now she was exhausted *and* she had a dehydration headache from crying yesterday.

"I thought you were going to send that to me today for stress testing."

"I know. I am." Esther tried to keep the irritation out of her voice and failed. Which only made her feel worse. Yemi didn't deserve to be snapped at. He was only trying to help.

She reached for her headphones and put them on. Maybe it would be easier to concentrate on work if she was listening to music. She had a whole playlist of soothing, unobtrusive songs she liked to listen to when she was working and needed to shut out the distractions of the earthly plane.

Yemi kicked her chair, and she took off her headphones again. "What?" There she went, sounding irritated again. She turned around and forced a smile to make up for it.

"What time are we going to lunch?"

Shit. Lunch. Would Jinny be there? Would she be able to talk to her? Or would she skip lunch entirely to avoid confrontation?

No way to find out but show up and see what happened. "The usual, I guess. Noon."

"Okay," Yemi said. "That gives you two whole hours to finish those changes. Good luck." From anyone else, she would have assumed it was sarcasm, but Yemi didn't have a sarcastic bone in his body. If he wished you good luck, he meant it.

She could use all the good luck she could get at this point. She put her headphones back on and tried to focus.

JINNY WASN'T in the cafeteria when Esther and Yemi got there a little after noon. There wasn't any sign of her by the time they'd gone through the line and sat down with their food either.

"Where's Jinny?" Yemi asked after five more minutes had passed with no sign of her.

"Avoiding me." Esther stabbed half-heartedly at her Chinese chicken salad. She didn't have any appetite today. Everything tasted like wet paper in her mouth.

Yemi's brow furrowed over his glasses. "Why?"

"She's mad at me."

"What did you do?"

Of course he'd assume it was all Esther's fault. Which it was, but that wasn't the point.

She scowled. "I don't want to talk about it. I did something stupid and now she's not talking to me. Let's just leave it at that."

"You should apologize." So much for not talking about it.

"I did."

"You should apologize again. You should keep apologizing until she stops being mad."

Esther set down her fork and reached for her Mountain Dew. She didn't usually indulge in this much caffeine, but today she needed it. She twisted the cap off the bottle and swallowed a mouthful, grimacing at the sweetness. "Doesn't that just make people *more* mad, if they want you to leave them alone and you don't?"

She'd been trying to decide whether to go to knitting that night. She almost never missed knitting; it was one of the high-lights of her week. But Jinny might be there, and Esther wasn't eager to rehash their fight in front of everyone. The others would almost definitely take Jinny's side. She could already imagine the looks on their faces when they heard what Esther had done. The judgment. She couldn't face that right now, on top of everything else.

Yemi tilted his head. "Sometimes. It depends if they really want you to leave them alone or if they're just saying that because they want you to work to win them back."

"How do you know which is which?"

"I couldn't tell you that." He shrugged. "I tend to get it wrong a lot."

Esther sighed and picked up her fork again. Yemi probably wasn't the best person to turn to for advice. But at least he wasn't judging her. When she looked at him all she saw in his expression was sympathy. It made her feel a little better. Until his thick-framed glasses and his furrowed brow reminded her of Jonathan, and then she felt miserable all over again.

"You should try anyway," Yemi said. "It's better to try and get it wrong than do nothing."

"Is it?" Esther wasn't so sure. Trying and getting it wrong was what had landed her in this situation to begin with. If she'd done nothing and let Jinny manage her own love life, they wouldn't be in the middle of a fight right now.

But then she and Jonathan never would have been friends. The thought made her even more depressed.

ESTHER SKIPPED KNITTING on Monday night. She decided what Jinny needed from her right now was space. It wouldn't do any good to force a confrontation before she was ready to talk—and listen. Jinny didn't react well to being pushed, which was what had gotten them in this fight in the first place. It wasn't about the fact that Esther had slept with Jonathan; Jinny was upset that Esther had tricked her into dating him.

Jinny's mother was always trying to control her: pressuring her into dressing a certain way, dating a certain kind of man, being a certain kind of person. Buying her clothes she didn't want, setting her up on dates she hadn't agreed to. She'd even gone through Jinny's purse once and thrown away a bunch of expensive lipsticks she'd pronounced "too slutty." Esther knew exactly how much Jinny resented it—and yet she'd turned around and done the exact same thing to her. No wonder she was mad.

The rest of the week went by without a word from her. Wherever Jinny was eating lunch every day, it wasn't the cafeteria. And since they worked in separate parts of the building on totally different projects, the cafeteria was the only place they were likely to run into each other.

This was exactly what Jinny had done the last time they'd had a fight. Gone silent for a week until she'd cooled off. Then they'd talked and patched things up. That's what Esther was hoping for. It might take some time, but hopefully it would blow over eventually.

Meanwhile, Esther's mother had started calling to beg for more money. She called on Tuesday and again on Thursday. "It's just impossible to find anything for that price," she pleaded. "You don't understand what the rental market up here is like."

Esther understood perfectly. She'd spent time on the internet searching for apartments around Seattle. Putting in different search parameters, trying to find something in her mother's budget that didn't look like a crack den. There wasn't much. For once, her mother wasn't exaggerating.

"I'm already giving you as much as I can afford," Esther said, feeling wretched. That wasn't strictly true, but she'd made a promise to Eric.

When she got home from work on Friday, Esther's eyes lingered on Jonathan's car in the space beside hers. She hadn't seen him all week. She kept hoping she'd run into him coming or going, but so far she'd been forced to content herself with gazing longingly at his car.

She'd thought about texting him, but she couldn't think of anything to say. Not anything that he'd want to hear, anyway. He'd probably reject any overtures of friendship at this point.

She went to check her mail, and her heart dropped like a stone when she saw the package waiting for her.

It was the new drip coffeemaker she'd ordered for herself last week. She'd intended to surprise Jonathan by offering him a decent cup of coffee the next time he came over. She wasn't ready to commit to a Chemex, but she'd decided it was time to move up to a real coffeemaker. She'd been planning to ask him for coffee recommendations.

But now she couldn't. She couldn't ask him for coffee suggestions, and she couldn't make him a cup of coffee in her new coffeemaker, because he wasn't going to be coming over anymore.

She picked up the box and carried it upstairs to her apartment. She didn't feel like unpacking it, so she left it on the dining table and went to go change into her pajamas.

Yes, she was putting on pajamas at six o'clock in the evening. Why not? It wasn't like anyone was coming over. The only two people who ever came to her apartment weren't speaking to her currently.

She sank down on the couch and flipped on the television. Sally jumped up beside her and promptly fell asleep. Rough life that cat had, sleeping all day, followed by an intense bout of evening napping. Must be nice.

As Esther flipped through the channels, looking for something to watch, the coffeemaker glared at her from the dining table. To the extent that an inanimate cardboard box could glare.

After a few minutes, she pushed herself to her feet, snatched it off the table, and dumped it on the floor in the coat closet where she wouldn't have to look at it anymore.

The stupid thing reminded her too much of Jonathan and how much she missed him.

What had happened to her? How had her feelings for him changed so much in just a few short months? How had she gone so quickly from hating him to liking him? Depending on him, even.

She missed the way he used to hang around outside, waiting for her to get home from work. She missed telling him about her day and hearing about his. She missed ordering pizza together and arguing about movies. She missed his sense of humor, and how fussy he was about his coffee. She missed the way he ran his hands through his hair when he was nervous, and the smile he only showed his friends. She'd probably never get to see that smile again.

She'd *liked* being his friend, dammit. Knowing he was right next door if she wanted company.

She wanted company *now*, and didn't have anyone to talk to.

The weekend loomed ahead of her, bleak and barren. No Jinny, no Jonathan. Not even knitting to look forward to on Monday. Just Esther and her cat.

She'd never felt like her social circle was small before, but tonight it felt microscopic. Nonexistent, even.

Chapter Twenty-Two

_B_y the time Monday morning came, Esther was actually glad to be back at work, just to have some human contact again.

She'd spent the whole weekend alone in her apartment, trying to ignore the sounds of Jonathan moving around next door. Trying not to wonder what he was doing, or whether he was thinking about her. _What_ he was thinking about her.

Instead of wallowing in self-pity, Esther had distracted herself by tackling a long overdue wardrobe purge. By Sunday night, she had a garbage bag full of old clothes earmarked for donation, and her closet looked like it had been set upon by a pack of obsessive-compulsives, right down to the spectrum of color-sorted shirts. It was so beautiful, she actually considered taking a picture and submitting it to _Apartment Therapy_.

But then she heard Jonathan's coffee grinder fire up next door, and spent the rest of the night on the couch eating cheese until she felt sick.

Now it was Monday and she was back in the land of the living, sitting at her desk in a form-fitting sheath dress and fancy shoes, feeling like an imposter. As a result of her closet purge, and in an effort to break out of her funk, she'd vowed to start dressing up more for work. Dress for the job you want, like the career counselors advised. One area of her life might be a dumpster fire, but she could at least focus on improving another area. Maybe if she made an effort to dress and act more professionally at work, she'd get more respect.

Only this form-fitting dress she was wearing had fit her form a lot better two years ago when it was new. Not only was it uncomfortably tight across the bust and hips, but it kept trying to ride up dangerously high on her thighs. It was also itchier than she remembered, which was probably why it had been buried in the back of her closet. Instead of feeling like a confident, grown-up career woman, Esther felt like squirmy kid chafing in her Sunday best. Total professional dressing fail.

"What's wrong with you?" Yemi asked. "You look weird today."

"Thanks," she muttered irritably. So much for New Improved Work Esther.

He narrowed his eyes at her. "Do you have an interview?"

"No, I'm just trying to dress a little nicer."

"Why?"

"No reason, apparently." She tugged her skirt down for the one thousandth time that morning. "What time do you want to do lunch?"

"Um." Yemi's shoulders hunched as his eyes skated away.

"What's wrong?"

"Why do you assume something's wrong?"

"You're making your turtle face."

"I'm not—I don't have a turtle face."

"Yes, you do. Whenever you don't want to do something, your head starts trying to retract into your body like a turtle. What don't you want to do?"

He pressed his lips into an expression that might have been

intended as a smile, but looked more like a rictus of pain. "I told Jinny I'd eat lunch with her today."

"Oh." Esther felt like someone had pulled her chair out from under her, right as she was about to sit down.

Yemi looked miserable. "I'm sorry if—"

"No. Don't be." She shook her head. "You should have lunch with Jinny." They were work friends too. The three of them had been eating lunch together for the better part of a year. It wasn't like Esther had a monopoly on Yemi.

"Are you sure?" He was clearly having a hard time with this. Navigating interpersonal drama made him uncomfortable. It wasn't exactly Esther's favorite pastime either.

"It's fine," she told him, trying to sound more sincere.

Yemi looked down at his shoes. "There's something else I should probably tell you."

Esther watched him squirm and waited for the other shoe to drop. Whatever it was, he *really* didn't want to have to say it.

"Jinny asked me out last week. We're sort of…dating, I guess."

"Oh. Wow. That's—wow." Esther couldn't form a better response. She should be happy for them. She should be ecstatic. Two weeks ago, she would have been jumping up and down at the news. She would have thrown them a party to celebrate. Now she just felt emptier than before. Abandoned.

Yemi's mouth turned down unhappily. "This is weird, I know."

"It's not," Esther said, doing a poor job of selling it. "It's great." It *was* great. "I'm happy for you both." She was trying to be, anyway.

"You should really talk to her."

"I've tried."

"Maybe I could—"

"Don't. Don't try to get in the middle."

"We could eat lunch tomorrow," Yemi suggested.

"I don't need a pity lunch." The words came out sounding

bitter, and Yemi flinched. She forced herself to smile. "I mean, we see each other all day, right? You should spend lunch with Jinny."

Yemi looked uncertain. "Okay."

"It's fine." Esther smiled wider. She was smiling so hard her cheeks hurt. Maybe if she kept doing it they'd freeze that way. "Really. Enjoy your lunch."

She turned around and went back to work. Or tried to, anyway. What she actually did was spend most of the morning staring into space and feeling sorry for herself.

She shouldn't be this upset. Yemi was just a work friend. It wasn't as if they hung out regularly outside the office. Nothing had to change between them. They'd still sit beside each other all day, and still be able to talk about work stuff.

So why did she feel like she'd lost something important?

Because Jinny had staked her claim on Yemi. She'd played a trump card that beat everything Esther was holding. If push came to shove, he would choose Jinny now. As he should.

At 11:55, Yemi got up to go to lunch. "I'll see you later," he said, sounding sheepish.

Esther nodded. "Yep."

She didn't go to the cafeteria. Instead, she cobbled together a measly lunch of snack foods from the vending machine down the hall. She stayed at her desk, munching on salt and vinegar potato chips and Famous Amos cookies while she caught up on the work she should have been doing all morning.

Yemi came back an hour later. He looked happy. Glowing, almost. The glow faded a little when he saw Esther. His eyes took in the empty potato chip bag on her desk and he frowned.

"How was lunch?" she asked, pushing the evidence of her own dismal, solitary lunch into the trash.

"The enchilada pie was under-salted today."

"That sucks."

"I'll eat lunch with you tomorrow," Yemi offered again. A consolation prize.

Esther didn't want it. She shook her head. "Thanks, but I can't tomorrow. I've got a call with one of the offsite testing teams." It was a lie, but Yemi wouldn't know that. He'd be off at lunch with Jinny tomorrow. And every day after that, probably.

ESTHER PACKED her own lunch on Tuesday, even though it was kung pao chicken day. Instead of enjoying delicious kung pao chicken and egg rolls with everyone else, she'd be eating peanut butter and jelly at her desk. A sad, pathetic lunch for a sad, pathetic loser.

She'd already abandoned her dressing-up initiative and reverted back to her old, comfy work wardrobe. What was the point? If she was going to be miserable, she might as well be *comfortable* in her misery.

At 11:55 on the dot, Yemi got up from his desk and gave Esther a sheepish nod on his way to lunch. She nodded back. Neither of them said anything.

When he came back an hour later, Esther had her headphones on. She pretended to be engrossed in her work so she wouldn't have to see the pitying look on his face.

They didn't talk the rest of the day. Esther kept her headphones on and buried her head in a spreadsheet. When five o'clock rolled around, Yemi packed his stuff and stood up. He tapped her on the shoulder and waved. She waved back, and he left.

Wednesday was meatloaf day. The meatloaf wasn't anything special, but they served it with macaroni and cheese. Esther loved the cafeteria macaroni and cheese.

She figured she couldn't hide from Jinny and Yemi forever, so she worked up the courage to brave the cafeteria alone.

She had a strategy all worked out. First, she waited for Yemi to leave, and then she let him get a five-minute head start before heading down herself. By the time Esther got in line, Jinny and

Yemi had already gotten their food and were sitting at a table by themselves.

It was the first time Esther had seen Jinny since their fight. She and Yemi were huddled together talking and smiling at each other —beaming, more like. In their own little world. So caught up in each other they hadn't noticed Esther walk in. Jinny had her full-on smitten face going, and Yemi was gazing back at her with his heart in his eyes. Esther had never seen him like this before. It was a revelation. She never would have pegged him for such a hopeless romantic.

They both looked so happy.

By the time Esther got to the front of the line, they were out of macaroni and cheese.

She got her meatloaf to go and took it back to her desk to eat alone.

ESTHER'S HEADPHONES were on again when Yemi returned from lunch. She'd cleaned up the remnants of her lunch, carrying the trash into the ladies' room. She told herself it was so she wouldn't have to smell meatloaf for the rest of the day, but it was also so Yemi wouldn't know she'd eaten at her desk. She wasn't sure why she cared. But she did.

She purposely didn't look up when he sat down. After a few minutes, she felt him kick her chair.

Spinning around, she lifted one headphone off her ear—just the one, to send the message she didn't want to talk. Jesus, she was being petty. She couldn't seem to help it though.

Yemi frowned at her. "You're upset with me."

Esther forced a smile that probably looked as fake as it felt. "No, I'm not. I'm just behind on these design notes."

Yemi's frown got deeper. "Are you mad that Jinny and I are dating?"

"No, of course not." Esther smiled wider. It felt like her face was going to crack and fall away, revealing a hideous lizard monster underneath.

"What do you want me to do?" Yemi asked.

"I don't want you to do anything. You're not doing anything wrong."

"I could talk to her for you," he offered again.

"Please don't." The last thing Esther wanted was to be responsible for causing tension in their brand-new relationship. "It's better if you leave it alone. I'm glad you're together. I'm glad you're happy."

The words rang hollow in the air between them, but it was the best she could mange. She *wanted* to be happy for them. That should count for something, shouldn't it?

Before Yemi could say anything else, she yanked her headphones on and turned her back on him.

THAT NIGHT, Penny called to check on Esther. "You've missed knitting two weeks in a row. Are you okay?"

"I'm fine," Esther said, brushing pizza crumbs off her pajama pants.

It was seven o'clock and she was already in her pajamas, eating pizza on her couch and watching mushy Hallmark movies. Because she was a loser with nowhere to be except at home with her cat. Not that she'd made a habit of going out much on weeknights before. But still. What a cliché she'd become. She didn't even have the heart to watch any of her favorite horror movies, because they reminded her too much of Jonathan. Instead, she was watching some heartwarming atrocity staring Melissa Joan Hart and Joey Lawrence. Which was a different sort of horror movie, but a horror movie nonetheless.

"Are you ever coming back?" Penny asked.

"Has Jinny been coming?"

Penny hesitated. "She came on Monday."

"Did she tell you she's not currently speaking to me?"

"She...might have mentioned something about that."

Esther squeezed the phone. "Did she tell you why?"

"Yes, and I'm not taking sides, but you guys need to make up."

"I've tried. She doesn't want to talk to me."

"It's not the same without you there. Everyone misses you."

"Jinny doesn't."

"She does. Even if she's too proud to say it."

"Well, the ball's in her court. I'm trying to respect her boundaries and give her space. Which is why I've given her full custody of you guys."

It was fine. Okay, so maybe her life felt a little like a movie montage about a lonely spinster who did nothing but go to work, eat lunch by herself at her desk, and spend her evenings knitting in front of the TV with her cat—which wasn't all it was cracked up to be, because Sally always tried to bite her yarn ends.

She'd finished Jonathan's hat last week, but she obviously couldn't give it to him, so she'd stuffed it in the bottom of her dresser and started a new pair of socks for herself. They didn't follow any kind of pattern. She was using up all the leftover sock yarn from other projects—all the random, miscellaneous bits and pieces in all different colorways. She'd reach into her stash and grab the first thing that came to hand, knit until she got tired of it, and then switch to something else. They were the ugliest socks she'd ever seen. Messy and tragic, like Esther's life.

"I hate this," Penny said unhappily. "Drama stresses me out."

Esther scowled at the Hallmark movie on her TV screen. "I'm not exactly a fan either."

"We're your friends too, and you'll always be welcome. You can come back whenever you want."

It was a nice sentiment, but Esther couldn't imagine going back as long as Jinny was refusing to speak to her. It would be awful and uncomfortable for everyone. They didn't deserve to be dragged into the middle of it.

"Promise you'll call if you need anything," Penny said.

"I will." Hearing Penny's voice drove home just how much Esther had missed the group. Vilma was like the mother figure she'd always wanted, and the others were like sisters. They were like a little family. The only family Esther had in LA. "I'll be back eventually. Assuming the divorce isn't permanent."

"You're not getting divorced," Penny insisted. "You two will work it out."

Esther wished she could believe that. She hadn't expected the fight with Jinny to go on this long. It had already been a week and a half. She'd tried texting Jinny again on Monday as a test balloon, but it had gone unanswered, like the others.

She toyed with the idea of going over to Jinny's apartment and seeing if she'd let her in. It was a trigger she might have to pull eventually, but for now it seemed like an endeavor with a high probability of rejection. She'd give her a few more days, and then she'd reevaluate.

Esther got off the phone with Penny and went back to watching her terrible Hallmark movie and knitting her ugly socks.

An hour later, there was a knock on her door.

Her heart leapt into her throat as Sally bolted for the bedroom. What if it was Jonathan? She couldn't talk to him right now. Not in her pajamas. There was probably pizza sauce on her chin and she wasn't wearing a bra.

She got up and peered through the peephole. There was no one there. Creepy. This was exactly how a lot of horror movies started. She waited, listening for any sounds of murderers skulking nearby. When she didn't hear anything, she opened the door a crack.

There was a manila envelope lying on the doorstep with her name written on it in a familiar black Pilot gel pen scrawl.

Jonathan had left her something.

Chapter Twenty-Three

*H*er heart thudded in her chest as she stooped to retrieve the envelope. There was no sign of him. He must have hightailed it back into his apartment, so he wouldn't have to face her.

She carried the envelope inside and closed the door. Inside it was a copy of Jonathan's first script. *American Dreamers.* The love story he'd promised to show her when it was finished.

Esther sank down on the couch and flipped to the first page. The Hallmark movie she'd been watching faded into distant background noise as she pored over every word. Fascinated. Mesmerized. Stunned.

The more she read, the louder her pulse pounded in her ears.

It was about her. About *them.*

Jonathan had completely rewritten the female lead, Emily, and remade her in Esther's image. Instead of a Manic Pixie Dream Girl, she was grounded, sarcastic, pragmatic, and a little closed off. Distrustful and averse to emotional attachments. She even had a degree in engineering and a disdain for good coffee.

Jonas, the male lead, was mostly unchanged. He was still loosely autobiographical, but with a lot of the character's annoyingly quirky traits excised. Instead of a busker, he was a writer now, like Jonathan. He was less smug in this draft, and kinder. More vulnerable. He wore his heart on his sleeve, quick to love and unafraid to express it.

The whole story had been overhauled. For one thing, there actually was one now. Jonas and Emily still met the same way— only in an airport instead of a train station, like Esther had suggested—but there was more purpose to their interactions. In this new draft, Jonas fell head over heels for Emily in the first act, and spent the rest of the screenplay trying to convince her that love at first sight was real, despite Emily's insistence that love was a fantasy. She even called it "a delusion caused by rising cortisol levels and depleted serotonin," like Esther had.

A *lot* of the conversations in the script mirrored conversations she'd had with Jonathan. It was almost like reading a diary of their friendship.

In the last act, Jonas begged Emily to postpone her trip and stay one more day. If she'd just give him one more day, he told her, he could prove they were meant to be together. She just needed to take a chance on him. Open herself up to the possibility of love.

It ended on a cliffhanger, just before Emily—clearly torn— made her decision. You didn't know whether or not she was going to say yes.

The words blurred before Esther's eyes as she stared at the page. Jonathan was using this script to tell her how he felt about her. Every page, every word, was about them. He was asking her to give them a chance.

Esther's stomach hurt. She felt like she couldn't get enough air into her lungs. It was possible she might be hyperventilating.

This thing between us is real, Jonas pleaded with Emily on the last page. *I know you can feel it too. Don't walk away from us.*

Esther closed her eyes and waited for her breathing to go back to normal. Then she picked up her phone and scrolled to Jonathan's name in her contacts. She needed to talk to him. He'd bared his soul by sharing this with her. She couldn't ignore that. It would be cruel. Heartless. She wasn't heartless. If anything, her heart was too full to fit inside her chest.

He answered on the first ring.

"Esther?" The sound of his voice made her eyes burn all the way down the back of her throat to the pit of her stomach. God, she'd missed him. *So much.*

She swallowed and stood up, pacing back and forth across her living room. "I read *American Dreamers.*"

"Yeah?" He sounded wary.

"I loved it."

He didn't say anything.

She stopped pacing. "Jonathan?"

"I'm here." His voice was hoarse. "You really liked it?"

"No, I *loved* it. It's so good. Your professor has to give you an A." She started pacing again, making circuits of her apartment from the living room to the kitchen and back.

"It's about you," he said. "About us."

She blew out a breath. "Yeah, I figured that out."

"Esther—"

"Don't," she said, her voice breaking in two. "Please. I can't."

"Can't what?"

"Do this. With you."

"Why?"

She swallowed around the lump in her throat. "I can't be what you need me to be. I don't feel what you want me to feel." She stopped pacing and stared at the floor. Grasping for something to say. "The screenplay was amazing, but it doesn't change anything. I'm sorry."

She missed being his friend—*so* much. But she couldn't give him more than that. And he deserved more. He deserved someone who could return his feelings unreservedly. As much as he thought he wanted her, she'd only end up hurting him even more. She owed him better than that.

He exhaled a long, slow breath. "Okay. I guess that's it, then." He sounded deflated, like an old helium balloon.

"I'm sorry," she said again. Final this time. A goodbye.

"Wait, don't hang up."

She waited.

"I miss you."

Her gaze went to the wall between their apartments. The only thing physically standing between them. Just a few inches of drywall and insulation.

There was a tremor in her voice when she spoke. "I miss you too."

"There's something real here. Don't throw us away." It was almost exactly what Jonas had said to Emily.

She pressed her palm against the wall that separated them. She didn't speak. She wasn't sure she could anymore.

"I love you," Jonathan said.

Her stomach dropped like she'd just done a corkscrew on a rollercoaster, and she jerked her hand away from the wall.

No man who wasn't related to her had ever said those words to her before. It felt as if the sky had reached down and smacked her in the face. "What?" she said, squeezing her fingers around the phone.

"You heard me."

"Jonathan." His name came out in a strangled whisper. "Please don't."

"Don't love you or don't say it?"

"Both." She felt faint. Her hand reached out for the wall again to hold herself up.

"I can't change how I feel. And don't try to tell me you don't have feelings for me, because I know you do."

"Of course I care about you, but..." It was too much pressure. She felt paralyzed. Unable to think of anything to say.

"But not enough, is that what you're saying?"

She blinked at the wall separating them. She could picture his face perfectly. The dark eyebrows, drawn together. That crinkle he got in his forehead when he was being serious. His eyes, soft and earnest behind his glasses.

She reached up to wipe the tears from her face. "I'm sorry."

"Okay," he said. Bitter. Resigned. "I guess that's it."

He hung up.

Esther sank to the floor and hugged her knees to her chest, still clutching her phone.

He didn't really love her. He was in love with the idea of being in love. He'd been looking for someone to fill the empty space in his heart for so long, he'd settled on the first person who came along. He'd only fixated on her because she was there. Because she was convenient.

That was what she tried to tell herself, anyway.

But deep down, she knew it was a lie.

Chapter Twenty-Four

*N*o one had ever fallen in love with Esther before. Not once, not in her whole life. She'd thought it would feel...better. And less vomit-inducing.

Maybe it would, if she wasn't so broken. If she was capable of responding the way she was supposed to. Normal people probably didn't feel like they were having a panic attack when someone they cared about told them they loved them.

Esther went to work the next day and tried not to think about it. There was a meeting coming up she needed to prepare for. A conflict had been identified between some of the power and payload sub-assemblies, and there was a roadblock meeting Monday to go over the problem and decide what to do about it.

It was a chance for Esther to ingratiate herself with both assembly teams. If she could come up with a solution and convince them to implement it, it would go a long way to proving her value.

Except she couldn't concentrate. Every time she tried to think about the problem, she wound up thinking about Jonathan instead. Replaying their phone conversation in her head, or remembering lines from his script. And then her stomach would start to hurt and her chest would feel too tight, and she'd have to squeeze her eyes shut to keep from crying.

At lunchtime, she went down to the cafeteria to get her food to go, like she always did. Yemi and Jinny were already there, at a table in the far back corner. Heads together. Huddled. Smiling at each other like there was no one else in the room. Esther watched them while she waited in line. They were in love. They might not know it themselves yet, but it was there to see, plain as day.

They looked so happy, it made her stomach hurt even more. She wasn't just feeling left out, she realized. She was envious of what they had together. That they could let themselves love like that.

She spent the rest of the afternoon struggling to focus on work. It was a relief when five o'clock rolled around and she could bolt for the door.

Jonathan's car wasn't there when she got home. She felt disappointed. Her daily glimpses of his car were as close as she was able to get to seeing him. She wondered where he was, and if he was okay after their conversation last night. A fresh pang of guilt stabbed at her.

As she was letting herself into her apartment, her phone rang. Great. Her mother. Another source of stomach-grinding stress.

"You answered your phone," her mother said. "You never answer you phone."

"Hi, Mom," Esther said, grimacing as she slammed her door shut. She'd ignored her mom's call the other night, and never gotten around to calling her back. One more thing to feel guilty about.

"I just don't know what I'm going to do about this apartment situation, sweetheart."

Just once, it would be nice if her mother would call to see how she was doing. Or at least *ask* how she was doing before jumping straight to her own problems.

"Eric said you had more apartments to look at today." Her

brother had been helping their mom search for a new place, but so far there hadn't been any she'd deemed tolerable. And the clock was ticking down to the end of the month.

"They were all a nightmare. One of them had a sink in the bedroom."

Esther went into the kitchen to feed Sally. "I know it sucks, but you might have to lower your standards a little."

"You didn't see these apartments, honey. No one would want their mother to live like that."

Eric had sent Esther the links, and she'd looked at them online. None of them had seemed that bad. They were about as nice as Esther's place.

"If I could just have a little bigger budget, it might be possible to find something fit for human habitation."

Esther sank down on the couch and rubbed her temples. "I can't give you any more money than I already am."

"But I know you make good money at that job of yours."

"I'm only in my second year, and living in LA is expensive."

"Well, if you moved back to Seattle—"

"Seattle's expensive too," Esther snapped. "And my job is in LA."

"You know I don't like having to beg my daughter for money."

Esther gritted her teeth. "I know."

"You're being unreasonable. I need your help."

"I can't help you," Esther said. "I'm sorry."

"What did I ever do to deserve this? How did I end up with a daughter who's so unfeeling? One day I'll be dead and you'll regret treating me so coldly." Her mother hung up angry. She always hung up angry these days.

Esther didn't know how much more of this she could stand. She went into the kitchen for a beer, and then she called her brother. "I'm offering Mom more money the next time she calls."

"Don't you dare."

"I can't deal with her anymore. Please let me throw money at the problem to make it go away."

"How much money are you willing to throw at her? An extra thousand dollars a month? Because that's what she thinks she needs. She wants this apartment in Maple Leaf that's eighteen hundred bucks a month, because the light has a positive energy or some feng shui shit."

Esther couldn't afford an extra thousand a month. Not and keep her current apartment. She could afford a couple hundred more, max.

"Besides," Eric said, "it won't stop there. Not if you give in now. Next year she'll want a little more, and even more the year after that. You'll end up fully supporting her. Is that what you want? Is that something you can afford?"

"She's our mother."

"She's not sick or disabled. She is perfectly capable of solving her own problems and supporting herself, she just doesn't want to. Don't let her manipulate you, Es. You're not doing her any favors by giving in."

Esther knew he was right, but it didn't make it any easier. It didn't make her feel any better.

She was getting a stomach ulcer. She could feel the acids churning around like a blender, eating away at her from the inside out. Every time her phone started blaring the ringtone she'd given her mom—"Mother's Little Helper" by the Rolling Stones—she had a visceral negative reaction. Her heart started pounding and her stomach tried to turn in on itself.

It was all too much. Maybe she'd be able to deal with it better if she had someone else to talk to. Jinny, or the knitting group, or Jonathan. Or Jonathan.

God, she missed Jonathan so much. He'd know exactly what to say to cheer her up. He'd be able to understand, because he had issues with his parents too. His eyebrows would draw together like a fuzzy caterpillar and he'd blink those long lashes at her as his eyes softened in sympathy. Even if he couldn't solve her problem, he'd make her feel better, just by listening.

But Esther had lost Jonathan. She'd pushed him away. The only person she could talk to was Eric, and he was already harried enough. He was the one telling her not to do the thing she wanted to do.

There was one potential solution to her mother's problem that Esther had yet to explore. Something she knew Eric wouldn't approve of.

Their father owned a couple of rental houses. He might be convinced to offer one to their mother at a discounted rent. It was a long shot, but maybe he'd do it for Esther's sake. If she explained that she and Eric were at their wit's end, that she was stressing herself into an early grave, maybe he'd agree to help them out.

She let the idea sit for a few minutes, rolling it around. Then she gave in and called her dad.

"Esther?" He sounded surprised when he answered the phone. No wonder. She almost never called him. They hadn't talked in months.

"Hey, Dad," she said, pacing around her apartment.

"Is everything okay?" It wasn't a holiday or anyone's birthday, so of course he'd assume she was calling because something was wrong. Because she needed something. Which she did.

She was treating her dad like her mother treated her. The realization made Esther feel even sicker.

"Yeah," she lied, "everything's fine."

"What is it? You can tell me." Even her absentee father could see through her lies. She'd meant to start out by asking how he was doing and pretending to be interested in his life, but that was out the window now.

"I, um...I had a question about those two rental properties you own. In Fremont."

"What about them?"

"Do you still have them?"

"Yes."

"I don't suppose there are any vacancies." She knew it was a crazy pipe dream as soon as she said the words out loud. The two properties only had eight units between them. What were the odds one would be available? Much less that her father would be willing to let her mother live there.

"What's this about?" he asked, impatient for her to get to the point.

"Mom's losing her apartment."

"Oh. Of course." His voice had gone flat. He was already distancing himself, the way he always did when the subject of her mother came up.

Esther barreled on, even though she knew it was hopeless. "She's having trouble finding a new place in her price range, and I was just wondering—hoping, really, that you might be able to rent her one of your properties."

"I doubt she'll be able to afford the rent."

"I thought maybe you could give her a discount on it..." She chewed on her lower lip as she waited for his answer.

"Esther." His voice was even flatter now, like a penny left on a railroad track. "I can't do that."

"You mean you won't."

"I have renters in those properties with leases. I can't break them."

"Okay, but—"

"Even if I could, I wouldn't."

And there it was. Why had she ever thought there was a chance this would work? Her father would never go out of his way to help her mother.

"Dad, please," she said, making one last Hail Mary. "I'm asking you to do it for me. Eric's been trying to help her find her a new place, but they haven't had any luck. She's got to be out by the end of the month. We're desperate."

"Listen, pumpkin..." It grated on her that her dad still called her pumpkin, like she was nine. Not so coincidentally, that's how old she was when he last spent any real time around her. "This is your mother's problem to solve, not yours, not Eric's, and definitely not mine."

Esther sat on the couch. Her free hand squeezed the edge of the cushion in a death grip. "That's great in theory, but it doesn't stop Mom from ending up on the street."

"Your mother will get by. She always does. Once she realizes she can't get someone to step in and do the hard work for her, she'll figure something out for herself. That's how she works."

"It's different this time. You know what the rental market is like right now."

"There are plenty of people in the greater metro area getting by on modest salaries. If she wanted to make it work, she could."

"Spoken like someone who lives in Laurelhurst."

"Your mother made her own choices."

"She didn't choose for you to leave her for your dental hygienist." It was a low blow, but the low road seemed to be Esther's preferred mode of transportation these days.

"She had a very comfortable alimony from me," her father replied, quietly terse. "No one forced her to marry and then divorce that painter, throwing it all away. Just like no one is keeping her from getting a full-time job to make ends meet. Those are her choices, and what's happening now is the consequence of those choices."

Esther's foot kicked the leg of the coffee table. "They're not just her consequences though. They're mine and Eric's too, because we're the ones left to take care of her."

Her father sighed the beleaguered sigh of someone who had spent years of his life taking care of her mother. "Your mother needs to stand on her own two feet. If we keep picking her up every time she falls down, she'll never do it for herself. How do you think your mother got like this? Her parents babied and protected her, and then I picked up where they left off."

"And now I'm the one who's supposed to turn my back on her?" Esther kicked the coffee table again. Hard enough to hurt this time.

"I'm not saying it's fair. But yes."

"Easy for you to say."

"Maybe it is now, but believe me, it wasn't easy when I left her. It wasn't easy to extricate myself from her web of dependency, but that's what I did, and it's what you need to do now."

"Was it easier or harder than leaving me and Eric?" she said in a cold, flat voice.

"Esther—"

"Never mind, don't answer that. Thanks anyway, Dad." She ended the call before he could say anything else.

It was just like she'd thought. She was on her own.

Chapter Twenty-Five

*E*sther got up the next morning and got ready for work, determined to put everything except work out of her mind. She wasn't going to think about any of that other stuff, because there was nothing she could do about it. Instead, she was going to focus like a laser on the one thing she could control: her job.

Until she stepped out of her apartment and came face to face with Jonathan.

Esther's heart leapt into her throat at the sight of him. A bottle of laundry detergent dangled from one of his hands; the other clenched the doorknob of his apartment. He was wearing sweatpants and flip-flops, his hair fluffy and disheveled, his stretched-out T-shirt baggy on his frame.

He stared at her, frozen. Eyes wide with horror. A marble sculpture entitled "An Unwelcome Encounter."

She'd been aching for a glimpse of him for days, but now that they'd come face to face, all she wanted to do was flee. She wished she could rewind time and take an extra few minutes leaving her apartment, so she'd never have to see the way he was looking at her right now.

Esther's mouth opened—to say what, she wasn't sure—but before anything could come out, he recovered his motor control and went into his apartment without a word. She deflated like a punctured air mattress as the door slammed behind him.

So much for focusing on work.

She locked her apartment with a shaking hand and went down to her car, eyes locked straight ahead as she walked past his window. Her stomach did a small heave at the sight of his Lexus in the space next to hers. She got behind the wheel of her Prius and clenched the steering wheel with both fists, taking deep breaths until she could trust herself not to cry on the drive to work.

She might need to move. Living in such close proximity to Jonathan was torment.

An hour later, she sat at her desk with her headphones on, still haunted by the stark expression on his face.

He'd looked like someone in agony. Like the very sight of her hurt him.

That was what came of loving her. Pain and unhappiness.

No. *Enough.*

Fuck wallowing. There was nothing she could do about Jonathan, but she could damn well fix this problem with the project.

She already had an idea, she just needed to flesh it out a little more and double-check a few things. It was a good idea. Actually, no, it was great. She was going to knock their damn socks off at that meeting on Monday and show them what she was worth.

What she needed was some motivating jams to drown everything else out. She started up her Rihanna playlist, cranked the volume, and got to work.

SHE SPENT the entire weekend working on her presentation for the roadblock meeting. She was going to rock this. The solution she'd come up with was efficient and innovative: designing a single composite part to hold both sub-assemblies in the same space. It would be a little more expensive, but save both weight and space. She had a killer PowerPoint deck to illustrate her proposal, and detailed data to back it up. The only other person who had submitted a proposal was Dan, and his solution wasn't anywhere near as elegant as hers.

Esther got to the conference room earlier and chose a seat by the whiteboard. Dan showed up a few minutes later with a dozen doughnuts. Not cheap doughnuts either, but expensive gourmet doughnuts from a shop in Manhattan Beach. He'd even made sure to get a couple vegan doughnuts for Bhavin.

"Hey, my favorite doughnuts!" Dmitri said when he arrived. He had the friendly, slightly slick demeanor of a car salesman. The fact that he was almost always smiling helped counteract the fact that his Lithuanian accent made him sound a little like Dracula. He clapped Dan on the back, grabbed a chocolate doughnut out of the box, and shoved it halfway into his mouth as he took his seat.

Esther's proposal was up first in the bake-off, and she presented it in a calm, unemotional, professional manner. She fielded questions from the other designers, and when Dmitri asked about the grounding path, she got up and walked him through it on the whiteboard.

Dan didn't say a word or ask any questions. He just sat there silently with that same smug expression on his face.

"Well, that's certainly an interesting idea," Bhavin said when Esther had finished. "We've never done anything like this before."

"That's true," Esther said. "But it's not entirely untested. It's just a new application of processes we've used on other projects."

"Here's the thing." Dmitri leaned forward, flashing his jovial salesman grin. The one he used to let people down easy. "We talked about your idea, and it sounds risky. There's a reason we do things the way we do them."

Beside him, Bhavin bobbed his head in agreement.

Dmitri stood up and helped himself to another doughnut. "Why don't we hear what Dan's got to say?"

Esther capped the whiteboard marker and took her seat again. She listened quietly, keeping her expression neutral, as Dan launched his proposal. He talked a good game and made an impressive PowerPoint deck, but it was obvious he'd hand-waved some of the science. She kept waiting for someone to call him on it, but no one did. Bhavin wasn't technical enough to realize Dan was blowing sunshine up his ass. Dmitri was, but apparently he didn't care because Dan was his bro.

When Dan finished, Dmitri was nodding his head. "Thanks very much, Dan. I think we've heard all we need to." He turned to address the whole table. "Esther, I like the innovation, but in this case I think we need to stick to the solution with the tried and true application that offers the most cost savings. Everyone agree?"

There were nods and a murmur of approval around the table. Esther sat there in shock as the meeting was adjourned and everyone began shuffling out of the room.

"Better luck next time," Dan sneered on his way out the door.

"It was a good idea," Bhavin told her as he took the last vegan doughnut. "It showed a lot of initiative."

Not good enough to implement though. "Dmitri said you'd talked about my proposal." It was an effort to keep her voice from shaking. "When was that?"

"At trivia on Friday," Bhavin said around a mouthful of doughnut. "I'm on a team with Dmitri and a couple of his devs." He finished chewing and swallowed. "It's not like it was a planned meeting or anything. It just came up in conversation."

Esther nodded. "Was Dan there?"

"Yeah. I mean, he's the one who organized the team."

Of course he was. It was no coincidence the team included both Dmitri and Bhavin. What better way to suck up to them outside work?

If Esther had thought to organize a trivia team and invite Dmitri and Bhavin to join, would they have picked her proposal instead? Probably not. They probably wouldn't have joined her trivia team, because she wasn't "one of the guys" and she never would be. Not even if she learned to play Magic: the Gathering or forced herself to care about fantasy football.

The one thing she'd thought she could control in her life was her job, and it turned out she couldn't control that either. No matter how good she was, or how hard she worked, she'd never be appreciated. Like everything else, it all came down to being liked —something Esther wasn't any good at.

She'd just needed something in her life to go well. It hadn't seemed like too much to ask.

She spent the rest of the afternoon fuming silently at her desk with her headphones on. Instead of going home when five o'clock rolled around, she took herself to the movies. She couldn't bear the thought of another night alone in her apartment, knowing that Jonathan was right on the other side of the wall. It was excruciating.

The air inside the movie theater was hot and stale and thick with the smell of artificial butter. She bought herself a small popcorn, which turned out to be as big as her head, and a five-dollar bottle of Diet Coke. Dinner of champions.

She'd thought the movie would be a distraction, but she'd made the mistake of picking a sci-fi movie and every frame reminded her of Jonathan. She'd never gotten to read the final version of his sci-fi script. She wondered what he'd ended up doing for the turning point in act two. Now she'd never find out.

She got up and left before the end of the movie. It was obvious some of the characters were going to die, and some would live happily ever after, and she didn't particularly care to find out which were which. Besides, the popcorn was making her feel sick to her stomach.

When she got home, Sally refused to greet her. She was mad

that her dinner was late, so she walked to the far corner of the living room, turned her back, and petulantly groomed herself. *Et tu*, cat?

Esther gave Sally her food and crawled into bed. She didn't even bother putting on pajamas, although she did take off her shoes. So what if she fell asleep in her clothes? Who was there to know? Or care? She was all alone in the world. She could die in her sleep and it would be days before anyone found the body, probably.

God, she was pathetic.

Esther rolled over and grabbed her phone off the nightstand. It was only nine thirty.

She called her brother.

"Hey," he answered gruffly. The sound of his voice triggered an overwhelming wave of homesickness, and she hugged her pillow against her stomach.

She was so tired of being alone. It felt like her whole life in LA had fallen apart. Or maybe she'd never had much of a life here to begin with.

"I figured out a way to help you with Mom," she said. "What if I moved back to Seattle?"

Chapter Twenty-Six

---

*E*sther didn't *have* to stay in LA. She was an adult in charge of her own destiny, and she had family back in Seattle who would be glad to have her nearby. Eric, Heather, Gabe, even her mother. If she moved back home, she could see them more often. Get to watch her nephew grow up and be a regular presence in his life instead of a distant figure who visited a couple times a year. She could be part of a family, instead of being alone.

"What time is it?" Eric sounded dazed. Muddled.

"It's nine thirty. Were you sleeping?"

"I fell asleep putting Gabe to bed."

This was exactly why she needed to move back home. To take some of the load off Eric. He had his hands full with his own family. He shouldn't have to take on all of Mom's problems too. Esther could take some of the Mom stuff off his shoulders *and* she could help out with Gabe. It was win-win.

There was a rustling sound on the other end of the line, like Eric was moving around. "What are you talking about moving back here for?" He sounded a little more awake now.

"To help you. To help Mom. To help you help Mom."

"Don't be stupid."

"I'd get to see more of my nephew. You and Heather too, obviously, but mostly I just care about your offspring."

"You're not moving back here."

"Gabe's toilet trained now, so I've missed the most unpleasant parts. It's the perfect time to show up and start playing the indulgent aunt."

"What's going on?" Eric didn't have any patience for her deflections tonight.

She sighed and rolled over onto her back. "I called Dad and asked him if he'd let Mom have one of his rental units."

"That was dumb." He didn't need to ask what Dad's answer was.

Eric had been older when their father left. He had more memories of their time as a whole family—and fewer illusions about what it had been like. Esther still held out hope that one day her father would be more of a father. Eric was right—she was dumb.

"I didn't hear you coming up with any better ideas. I figured it was worth a shot."

"It never is, with Dad."

Sally butted her head against Esther's hand, demanding affection. Esther scratched her behind the ears. "What are we going to do?"

"I told you I'd figure something out. You don't have to worry about it."

"Easier said than done."

He sighed. "I know."

She missed her brother. He was the only *real* family she had—the only family she'd ever been able to count on. It would be nice to live near him again. To get to know Heather and Gabe better. To have people around who loved her no matter how badly she screwed up. No matter how hard she tried to push them away.

"I've got a couple more leads on some places for Mom," Eric said. "Something will work out."

Esther chewed on her thumbnail. "By the end of the month?"

"If we have to, we'll put her stuff in storage for a few weeks and she can stay with us until she finds a new place."

That was a terrible idea. The worst. It was exactly what she was afraid would happen. "Eric—"

"It's fine."

It wasn't fine. His house was too small. Mom would drive him nuts. She'd drive Heather nuts.

"You don't even have a spare room."

"Then she won't be able to get comfortable. It'll motivate her to get her own place."

"Yeah, right." Her mother was like a lamprey eel. Once she'd clamped onto you, there was no shaking her off. Give her an inch and she'd take a second inch. And then a third, and a fourth, until you were all out of inches. She'd been dying for an invitation to move in with Eric and Heather since Gabe was born. Once she was ensconced in their house, she'd never move out. The appeal of being taken care of would be too great. She'd start wheedling them to get a bigger place. Suggesting they pool their money and go in on something together. He'd never be rid of her. For the sake of Eric's sanity—and Heather's—Esther couldn't let that happen.

"Forget it, I'm moving back. I can put in for a transfer to the Seattle office, get an apartment with a spare room, and move Mom in with me." She owed it to Eric, after everything he'd done for her. Coming back to Seattle after college, looking after Mom so Esther could take a job out of state and start living her own life. It was her turn now. Time for her to start doing her share again.

"Absolutely not."

She knew Eric still felt guilty for going to college out of state and leaving her alone with their mom. Esther had spent three years of high school and one year of undergrad dealing with their mother on her own while Eric was away, and he'd been doing this stupid self-imposed penance ever since.

"You're not the boss of me. I can do what I want."

"Tell me what's really going on," Eric said. "What are you trying to run away from?"

She elected to play dumb. "What do you mean?"

"This is what you do whenever things get too real. You run."

"I'm trying to run toward a problem, not away from it."

"You love living in LA. You've got a life there."

"I did. I do." She tried to keep her voice light, but the words landed with a leaden thunk.

"What's changed?"

She crossed her arms stubbornly, even though he wasn't there to see it. "Nothing. I'm just trying to do the right thing here."

Eric wasn't having it. "Sis."

"What?"

"I can always tell when you're hiding something. Spill, before I fall asleep again."

Esther sighed and stared up at the popcorn ceiling of her bedroom. She'd always hated that popcorn ceiling. It was one thing she definitely wasn't going to miss. "Los Angeles is fine. There's just not as much keeping me here as there used to be."

"What does that mean?"

"I don't know. My job isn't going like I thought it would, my best friend stopped talking to me, and all my other friends went with her."

"What happened with Jinny?"

Esther filled her brother in on the highlights. He listened without comment until she'd gone through the whole sorry tale.

"So, it was about a guy," he said when she was done.

"It wasn't about the guy, it was about trust."

"Sounds like it was a little about the guy."

"It doesn't matter. The point is nobody would miss me if I moved back home." She sounded petulant and snotty, like a child.

"So your solution is to run away from your problems?"

"Mom's my problem too. You're already taking on more than

you can handle and you've got your own family to think about. I don't."

"That doesn't make your life any less important than mine."

She squeezed the phone against her ear. "Maybe a fresh start would be good for me."

Eric made a sound in the back of his throat. "There's no fresh start for you up here. I can handle this thing with Mom. Don't use us as an excuse. You need to fix your own shit."

"I can't. I've tried talking to Jinny, but she won't take my calls. I don't know how to get her to forgive me."

"You can't manage people into behaving the way you want."

"That's not what I'm doing."

"That's what you always do. That's what got her mad at you in the first place, right?"

She hated it when her brother was right. "Tell me what I'm supposed to do, then. Because giving her space doesn't seem to be working."

"In all the time you guys have been friends, have you ever told her how you feel about her—how important she is to you?"

"I tell her all the time."

"I mean *literally* tell her. Using actual words." Eric knew her too well. It was annoying.

"She knows how I feel about her," Esther said, feeling defensive.

Her brother sighed. "Look, I know you're allergic to expressing your emotions, and I understand why—better than anyone. But sometimes people need you to actually come right out and tell them how you feel. I don't think you realize how much distance you keep people at."

I don't do that, Esther wanted to protest. *Not with Jinny. Not with my friends.*

But maybe she did.

Her brother was right that she wasn't big on expressing her emotions. Why talk about your feelings when you could shove them all deep down inside? Keep calm and carry on. Like Queen Elizabeth.

But that didn't mean she was unfeeling or cold. She showed people she cared through her actions. Wasn't that better anyway? Showing rather than telling? That's why she was always taking care of people. She was the "mom friend." The one who could be counted on to help you out of a jam. That wasn't keeping people at a distance, was it?

Only…Jinny hadn't wanted to be mothered. She got enough of that from her actual mother.

"You still there?" Eric said. "Or did you faint at the prospect of sharing your emotions?"

Esther ignored the gibe. "So, what—if I tell her I care about her she'll magically forgive me?"

"Probably not, but you should tell her anyway. She deserves to know."

"What's the point? If she's not going to forgive me anyway?"

"The point is to do something that's hard for you because it's meaningful to someone else. Expose your soft underbelly. That means a lot more than saying you're sorry."

"And if she still doesn't forgive me? If she just doesn't want to be my friend anymore?"

"Then she doesn't. But at least you tried. And you learned something in the process. You pick yourself up, make some new friends, and don't repeat the same mistakes."

"You say that like it's easy."

"I know it's not easy, but you're tough. You can handle it."

"But Mom—"

"Mom will be fine. Don't use Mom's issues as an excuse to ignore your own. You fix your shit and let Mom fix hers. I know you like to swoop in and solve other people's problems, but she'll never learn to stand on her own two feet if we keep picking her up every time she falls down."

It was almost the exact same advice their dad had given her.

Esther considered telling Eric that, but decided against it. He'd long ago reconciled himself to their father's limitations as a parent and didn't need her upsetting the balance.

"I'm going to bed," Eric said. "Don't make any stupid decisions while I'm asleep."

"Fine," Esther muttered.

"Goodnight."

"Hey," she said before he could hang up.

"What?"

"Thanks."

"It's gonna be okay, Es. You'll see."

She wasn't convinced, but it was nice to hear someone say it anyway.

After she got off the phone, Esther lay in bed petting Sally and thinking about the things Eric had said. How she kept people at a distance. What had he said? She was allergic to emotions.

He wasn't wrong. Their family had never been particularly demonstrative or affectionate with one another—with the exception of their mother. But Esther had learned at an early age that her mother's affections had an ulterior motive. She only deployed them when she wanted something. They were a means to an end. She flattered and charmed people to manipulate them. Unless she needed something from you, it never occurred to her to pay a compliment.

Was it Esther's fault, then, that she was distrustful of open displays of affection? Afraid of expressing her feelings? Closed off and frigid? Jesus, she really was broken inside. She probably needed therapy, but the thought of it made her want to die. Opening up to a stranger, talking about all her innermost feelings and deep-seated fears. She'd rather peel off her own skin.

She remembered what Eric had said about making herself vulnerable. Showing you care by doing something for someone else that's hard for you.

Jinny was her best friend, and the idea of telling her how much she cared about her made Esther feel itchy all over, like she was breaking out in hives. How fucked up was that?

The fact that it was so terrifying probably meant she should do it. That Eric was right. She needed to tell Jinny how important she was to her. Maybe Jinny still wouldn't forgive her, but she owed her that much at least. She had to fight for her.

But how? Walk up to her at work and blurt it all out? Take a big feelings dump in her lap, right there in the middle of the office? Seemed like a terrible idea.

How were they supposed to talk when Jinny still wasn't taking her calls? She could show up at her apartment unannounced, she supposed. But what if Jinny shut the door in her face?

Esther thought about Jonathan's screenplay. How he'd left it on her doorstep. And how it had made her feel to read all those words he'd written for her—about her. No one had ever done anything like that for her before.

Esther couldn't write a screenplay, but she could write Jinny a letter. An actual, physical letter on a piece of paper. An email, Jinny might delete without reading. But if Esther sent a real letter through the mail, Jinny would almost certainly read it—out of curiosity, if nothing else.

That was what she was going to do. She was going to write a letter.

Now she just needed to figure out what to say.

Esther moved Sally off her chest and curled up on her side, turning over phrases and sentiments in her mind. She was still composing in her head when she finally drifted off to sleep an hour later.

SHE WOKE up before her alarm in the morning, and sat down at the dining table with a stack of stationery. Her grandmother had given it to her in high school as a not-so-subtle hint to write more often. Esther had never used it; she'd sent her grandmother emails instead.

The stationery had strawberries around the edges of the page. She stared at them, squeezing the pen in her fingers. Paralyzed.

Just start. Just say something. Anything. The words didn't have to be good, they just had to be true.

She started to write.

It had been years since Esther had handwritten a letter. Or even written more than a few words by hand. She had the handwriting of a third-grader.

Every word she scratched onto the page felt like it weighed a thousand pounds. Like it was being hauled up from the bottom of deep, dark well. *Like drawing blood from a stone.* That's how Jonathan had described writing once. She'd thought he was being overly dramatic, but now she understood. She was bleeding all over the paper, pouring her heart out to Jinny. Every drop was agony, but she pushed through, putting one word after the other.

Her hand started to ache by the end of the first page, but she kept going until she'd said everything she had to say. Until she'd bled herself dry. She'd filled six full pages by the time she was done.

It wasn't poetry, but it was honest. More honest than she'd ever been, maybe.

Her hands shook as she read over it. Was she really going to send this to Jinny? What if she read it and decided Esther was crazy? What if it drove her even farther away?

Fuck it. Then at least she'd have tried, right? She'd have said what was in her heart, and if it wasn't good enough, then it wasn't. But she'd have done it.

She felt drained, but also accomplished. Lighter. Maybe there was something to be said for expressing your emotions after all.

It took five minutes of searching through every drawer in her apartment to find a stamp. She wrote Jinny's address on the envelope, then deliberated for five minutes over whether to put a return address. What if Jinny saw it and threw it away unread? On the other hand, what if she assumed it was junk mail without a return address?

In the end, she elected to write her name and address in the top left corner. The whole point of this exercise was to be open and honest. No more deceptions. No more manipulations. If Jinny saw it was from her and didn't want to read it, there was nothing Esther could do about that.

She stopped at the post office on her way to work and pulled her car alongside the drive-up mailbox. She almost got cold feet again as she held the letter over the gaping maw of the metal box. There were no take-backsies. Once she let go, it was gone. Out of her hands.

So what? Let it be out of her hands.

What did she have to lose? You can't lose something you've already lost.

But maybe you can get it back again.

She dropped the letter in the slot and drove to work.

Chapter Twenty-Seven

*E*sther figured it would take a few days for the letter to reach Jinny. In the meantime, she had a fence to mend at work.

"Hi," she said to Yemi when she got to her desk that morning.

He looked up and nodded. "Hello." Then he went back to work. That was what they did now. Offered the basic common courtesies and then went back to pretending they were strangers.

Esther sat down at her desk. After she'd put her stuff away, she spun around and kicked the bottom of his chair. "Hey."

He swiveled to look at her, his expression one of polite yet guarded inquiry. "Yes?"

"I'm really sorry," she said.

He blinked behind his thick-framed glasses. "For what?"

"For avoiding you last week."

"Oh." He nodded, shifting in his seat like he didn't know what to do with that. "Okay. Thank you."

"Are you mad at me?"

"I thought you were mad at me."

"I wasn't."

"Then why have you been avoiding me?"

Esther didn't have a good answer for that. *Because I'm a giant baby who got her fee-fees hurt* didn't make a convincing case for winning him back. "I didn't want you to be caught in the middle," she said. "I didn't want to make you choose between me and Jinny."

"So you chose for me?"

She hung her head a little. "Pretty much."

"You shouldn't have done that."

"I know."

He pushed his glasses up, frowning. "I can be friends with Jinny and still be friends with you."

Esther stared at her hands. "I wasn't sure you'd want to be."

He kicked her chair to make her look up again. "I do." His eyes were so deep and kind, she felt like an even bigger ass for pushing him away. She shouldn't have given up on him so easily. She should have known he'd still be there for her, because that was the kind of person he was.

"I was dumb and I'm sorry," she said. "Can we go back to being friends?"

A smile spread across his face. "I'd like that."

She smiled back. "Me too." She felt lighter already. Like some of the poison that had been building up inside her had drained away.

His smile faded. "We don't have to hug, do we?"

Esther laughed. "God, I hope not."

Things were better after that. She told Yemi what had happened at the roadblock meeting, and he agreed that it was stupid and unfair. Having someone take her side made the situation feel more bearable.

Now that she had Yemi to talk to again, she didn't think about Jonathan quite as much during the day. Only once every fifteen minutes or so, instead of every thirty seconds. It was progress.

Evenings were a different matter, of course. Esther still thought about Jonathan obsessively when she was at home. It was hard not to, knowing he was so close. Hearing his coffee grinder through the wall and his wind chimes on the balcony. Walking past his window at least twice a day. Wondering if she was going to bump into him again.

She tried not to think about Jinny or the letter at all. Tried not to wonder when it would arrive. If she'd read it. If it would do any good.

It would happen when it happened. Or it wouldn't.

TWO DAYS LATER, an hour after Esther got home from work, Jinny called.

She stared at the screen of her phone, relieved and terrified all at once. It took her until the third ring to work up the courage to answer it. "Hi."

"You wrote me a letter," Jinny said.

"Yeah." Esther's mouth felt dry. It was hard to get the word out.

There was a pause. "Who even writes letters anymore?"

"Nobody does."

"Your handwriting is terrible, by the way." That was when Esther knew it was going to be okay. If Jinny was mocking her, she couldn't be that mad. Jinny was relentlessly nice to people she couldn't stand. Insulting people to their faces was something she reserved for her friends.

"I know," Esther said, letting out an unsteady breath. "It really is."

"It made me cry."

"My handwriting?"

"No, dummy, the letter."

Esther blinked against the stinging in her eyes. "I'm so sorry, Jinny. I wish I could go back and undo all of it."

There was another pause, and then Jinny said, "It's possible I may have overreacted a little. You didn't deserve two weeks of the silent treatment."

Esther sagged with relief. "Can I come over so we can talk about it?"

"Yeah. Of course."

She'd already changed into pajama pants for the night, so she had to change back into outside-the-house pants. She pulled on the first pair of jeans she could find, put her bra back on, and drove straight to Jinny's.

Jinny's apartment was newer than hers, with a lobby and indoor hallways that smelled like disinfectant. Esther knocked on her door and waited while her stomach tried to twist itself into elaborate nautical knots.

"That was fast," Jinny said. She looked almost as nervous as Esther felt.

"I may have run a stop sign or two." Esther's stomach hurt so bad she wanted to curl up in the fetal position. It was one thing to put her feelings into a letter, but now that she was looking into Jinny's eyes, faced with the prospect of having to talk about those same feelings out loud, she was terrified. Like, the-first-five-minutes-of-the-original-*Halloween* terrified. She wondered if you could actually die from talking about your feelings. Because her stomach definitely felt like it was trying to commit suicide.

Jinny didn't say anything. She was standing in the doorway watching her, and Esther didn't know if she was going to let her inside or if she should start talking out here in the hall.

Just as Esther opened her mouth to apologize again, Jinny stepped forward and hugged her. Hard.

Esther clung to her, burying her face in Jinny's hair. She smelled like lavender laundry detergent and Tory Burch perfume. Like Jinny.

"I thought you didn't care we weren't friends anymore," Jinny said into Esther's shoulder.

Esther held her even tighter. She couldn't believe Jinny could think such a thing. "I cared, believe me. I cared a lot."

"I cared too."

Esther sniffled. Right in Jinny's hair, but Jinny didn't seem to mind. "I thought you didn't want me around anymore."

"I always want you around," Jinny said. "Even when you piss me off."

"I shouldn't have fixed you up with Jonathan and lied to you about it. That was shitty. You were right to be mad."

Jinny let go of her and reached up to wipe her eyes. "I should have taken your calls. That was pretty shitty too."

Esther looked down at the scuffed linoleum floor and shuffled her feet. "I've been doing some soul-searching lately, and I've come to the conclusion that I might be broken in some crucial ways. I should probably be in therapy."

"Probably," Jinny agreed. "But you're not broken."

Esther looked up tentatively. "You think?"

Jinny shrugged. "You're no more broken than I am."

"Are we okay?" Esther asked.

"Yeah," Jinny said, nodding. "We're gonna be fine."

Esther blew out a ragged breath. Jinny was still her friend. Everything was going to be okay.

"Come on." Jinny grabbed her hand and dragged her into the apartment. "Get in here before any of my neighbors sees us crying in the hallway like weirdos."

THEY'D TALKED until late into the night, clearing the air between them. Jinny hadn't held anything back, and neither had Esther. It was painful, but it also felt good. Like draining the poison from an infection. For the first time in weeks—for the first time since they'd known each other, actually—they'd *really* talked. Openly and honestly. About everything.

Not just about their friendship, but about their relationships with men and with their mothers. About Esther's abandonment issues and how they made her keep people at a distance, and about Jinny's low self-esteem and how she needed to value herself more. How Jinny's mother had screwed her up by making her resentful of being managed, and how Esther's mother had screwed her up by making her feel like she needed to manage everyone else. And how that was all stuff they were going to have work through, and find a way to navigate.

Esther hadn't gotten home until almost two a.m., and she'd been so amped up it had taken her another hour to fall asleep.

Her alarm hit her like a ball-peen hammer to the brainpan when it went off at six thirty in the morning.

Groaning, she shoved Sally off her chest, silenced her shrieking alarm, and staggered out of bed. In the kitchen, she downed two ibuprofen with a full glass of water, and followed it up with a cup of coffee from her new drip coffeemaker.

She was getting used to making herself coffee in it every day, even though the coffee always tasted a little bitter, because it reminded her of Jonathan and how much she missed him. But having Jinny back mitigated the sadness somewhat. Her coffee only had a level teaspoon of sadness and regret in it this morning, instead of a heaping tablespoon.

Yemi looked up when Esther walked into the office. "You're six minutes later than usual," he said, grinning at her weirdly.

"The traffic light at Overland was out again. And why are you smiling like that?" She sat down at her desk and docked her laptop.

He swiveled his chair all the way around, grinning even wider. "Because you and Jinny made up."

"She told you already?"

"She called me first thing this morning."

Of course she had. She was his girlfriend. That was what girlfriends and boyfriends did—talked to each other about the people in their lives.

Esther tried not to feel weird about it, but this was all uncharted territory. She'd never been friends with one of Jinny's boyfriends before. She couldn't help wondering how much Jinny had told him, exactly. Had she given him an exhaustive recap—including every gory detail and teary confession—or just the condensed version? How much of Esther's private angst was Yemi now privy to?

"I'm glad you worked things out," he said. "I hated that you two weren't talking."

"Me too." Esther decided not to care if Jinny talked to Yemi about her. What mattered was that they were all friends again. They'd figure out the rest of it along the way.

"You should really take the freeway though," Yemi said, spinning his chair back to his computer again.

Esther smiled at the back of his head. "I'll take it under advisement."

His phone vibrated on his desk, and he picked it up. "Jinny wants to know what time we're going to lunch."

"What's the special today?"

"Lasagna."

"Better go at eleven forty-five, then."

"Fine," Yemi said as he typed a reply.

Still smiling, Esther started up her computer and went to work.

ON SATURDAY, Jinny came over to hang out at Esther's pool, just like old times. They were having mimosas to celebrate.

"You cannot move to Seattle to take care of your mother," Jinny said as she took the orange juice out of the fridge. "I forbid it."

Esther got down the champagne flutes. "Don't worry, I'm not." The glasses were dusty with disuse. She took them to the sink and rinsed them out.

"I can't believe you were even considering it. She'd drive you insane." Jinny shook her head as she picked at the foil around the champagne cork.

"Okay, but seriously, what am I supposed to do? Nothing? Just let her lose her apartment?"

"Your brother's right. She's an able-bodied, grown-ass adult. She shouldn't need her kids to take care of her. That part comes later, when she's old and infirm. She's cashing in her markers too early."

"She's my mother. She doesn't have markers."

"Everyone has markers." Jinny winced as she popped the cork off the champagne. Whenever she opened champagne, she always made a face like that scene in *Elf* when Buddy was testing the jack-in-the-boxes.

Esther went into the bathroom for sunscreen. She was wearing shorts and a tank top to try to get some color in her paper-white skin, but she'd wind up crispy-fried if she didn't slather herself in sunscreen. "You say that like you don't always do exactly what your mother asks you to do," she called over her shoulder as she dug around under the sink.

"I can say that *because* I always do exactly what my mother wants," Jinny called back. "I recognize a master manipulator when I see one."

Esther came back out and stuffed the sunscreen in her pool tote with the towels. "Speaking of your mother, how does she feel about Yemi?"

Jinny's mouth twisted. "You mean because he's black?"

"I wasn't going to come right out and say it, but yeah."

"Weirdly, she seems okay with it."

"Really?" Jinny's mother had never liked any of the men Jinny had dated. The only men that seemed to meet with her approval were Korean doctors and lawyers.

"I think it's because he's Catholic." Jinny shrugged. "Maybe she's finally given up on me ever settling down with a nice Korean boy and has reconciled herself to taking what she can get."

"You've got to admit, after the parade of douchebag mouth-breathers you've dated, Yemi is definitely an upgrade." Esther froze after the words left her mouth, afraid that maybe she'd gone too far and touched on a sore spot. Maybe they weren't to the point yet where she could make jokes about Jinny's taste in boyfriends.

"God, you're such a bitch," Jinny said, breaking into a smile. "I totally missed this."

Esther smiled back at her. "Yeah, me too."

"You ready to head down?"

"Mmmm hmmm." Esther scooped up her bag and the two glasses while Jinny grabbed the OJ and champagne.

As they walked toward Jonathan's door, Esther tried not to peer through the blinds in his front window—which were always shuttered these days. It was torture every time she had to walk by his apartment, and she hurried her steps to get past as quickly as she could.

Except this time, Jonathan's door opened and he stepped out into the breezeway. Right in front of Esther and Jinny.

All three of them froze in a diorama of mortification. No one seemed to know what to say. Or to be able to move.

And then a woman emerged from Jonathan's apartment behind him.

Chapter Twenty-Eight

*T*he woman who stepped out of Jonathan's apartment was beautiful. Tall, slim, blonde, with miles of unblemished, honey-gold skin. Her hair was twisted into a picture-perfect messy bun, and she was wearing a striped jersey tank dress that showed off her perfect figure.

Esther felt like she'd been kicked in the back of the knees. Her free hand fumbled for the railing to steady herself.

The woman smiled at Esther and Jinny, her eyes taking in the champagne and glasses. "Hello." She had a radiant smile. Glowing with vitality. She wasn't wearing any makeup and still managed to look like a model in a Neutrogena ad.

Jonathan turned away and locked his apartment door.

"Hi," Jinny said, smiling as if this was a perfectly ordinary interaction that was in no way fraught with awkwardness and resentment.

"Let's go," Jonathan said to the woman. He put his arm around her and guided her toward the stairwell without a backward glance.

Esther watched them walk away, still clutching the railing for support. She felt a physical compulsion to follow, like someone had hitched a tow rope to her stomach and was reeling it in. Then Jonathan stepped out of sight at the end of the corridor, and the rope snapped. Her stomach lurched back into place with the poise of a drunk girl in six-inch heels.

"That was hella awkward," Jinny said beside her.

"Yeah," Esther managed to say.

"Who was that woman with him?"

"I don't know." Esther's stomach was still reverberating from the shock. It felt like a bowl of Jell-O in the midst of an earthquake.

"Is he dating someone new?"

"I don't know," Esther said again.

Jinny looked at her, frowning. "Are you okay?"

She was not okay. Jonathan had a woman in his apartment. On a Saturday morning. With I-just-rolled-out-of-bed hair.

He'd already moved on. Replaced her. Which…he had every right to do. She'd told him in no uncertain terms there was no future for them. She just…hadn't expected him to move on so quickly. She'd thought maybe he'd need to spend some time licking his wounds before he invited someone else into his bed.

She forced a smile for Jinny's sake. "I'm fine. Why wouldn't I be?"

"I don't know," Jinny said, still frowning at her. "You tell me."

Esther started for the stairwell. "There's nothing to tell."

"You're acting weird," Jinny said, following her.

"Like you said, it was awkward." Esther's flip-flops slapped against the metal as she descended the stairs. "I'm not exactly his favorite person anymore."

"You're not, like, hung up on him, are you?"

Esther dumped her bag on one of the lounge chairs, studiously avoiding Jinny's eyes. "I feel guilty. I screwed up and now he hates me, and we still have to live next door to each other."

Even though she'd vowed to be more honest with Jinny from

now on, she couldn't make herself talk about Jonathan. It hurt too much.

Esther changed the subject before Jinny could interrogate her further. "What are you and Yemi doing tonight?"

Jinny's face broke open at the mention of his name. "He's cooking for me."

"Yemi cooks?"

She nodded happily. "Yemi cooks. He's kind of perfect."

While Jinny regaled Esther with tales of Yemi's superior boyfriend skills—strictly G-rated, thank god—Esther's mind wandered back to Jonathan and his mystery woman.

Was it serious between them? Or was she just a one-night stand?

It was probably serious. Jonathan wasn't the one-night stand type. Except for Esther, of course, but that hadn't been his choice.

How long had it been going on? Where had they met? She didn't look like a writer. She looked more like an actress. Was he dating an actress? Was she going to be around all the time? Because if so, Esther really did need to move.

"Hey," Jinny said. "Are you even listening?"

"Yeah," Esther said, gulping down a mouthful of mimosa. "Totally."

SEEING Jonathan with another woman hit Esther harder than she'd been prepared for. She'd thought she was starting to make peace with not having him in her life anymore, until she'd seen that woman step out of his apartment. The sight of him with that pretty, skinny nightmare on two legs had left her feeling like an open wound.

She spent Sunday in her pajamas, knitting in front of the TV and punishing herself with more Hallmark movies. She watched an entire marathon of them. Sickly sweet, inspirational, poorly acted, low production value movies with cardboard characters played by C-list actors reciting stilted dialogue. It was like a juice cleanse, but for her feelings. That was the idea, anyway. Wallow for a day, get it out of her system, then pick herself up and move on.

Only it didn't work. She had the wallowing part down; it was the moving on that wouldn't take. After she finally turned the TV off and went to bed, she wound up lying in the dark, still microanalyzing the encounter with Jonathan and that woman he'd been with. Feeling worse and worse.

So Jonathan had replaced her. So what? Esther had given him up. Voluntarily, no less. What had she expected? Of course he'd moved on. It was exactly what he should do. Good for him.

That was what she needed to do too. Move on.

So why couldn't she?

She'd never been this dejected over a man before. The closest she'd ever come was with the friends-with-benefits guy in college. But even that hadn't been this bad.

Was this what love felt like? Because this felt like being sick. Aches, nausea, loss of appetite. Insomnia. Persistent headache. It kind of felt like she might be dying, actually.

Oh, god.

She'd made a terrible mistake.

She done exactly what Jinny had said she always did: she'd pushed Jonathan away before he could get too close. Esther had told herself it was because she didn't care about him the way he wanted her to, but that was a lie. She cared about him plenty. Too much. So much it had terrified her. Things had gotten too real, and she'd run.

She wasn't incapable of love. She was just too afraid. She was so scared of being rejected that she made sure to do the rejecting first.

Jonathan was decent and kind and he'd actually liked her. And she'd liked him back. She hadn't just been attracted to him, she'd actually enjoyed his company. She probably could have loved him if she'd let herself. But instead she'd ruined everything between them. Thrown away their friendship by sleeping with him, then thrown away any chance of something more by pushing him out of her bed.

She'd been so afraid of getting hurt, she'd hurt herself.

And now it was too late to repair the damage. Even if he'd been willing to forgive her at this point—which seemed like a long shot—he was with someone else. Any chance she'd ever had of getting him back was lost.

Chapter Twenty-Nine

*M*onday morning, Esther stared at her computer screen, trying to remind herself that things weren't so bad. She was friends with Jinny and Yemi again. She was going to knitting tonight for the first time in three weeks. She had a job, a roof over her head, and a good health insurance plan. Not to mention her cat. There was a lot to be thankful for.

Okay, her mother was about to be evicted, and Esther had probably thrown away the best shot at love she'd had in years, but life wasn't perfect. *You can't fix everything,* she reminded herself. *Focus on the good. Concentrate on things within your control.* That was the ticket to happiness. Or at least survival.

She tried to focus on the assembly file on her screen. She was working on some of the parts for Dan's sub-assembly and in order to finish the schematics, she'd needed to pull up the 3-D model at the next higher level to see how her part fit with everything else. It wasn't something the designers did often, because it was a huge file that took a long time to load.

Esther spun the model around, studying the section where her parts went. Then she leaned forward, squinting at the screen.

That...wasn't right. Was it? She spun it around some more, looked at it more closely, and read all the design notes.

It wasn't going to work.

Dan's proposal, the one they'd chosen over hers in the bake-off, had a fatal flaw. To accommodate the more spread-out design, the data cables had to be longer. Which meant they'd pick up electromagnetic noise that would give a less useable output by the time it hit the antenna to be transmitted down. And the radio spectrometer they were using had a low power draw that made the signal extra sensitive to loss.

Esther leaned back in her chair. Yemi was on a conference call behind her, and had his headset on. He was in a peer review session which was likely to go on for another couple hours. If she wanted to get his opinion, she'd have to wait.

She didn't need his opinion though. She knew what she was seeing. She knew she was right. Once they started putting their components into the live model, it would be obvious to everyone.

Esther had two choices. One: do nothing. Wait for Dan to upload his parts to the assembly file, and let one of the other teams point out that he'd screwed up. He'd look incompetent in front of the entire project team, and Dmitri and Bhavin would both look bad for letting him get this far with a sloppy design.

Then there was option two: go tell Bhavin what she'd found so Dan could fix his mistake before anyone else saw it.

Option one was sorely tempting. It would feel good to watch them all squirm after they'd discounted her proposal—which would have avoided this issue entirely, by the way.

The problem was, it might be weeks before they noticed the issue. And once they identified the problem, they'd have to go back and fix it, which would eat even more time. It could cause them to slip their next delivery date, which could cause a bow wave that might slip the entire project.

It would also be all Dan's fault, and everyone would know it. It would be vindication. Sweet, sweet vindication.

The question was whether Esther was willing to let the project slip in order to finally prove to everyone else that she was right.

With a bone-deep sigh, she pushed her chair back and walked over to Bhavin's desk. "Can I show you something?" she asked him.

He followed her back to her cubicle, and she showed him the assembly file. His hand tapped nervously against his thigh as she spun it around for him, pointed out the problem, and let him read the requirements documents for himself. By the time he'd digested it all, his hand was twitching so fast it was almost a blur.

"I'm gonna need to talk to Dmitri," he said, and walked off.

Esther sat back down at her desk, and tried to work on something else while she waited to find out what they would do. When Yemi finally got done with his teleconference, she told him what she'd found.

"You did the right thing," he told her.

"I know," she said. "But I *really* wanted to do the wrong thing. What does that say about me?"

He shook his head, pushing his glasses up the bridge of his nose. "Nothing. Everyone has bad impulses. What matters is how you choose to act."

At four o'clock, Bhavin came back, and headed straight to Esther's desk. "Nice catch," he said. "You just saved all our asses."

Forty-five minutes later, Dmitri sent an email out to both teams, copied to both the project manager and the VP above him, announcing that they were scrapping the previous sub-assembly plans and going with Esther's proposal instead. Without naming names, he explained the interference that had necessitated the change, and reiterated to the designers the importance of checking *all* the requirements documents and taking into account the other systems involved.

The email concluded by praising Esther by name for discovering the issue before it became critical and providing an elegant fix. He even used the phrase "team player." *Take that, Diane.*

ESTHER WAS STILL RIDING the high when she got to knitting that night.

Jinny had arrived before her, and already announced that she and Esther had patched things up. Esther was welcomed back from her sabbatical with open arms, and caught up on all the news she'd missed. Vilma's younger son had made the varsity soccer team. Penny's cousin had had her baby, and yet another cousin was now expecting. Cynthia had finished all her tiny animal sweaters and had proofs from the photo shoot to pass around. And Olivia had bought herself a pair of clear Converse All-Stars that she'd apparently been dying to show Esther.

"They're perfect for wearing with hand-knit socks, because you can see the socks through them!" She stuck out her feet so everyone could appreciate them. "Aren't they badass?"

Esther agreed they were indeed badass and she needed to get herself a pair immediately.

As the ladies chattered around her, a feeling of contented belonging settled over her. She leaned forward to snag one of the peanut butter cookies Penny had brought, feeling keenly how lucky she was to have these women in her life.

Friends were important, and she needed to do a better job holding on to the ones she had. Esther mentally added it to her self-improvement to-do list, right under *Stop pushing away people who care about you. Let friends know they matter to you.* She hadn't fixed on a third item for her list yet, but she was considering *Be a nicer person.* Maybe. She still had some self-reflection to do on that one.

Esther was done sabotaging herself. She might have screwed things up with Jonathan irrevocably, but at least she'd learned from her failure. She was trying to be a better person. A less broken person.

Two hours later, as they were all walking out to their cars,

Cynthia fell into step beside Esther. "So what exactly happened with you and that guy?"

Esther assumed she meant Jonathan, and glanced across the parking lot, to where Jinny was getting in her car. "Nothing happened."

Cynthia gave her a *don't bullshit me* look. "Something happened."

"It doesn't matter anymore."

"Is that right?" Cynthia said, not buying it.

They'd reached Esther's car, and she unlocked her door and shoved her bag inside before turning to face Cynthia. "I fucked up. But it's over now. We've all moved on."

Cynthia's eyes narrowed. "It's not like you to do something like that."

"Sure it is," Esther said. "I have one-night stands all the time —I mean, not *all* the time, but—"

"I'm not talking about that." Cynthia waved her hand dismissively. "Look, I get why you thought you needed to trick Jinny into going out with that guy. We all knew Stu wasn't shit, and she was headed right back to him. I'm not saying you were right, but I understand the impulse, at least. But the fact that you'd sleep with this guy? Knowing it might hurt Jinny? *That's* what's not like you."

"Yeah, well." Esther looked down at her feet.

Cynthia touched her arm. "You've never been the type to lose your head over a man. So if you're losing your head over this one, maybe you should ask yourself why. What's so special about him?"

Esther was pretty sure she knew what was so special. But she wasn't ready to admit it to Cynthia or anyone else. New Improved Esther was still a work in progress. She hadn't recovered from her big heart-to-heart with Jinny yet. It would be a while before she was ready to let herself be that vulnerable again.

Besides, it didn't matter anymore, because Jonathan had moved on. It was great that she'd had this epiphany and all, but her life wasn't a rom-com. There wasn't going to be any running after the boy and winning him back with declarations of love. It was best to forget it and move on with her life.

"There's nothing special about him anymore," Esther said, meeting Cynthia's eye.

Cynthia raised a dubious eyebrow. "Mmmm hmmm." She headed off toward her car, lifting a hand in farewell. "See you next week," she called over her shoulder.

Esther got into her Prius and pushed the conversation with Cynthia out of her mind. It was fruitless to keep thinking about Jonathan. All it brought her was pain. And she wasn't going to turn into someone who spent the rest of her life pining over the one who got away. She wasn't going to be tragic.

Today had been a good day. Better to focus on that instead of the things that sucked. She started up her Rihanna playlist and blasted it on the drive home, singing along off-key, not caring that the other drivers around her could see her doing it.

Her brother called just as she pulled into her parking space. A feeling of grim foreboding stole over her as she stared at his face on the screen. The end of the month was only two weeks away, and her mom still didn't have anywhere to live.

"Hey, brother," she said, shouldering her bags as she got out of the car. Her eyes skated over to Jonathan's Lexus, parked beside hers. It was at a slightly different angle than it had been this morning, and there was a coffee cup in the console that hadn't been there before.

She was going to need to work on this stalker thing if she was serious about getting over him.

"You're not going to believe this," Eric said.

"What?" Esther tore her eyes away from Jonathan's car and headed toward the stairs.

"Mom found herself a place to live."

"*What*? How? Where?" Her voice bounced off the stairwell in front of her and echoed around the carport.

"You know that handyman the landlord always sent to fix shit?"

A vague memory of a pot-bellied man with longish gray hair and a predilection for tie-dyed shirts surfaced. "Jake?"

"Blake."

"Whatever." She'd only met him once, when he came to fix the disposal.

"She's moving in with him."

Esther stopped in her tracks, halfway up the stairs. *"What?"* The word reverberated back at her.

"She says they're in love, although I'm pretty sure it's his ability to pay rent she's in love with."

"But..." Esther didn't actually have a follow-up. She didn't know how to react at all.

"I know," Eric said.

She tried to remember what Jake—Blake—was like. He wasn't very memorable; she couldn't even picture his face. He'd seemed fine though? As best she could recall. Cheerful. Polite. He hadn't set off any alarm bells or given off serial killer vibes. Of course, she hadn't been evaluating him as a potential live-in love interest for her mother. He was just the guy who was there to install a new disposal.

"Is that— Are you okay with that?" she asked Eric as she started up the steps again.

"I'm okay with the fact that Mom isn't going to be sleeping on my couch. I've decided the rest isn't my business."

"Seriously?"

"That's my story, and I'm sticking to it.

"How's it going so far?" Her steps slowed as she approached Jonathan's apartment, torn between dreading another chance encounter and hoping for one. The blinds in the front window were drawn again, but there were lights on inside. She stared at them as she walked past, wondering what he was doing tonight, and who he was doing it with. Was his new lady friend in there right now? Was she drinking his coffee, and reading his scripts, and having sex with him in the same bed Esther had slept in?

"Look, Mom's gonna do what she's gonna do," Eric said as Esther fumbled her keys out of her purse and unlocked her door. "Even if I wanted to raise an objection, it wouldn't work."

It was a fair point, Esther conceded as she let herself into her apartment and flipped on the lights. Once their mother had set her sights on something, it was almost impossible to talk her out of it. When she'd announced she was marrying that artist, Ian, Esther had pointed out that she'd lose her alimony, and that she hadn't known Ian for that long. That maybe it would be better to wait, just to make sure this was really what she wanted. Her mother had responded by eloping to Vegas without telling anyone. The marriage had lasted for all of a year.

"Honestly, the person I'm most worried about is Blake," Eric said. "I'm not sure he knows what he's getting himself into."

"How much do you know about him?" Esther deposited her bags on the dining table and headed into the kitchen to feed Sally. "Is he a decent guy?"

"He seems okay. You know the kind of guys Mom goes for. He's probably fine."

Their mother had an affinity for men who wanted to take care of her. They tended to be kind, dutiful, and pliant. Susceptible to her charms and easily manipulated. Ian had been that way, and so had their father. Until they'd both reached their limits and grown a backbone. It had just taken her father thirteen years longer than Ian.

"So that's it?" Esther said, dumping a scoop of food into Sally's bowl. "We're letting her do this?"

"There's no letting involved. She's a grown woman. She makes her own decisions."

"Until she digs herself into a hole she can't dig herself out of. Then she'll come running back for help." Esther wandered into the living room, toed off her shoes, and sank down on the couch.

"What happens when the relationship combusts and she's out on the street again?"

"Then she'll have to figure something else out for herself. I'm done. That's what I told her."

Esther wasn't confident Eric's edict would stick, but good for him for making it. "Okay, then. Crisis averted, I guess." So, this thing she'd been stressing herself out about for weeks had just... resolved itself with no effort on her part. *See? You don't always need to swoop in and solve everyone's problems for them. Sometimes things work out just fine without your intervention.*

"I told you she'd figure something out on her own if we refused to do it."

"I told you so isn't a good look, brother."

"You should be happy. You don't have to worry about Mom anymore."

"For now." She was always going to worry about her mother. She was always going to feel responsible for her. That wasn't something she could just get over. But maybe she could try worrying a little bit less.

"How's everything else going?" Eric asked. "You and Jinny make up yet?"

Esther leaned back and propped her feet up on the coffee table. "Yeah, actually, we did."

"I knew you would."

She didn't tell him she'd taken his advice, because he was already being insufferably smug. She refused to give him the satisfaction.

"What about work?" he asked. "You're not still thinking of transferring, are you?"

"No, work's going better. I got praised by one of the team leads to the project manager today."

"Hey, congratulations. That's great."

"Yeah, it is."

"Sounds like everything's unicorns and rainbows. Funny how fast things can turn around, huh?"

"Yeah. Funny." Esther thought about Jonathan, the one thing that hadn't gotten better, and wouldn't.

"What about the guy?" Eric asked, like he could read her mind.

"There is no guy." She really needed people to stop asking her about Jonathan. It was making it harder to get over him.

"The neighbor. You know, the one you and Jinny were fighting over."

"We weren't fighting over him," she said a little too forcefully. "He's a non-issue."

"You sure about that?"

"Yes, I'm sure." He was out of her life. It would be a lot easier to accept that and move on if everyone would stop bringing him up. She didn't want to have to think about him anymore.

"If you say so."

She said so.

Chapter Thirty

"It says here, your best nude lipstick shade is the color of your nipples." Jinny was at Esther's place again, lying on the couch flipping through an *InStyle* magazine as thick as a textbook.

Esther was folding laundry on the dining table. "You know what I've never done? Seriously contemplated the color of my nipples."

"Kind of hard to test in the store, I'll admit." Jinny reached for the Frappuccino she'd brought with her. It was the same pinkish-purple color as her nails, and it looked disgusting.

The timer on Esther's phone went off. "That's the last load." They were going out for drinks as soon as Esther's laundry was done, and then meeting Yemi for dinner later, after he was done helping his parents around the house.

Jinny waved her off, sucking noisily on her straw.

Esther grabbed her laundry basket and headed downstairs. Tonight would be her first time going out with Jinny and Yemi since they'd started dating. Her first time officially being the third wheel to their perfect happy couple. She wasn't nervous about it, exactly—she knew it would be fine. But she was glad she and

Jinny were pre-gaming before they met up with Yemi. The alcohol would help smooth over any awkwardness that might present itself.

She got waylaid by Mrs. Boorstein in the courtyard, so it was fifteen minutes when before Esther let herself back into the apartment. Jinny was sitting on the couch reading Jonathan's screenplay.

Esther stopped in her tracks. "Where did you find that?"

Jinny looked up. "Under a J. Crew catalog in your bedroom. It's like you wanted me to find it."

"Well, I didn't." Esther dropped her laundry and walked over to snatch the script out of Jinny's hand.

"Hey!" Jinny stood up and grabbed it back, shaking it at her in accusation. "Why didn't you tell me about this?"

"Because it's nothing." Esther picked up her laundry basket and carried it into the bedroom. "It doesn't matter anymore."

Jinny followed, right on her heels, still shaking the script at her. "This is not nothing."

"I don't want to talk about it." Esther set her laundry on the bed and went to the closet for hangers.

"This script is about you!"

"Yes, I know." Esther concentrated on sorting her laundry. She didn't want to be having this conversation.

"He captured you so perfectly, it's freaking uncanny. Who knew the guy was such a good writer?"

Esther didn't say anything.

"Esther!"

"What?" When she looked up, Jinny was frowning.

"Jonathan wrote a whole screenplay about you and how much he loves you."

Esther's eyes skated away guiltily. "It's not that big a deal."

"It's a *big* deal. You didn't tell me he was in love with you." Her tone was accusing, and a little hurt.

They hadn't talked about Jonathan much when they'd had

their heart-to-heart. They'd talked *around* the subject a lot, but not directly about him. Jinny had assumed Esther's hookup with him had been nothing more than a drunken one-night stand, and Esther had avoided disabusing her of that notion.

"Because he's not." Even if he had loved her, he didn't anymore. It was a moot point.

"Clearly, he is. This Emily character is totally you, and the character professing his love to her is totally him. You don't write something like that about someone you're not in love with. You don't *give them a copy of it* unless you want them to know."

Esther grabbed one of her work shirts out of the basket and shoved it onto a hanger. "It's fiction."

Jinny let out an exasperated breath. "I know you're not that naive. Are you seriously in this much denial?"

"I doesn't matter. We're finished. He doesn't want anything to do with me anymore."

Shaking her head, Jinny sank down on the bed next to Esther's laundry basket. "I can't believe I didn't see it before."

"See what?" Esther focused on matching up socks, refusing to look Jinny in the eye.

"I thought you were acting weird about Jonathan because of me, but it wasn't about me—it was about him. You really like him, don't you?"

Esther stared at the socks in her hand. "It doesn't matter," she said again.

"Yes, it does. Tell me the truth." Jinny was using her stern principal voice. There was no denying her when she used that voice.

"I did like him," Esther admitted finally, her voice coming out thin and wobbly. "I do."

"Esther!" Jinny grabbed her arm, beaming at her. Her face glowed like one of those sun lamps for seasonal affective disorder.

Esther winced. "What?"

"You're in love!" Jinny said, beaming even brighter. Where did she get all that light from? It defied the laws of physics.

Esther shook her head. "I'm—" She stopped. She'd been about to insist she wasn't in love with him. But...why? Why was she so determined to pretend it wasn't true?

"I can't believe it!" Jinny stood up and hugged her.

Esther froze, bewildered, as she was enveloped in a cloud of Tory Burch perfume. "What's happening right now?"

Jinny stepped back, still gripping Esther's arms. "You have to tell him."

Oh, no. No no no. Esther shook her head. She would have pulled away, but Jinny's tiny hands held her in a vise grip

"You have to tell Jonathan how you feel," Jinny said. "You have to get him back."

Panic rose in Esther's throat. Her eyes widened like a rabbit caught in a snare. "I can't."

Jinny let go, and Esther spun away from her, grabbing two handfuls of clean underwear out of the basket. "You have to," Jinny said.

Esther shoved the underwear into the top drawer of her dresser without folding it. The drawer was already full, and she had to cram it to get it all in. She really needed to clean out her underwear drawer next.

"I'm serious." Jinny was using her principal voice again.

"That's not happening."

"Esther."

She could feel Jinny's gaze on her. She stared into her underwear drawer, refusing to meet it. "I can't date a guy you dated. That's gross. It's a violation of the Friend Code."

"Fuck the code," Jinny said. "I barely dated him. And it was under false pretenses, so technically it doesn't even count."

Esther turned around. "That's even more reason not to do it."

Jinny had her hands on her hips. It made her look taller than she was. She had an intimidating physical presence for someone who was only five foot two. "I care more about your happiness than some stupid code. I care about the fact that we've been friends two years, and I've never once seen you fall hard for a man. Now that you finally have, I'm not letting you throw it away. Especially not because of me. No way."

"It's not up to you. In case you forgot, he's already moved on."

Jinny rolled her eyes. "Bullshit. You don't write something like this and then just move on."

"He did. You saw her yourself." Esther's eyes watered at the memory.

Jinny stepped toward her, her expression growing softer. "Whoever that woman was, it can't be that serious. Not yet, anyway. That's why you've got to move fast."

Esther shook her head, but Jinny ignored her.

"You need to tell him, and you need to do it before he really does get over you and move on."

"I'm not doing that."

"Yes, you are." Jinny crossed her arms, and Esther knew she'd lost. There was no arguing with Hurricane Jinny. She was an unstoppable force. She'd get what she wanted, one way or another.

"What if it doesn't work?" Esther said, feeling nauseous. "He was pretty upset with me. What if I tell him how I feel and he doesn't want anything to do with me?" She wasn't sure she could survive being rejected by him. It would probably kill her on the spot.

"Then at least you tried. He wrote this amazing thing about you. You have to at least try. He deserves that much."

She was right, even though Esther hated to admit it. Jonathan had put himself out there for her, and she'd pushed him away. He deserved the chance to reject her back. Even if it killed her.

Esther exhaled a long, unsteady breath. "You're mean, you know that? You're a mean person."

A smile spread across Jinny's face. "You're my best friend and I want you to be happy."

"I don't need to be in a relationship to be happy."

"Of course not. But that doesn't mean you shouldn't let yourself love people. The more people you love, the happier and richer your life will be."

Esther couldn't quite bring herself to believe that. People were unreliable. If you went around giving out love to just anyone, you increased your chances of getting hurt. She'd already exposed her soft underbelly to Jinny. Hadn't she fulfilled her quota of letting people in for the month?

Jinny stepped forward and took both of her hands. "He loves you, Esther, and I'm pretty sure you love him back. That's too rare to throw away. Promise me you'll talk to him."

Esther opened her mouth, but nothing came out.

Jinny's eyes narrowed with determination, and her hands tightened on Esther's. "Promise me, or I will go knock on his door right now and tell him myself." She would absolutely do it too.

"Fine," Esther said. "I'll do it. But in my own time, my own way."

Jinny let go of her hands. "You've got a week. If you haven't done it by next Saturday, I'm doing it for you."

Great. A whole week until her imminent death. She better start writing up a will.

ESTHER SPENT the first five days of her allotted week agonizing over the looming conversation with Jonathan and giving herself an anxiety stomachache. She ran through all of the different things she could say to him in her head and imagined a hundred different responses—most of which involved him telling her he didn't want anything to do with her anymore.

"Have you talked to him yet?" Jinny asked every day at work.

"Not yet," Esther answered every day.

"You need to."

"I will."

"You have three days," Jinny reminded her on Wednesday.

"I know," Esther said.

"Only two days now," Jinny said on Thursday.

"I *know*," Esther said. She was well aware of how fast time was running out.

She really needed to do it tonight.

If Jonathan was seeing someone, he might not be home Friday night. He might be out with *her*. Or worse—she might be at his place with him. If Esther was going to talk to him, it would be safer—and better—to do it tonight. Otherwise she might miss her chance. And then Hurricane Jinny would make landfall.

When Esther got home that night, Jonathan's car was in his parking space. She was simultaneously relieved and disappointed. Her heart rate spiked as she walked past his window. If this didn't work out in her favor, she was definitely going to have to move. For the sake of her cardiac health, as well as her sanity.

She went inside her apartment but didn't change out of her work clothes. She needed to keep her bra on if she was going to go next door and try to talk to Jonathan. Instead, she set her stuff down, gave Sally her dinner, and—after a few minutes of nervous pacing—forced herself to go back out.

Her stomach felt like it was tied up in knots as she stood in front of Jonathan's door. Her insides were a knitting project gone awry that had been carelessly frogged and left in a hopeless tangle.

On the bright side, one way or another, this would be over soon.

Esther took a deep breath and raised her hand to knock.

Her hand froze in midair.

Maybe she should wait until tomorrow. Maybe it would be better that way. If he wasn't home because he was seeing some-one, it would render the whole exercise moot. She could tell Jinny he was out on a date and that would be that. Issue resolved.

Yeah, Jinny would never let her get away with that.

She would still insist that Esther talk to him. Either that or she'd talk to him herself.

Esther needed to do this. Jinny was right. She needed to be brave and face her rejection like a woman.

You can't lose something you've already lost, she reminded herself. But maybe—just maybe—there was a chance she could get it back again.

Before she could screw up the courage to knock, Jonathan's door jerked open in front of her.

Chapter Thirty-One

*J*onathan glared at her, wary and unsmiling. "What are you doing out here?" He was blocking the doorway with his body, his hand perched on the knob in case he decided to shut the door in her face.

Esther swallowed. "Hi."

"Hi." He didn't sound the least bit happy to see her, which shouldn't have been a surprise, but cut deeper than she was prepared for.

"Can we talk?" Her voice sounded feeble and paper thin. Exactly the way she felt.

He looked down at the ground, and she died a thousand tiny deaths while she waited for his answer. After a few seconds he nodded and stepped back.

Esther walked past him into the apartment. He'd made sure to step back far enough that there was a wide gap between them and no chance of her accidentally brushing against him. He shut the door behind her and waited, standing by the exit. Ready to throw her out again.

She fidgeted under his gaze. She wasn't used to having him look at her like this—like he didn't want her around.

"Well?" He was impatient. Annoyed. "You said you wanted to talk, so talk."

Esther didn't have a game plan. For all the time she'd spent fretting over this conversation, she hadn't actually settled on what she wanted to say. How best to begin. And now that she was here and he was looking at her like that, she was paralyzed.

What *could* she say? What could possibly make up for what she'd done to him? Why was she even here? He'd moved on, remember? He had a new girlfriend now. He didn't need her—or want her—anymore. That much was obvious.

As she stood there mentally flailing, Eric's advice came back to her: *make yourself vulnerable.*

"I was wrong," she said. "I was so wrong."

Jonathan's expression didn't change. "About which part specifically?"

"All of it."

His hair was a tousled mess, falling in puffs across his forehead and into his eyes. Her fingers ached to reach up and push it back for him. She took a tentative step toward him, and he backed up flat against the door, reminding her she wasn't welcome in his space anymore.

Esther's chest clenched painfully. The hand that had been itching to touch his hair worried at the collar of her shirt instead.

"I never meant to hurt you," she said.

He didn't react. "Okay."

"I'm sorry. And you were right."

Jonathan rubbed the back of his neck, grimacing. "About what?"

"I was scared to let myself admit I had feelings for you."

She caught a fleeting glimpse of...*something* in his eyes before they skated away from hers. Hope, maybe. She hoped it was hope.

"Do you have a girlfriend?" she asked, terrified of the answer. He was going to say yes, and that was going to be it. There'd be nothing left for her to do after that except leave. And she didn't want to leave.

He looked at her, his expression shifting to confusion. "What?"

"The woman you were with last week…"

His mouth twitched. "My sister."

Some of the knots in Esther's stomach loosened. "That was your sister?"

He nodded. The mouth twitch had turned into something that wasn't quite a smile, but might be the beginnings of one. An embryo of a smile. "I don't have a girlfriend."

Esther opened her mouth, then closed it again. She took a deep, unsteady breath and said, "Will you give me another chance?"

The embryo smile disappeared. "To do what?" He was gun-shy. She'd hurt him once, and he was afraid she'd do again.

"To show you that you're important to me. I know I have issues and I'm not any good at this stuff, but I'm trying to be better at it, because I really like you." She couldn't bring herself to use the word *love*. The broken parts of her were still too broken for that. "I miss you."

When she'd gotten all the words out, she held her breath, waiting.

Jonathan's mouth twitched again. "Do you want to sit down?"

"WHAT HAPPENED WITH YOUR ADVISER? Did you turn in your scripts?" They were sitting on his couch, at opposite ends. The upholstery felt like sandpaper against Esther's skin. It wasn't a very big couch. There was barely enough space between them for another person. It felt like a lot more space than that though. It felt like the Grand Canyon lay between them.

Jonathan nodded without meeting her eye. He was staring straight ahead with his bare feet up on the footlocker that passed for a coffee table. "I got an A. Fall classes start a week from Monday."

Esther broke into a grin. "That's fantastic!"

He was near enough she could smell the cigarette smoke on him, with just a hint of the woodsy Jonathan smell underneath. She'd missed that smell. She wanted to bury her face in it, but she figured she wasn't allowed anymore. She wanted to do a lot of things—hug him, hold his hand, kiss the ever-living shit out of him—but it felt like there was an invisible wall between them. A physical barrier she wasn't permitted to breach.

He glanced over at her, then away again. "Whatever happened with Jinny?"

Esther's smile faded. "We made up. She forgave me —eventually."

"Won't she mind..." His hand flicked, gesturing at the space between them.

"She gave me her blessing."

He scowled down at his lap. "Great." She didn't want him to be scowling. She especially didn't want to be the reason he was scowling.

"Jonathan." Her throat constricted as she said his name.

His eyes lifted to her face.

"I'm sorry," she said again. Helplessly.

He shook his head at his lap. "Don't be. I get it."

"You do?"

"Yeah, actually." He shrugged. "That was what made it so hard. I could understand why you were doing it, but that didn't make it hurt any less. It just meant I couldn't hate you for it."

"I don't know," Esther said, "I feel like I was a pretty big asshole. You're allowed to hate me if you want."

"I don't want to hate you." His eyes found hers and softened. "I like you too much."

Something fluttered in her chest. He hadn't said love, but like was pretty good, considering. She'd happily take like. "Still?"

"Still." He laid his hand on the couch between them, palm up. An invitation.

Esther twined her fingers with his, squeezing gratefully.

They sat there holding hands without speaking. A sense of possibility had opened up between them, and it needed time to soak in. Her thumb moved over his wrist, searching for his pulse. It was racing almost as fast as hers.

There was a smudge of black ink on his index finger. She wanted to kiss it. But she felt like it might be too soon. Baby steps.

"Do you want to go on a date with me?" she asked.

He smiled down at their intertwined hands. "Yeah. I'd like that."

Chapter Thirty-Two

*T*hey were going out on a date. A *real* date. They'd agreed to do it the very next night: Friday.

Tonight.

Esther couldn't remember the last time she'd gone out on an actual, honest-to-god date. Usually, she met someone, flirted for an hour or two, and then went home with him—always to his place, never hers. Easier to duck-and-run the next morning, thereby avoiding any attempt at awkward morning-after pancakes.

But that was the old Esther. Not only was she going on a date tonight, but she'd had to plan it, because she was the one who'd done the asking. She'd definitely never been the one in charge of planning a date before. But she'd spent the whole day thinking about it and had it all figured out.

"What about this one?" she said, holding a dress up in front of her phone's screen. Jinny was helping her get ready for the date via FaceTime.

"Yellow makes you look like you have malaria."

Okay, then. No more yellow dress. Esther tossed it into the corner to donate to Goodwill.

"It's the blue or the purple," Jinny said. "Those are the two best."

The blue one fit better, but the purple one showed off more cleavage. Esther remembered how much Jonathan had seemed to like her in the low-cut top she'd worn to the party. "Purple it is."

"Good choice. Wear the tan shoes."

The tan shoes were heels. Esther wasn't a fan of heels, but they did look the best with the purple dress. "Hair up or down?"

"Down."

Esther frowned into the phone. "Are you sure?"

"I love how nervous you are. It's adorable."

"Shit, should I get him flowers? I didn't get him flowers."

"Let's not go overboard. You don't want to emasculate him."

"That's patriarchal toxic masculinity bullshit, and I refuse to participate in it."

Jinny rolled her eyes. "Are you really going to run out and buy flowers in the next fifteen minutes?"

Esther checked the clock. "No, I don't have time."

"Then he's not getting flowers."

"Oh, god," Esther said, staring into her makeup drawer.

"What?"

"How am I supposed to pick a lipstick? There are too many to choose from."

"Relax, I've got you. Nothing glossy or sticky."

"They're all sticky."

"You want something matte for maximum kissability. Like the one you got last time I dragged you to Sephora."

Esther propped the phone on the counter and dug through her lipstick collection, looking for the liquid lip color Jinny had talked her into buying. "This is weird, isn't it? You helping me pick makeup to seduce a guy you've kissed."

"First of all, you're not seducing him with your makeup, weirdo. Second of all, yes, it's a little weird...but not insurmountably so."

Esther looked up at the camera and smiled. "What would I do without you?"

Jinny smiled back at her through the screen. "You would be a disaster, my friend. A fucking disaster."

AT EXACTLY SEVEN O'CLOCK, Esther let herself out of her apartment and locked it behind her. Her stomach was roiling like a ship on the high seas. She wasn't sure she'd ever been this nervous before, not even when she'd defended her thesis.

Last night, when she'd left Jonathan's apartment, she'd desperately wanted to kiss him, and he'd almost looked like he'd wanted to kiss her too. But as soon as she'd started to lean in, he'd turned his head away.

Her pride was still a little scorched from the burn. She couldn't blame him for not trusting her though. Obviously, she still had some work to do to win him back. That was fine. She was willing to do whatever it took to earn his trust again. That was the whole point of going on this date tonight. To show him how invested she was in rebuilding their relationship.

She wondered if he'd let her kiss him tonight. God, she hoped so.

As she walked the twelve feet to Jonathan's door, her heels rang out like gunshots on the cement surface of the breezeway, which did nothing to calm her nerves. He must have heard her coming—the entire building had probably heard her coming—because his door opened before she could knock.

"Hi," he said, smiling sheepishly.

Her heart swelled at the sight of him. She hadn't seen him in almost twenty-four hours, and she'd *missed* him. The last few weeks without him had been torment. Now that she was allowed to be around him again, she was starving for more. It was like setting a piece of chocolate cake in front of someone on a

Whole30 diet. Her mouth was actually watering, she wanted him so bad.

"Hi," she said, smiling back at him. Her heels put her a little closer to his level, but she still had to look up to see his face. "You look nice."

His hair had been tamed with product, and he was wearing a striped button-down, slim gray pants, and the same ankle boots he'd worn to the party. He was Date Jonathan tonight. She loved Date Jonathan.

"You look nice too." His eyes remained disconcertingly focused on her face, ignoring her cleavage. What an inopportune time for him to be gentlemanly.

He had his keys in his hand, and they jangled as he flipped them around his index finger. "What's the plan? Do you want me to drive?"

"Nope, tonight I'm wooing you. All you have to do is sit back and enjoy yourself."

He smiled a little wider. "Okay."

Esther waited while he locked his door, and they set off down the hall to the stairwell. He didn't try to hold her hand, so she didn't try to hold his either. Even though she wanted to.

But when they got to the stairs, and she started teetering down the steps in her heels, he offered his hand to steady her. "Thank you," she said, clutching it gratefully.

As soon as they got to the bottom, he let go of her hand again. Damn.

Esther unlocked her car, and they got in. It was the first time he'd been in her car, and he had to slide the passenger seat all the way back to make room for his legs. She briefly wished she'd had time to get it cleaned, but then she remembered the trash pile that was the interior of his car and decided he wouldn't care about a little dust on the dashboard.

"Where are we going?" he asked as he buckled his seat belt.

Esther checked her mirrors and backed out of the carport.

"Dinner and movie. Actually, a movie and then dinner, because the movie's at seven thirty."

"What movie?"

Her mouth curved into a grin. "It's a surprise." *Blood Simple* was playing at one of LA's vintage cinemas tonight. As soon as she'd seen the listing, she knew it was where she had to take him.

"Intriguing."

"You'll like it, don't worry."

"I have no doubt of that." When she glanced over at him, he was smiling. So far, so good.

Esther had the night all planned out. *Blood Simple* at the old Aero Theatre at seven thirty, followed by dinner at a popular Santa Monica restaurant down the block. It was perfect.

It *would* have been perfect, anyway, except there was an accident on the freeway, which she'd only taken because Yemi was always telling her how much faster it was. Only it wasn't faster when the two right lanes were closed because of a fender bender. They crept along, alternating between a dead stop and short bursts of movement reaching almost five whole miles an hour. As the minutes ticked away, Esther became increasingly anxious.

"We're going to be late," she said, squeezing the steering wheel so hard her fingers started to go numb. "I'm sorry."

"It's fine," Jonathan said. "It doesn't matter."

"It does. We're going to miss the beginning of the movie."

He reached over the console and laid his hand on her leg, squeezing gently. "I don't care about the movie."

With the weight of his hand warming her thigh, she didn't care as much about the movie either. She unclenched one hand from the steering wheel and tangled her fingers with his, trying to relax a little.

It was seven thirty-five when they finally neared the theatre. Jonathan broke into a grin as the marquee came into view. "We're seeing *Blood Simple*?"

"That was the plan. Sorry I screwed it up." At least she'd

bought the tickets online, so they didn't need to worry about it being sold out.

"There'll be previews first. We're fine."

Except it took five minutes of circling before she found a parking space, and another five minutes after that to walk from the car to the theatre. "Sorry," she said again as she limped into the lobby at seven forty-five, seriously regretting the stupid heels she'd chosen to wear.

He shrugged. "I've seen it before."

The usher admitted them with a judgy look. The movie had indeed started. "Sorry," Esther whispered for the third time as they slunk to their seats.

"Stop apologizing," Jonathan whispered back. He leaned back, gazing up at the screen, and reached across the armrest for her hand.

Okay, so maybe she hadn't ruined the date after all.

He held her hand through the whole movie, absently stroking her knuckles. Whenever something violent happened on screen, he'd hold on even tighter. Fortunately for her, it was an extremely violent movie.

Esther's eyes kept drifting to his face during the film. The worry lines in his forehead. The soft bump below the bridge of his nose. The inviting curve of his lips. He was gorgeous. She couldn't believe she'd spent so much time disliking him when she could have been appreciating the view instead. She should have called dibs for herself from the start, and saved everyone a world of trouble.

They stayed in their seats through the end of the credits, waiting until the lights came up before making their way to the aisle. Esther's feet had enjoyed their reprieve, but now that she was standing on them again, they were not happy. She was definitely getting a blister. Maybe two.

"What's next?" Jonathan asked as they emerged from the theatre.

"Dinner," she said. For emphasis, her stomach made an embarrassing pterodactyl screech.

He grinned and stuck out his elbow. "Lead on, my lady."

She wrapped her hands around his arm, relishing the opportunity to cozy up to him as they started for the restaurant. It was the closest they'd been physically since their ill-fated indiscretion, and her heartbeat quickened as she breathed him in. He didn't smell like cigarette smoke tonight. He smelled divine. She held on tight and leaned even closer.

The restaurant she'd planned to take him to was only a block away. But as they approached, she could see people spilling out onto the sidewalk from the front door.

"Looks a little crowded," she observed with a sinking feeling.

The wait for a table turned out to be an hour. Her stomach made another loud pterodactyl noise while they were discussing whether to stick it out.

"We'll find somewhere else," Jonathan said, leading her away. "I think we need to get some food in you before you turn into Low Blood Sugar Hulk."

They kept walking, to the increasing unhappiness of her feet. The next restaurant they came to was as crowded as the last. Goddamn LA and its high concentration of foodie hipsters. Finally, three blocks away, they happened upon an Indian restaurant that could fit them in. All the tables were taken, so they had to sit side by side at the bar. It wasn't exactly the romantic dining experience Esther had been hoping for, but at least they were off their feet with the promise of food on the horizon.

After they'd ordered, the conversation hit a lull. Esther squirmed on her stool, trying to get more comfortable. Her feet were dangling in the air, and her shoes had slipped off the backs of her heels.

"So, that was your sister the other day," she said, flailing for conversational topics. "The banker or the med student?"

Jonathan glanced over at her, then down at the counter. "The med student, Sarah."

"What's she like?"

"Competitive. Annoyingly smart. Perfect, basically." There was more than a hint of bitterness in his tone.

"All that and beautiful too. Sounds like a nightmare."

He offered a thin smile. "She's great, actually. It's just not much fun being compared to her all the time."

Esther wobbled on her stool as she shifted to face him more. "How much older is she?"

"Four years. And Rachel is four years older than Sarah. My parents wanted us well spaced out." A shadow passed across his face, as it always did at the mention of his parents.

"I'll bet your sisters mothered you a lot."

"You bet right." His knee was jiggling under the counter, like he was restless. Or bored. "What about your brother? How much older is he?"

"Three years."

"Did he try to parent you?"

"We kind of parented each other. It was always me and Eric against the world. Until he left for college, and then I was mostly on my own."

Jonathan's eyes softened behind his glasses. "That must have been hard."

Esther shrugged, regretting the conversational path she'd chosen. "I was used to fending for myself by then. It's kind of funny—you basically grew up with three mothers, and I grew up with none."

It wasn't really funny at all, and Jonathan's nod was half-hearted at best. There was another lengthy lull before he broke the silence. "You grew up in Seattle, right?"

She nodded. "I moved here after college when I took the Sauer Hewson job."

"What's Seattle like? I've never been."

"Rainy." She missed the rain. There was a lot to be said for Los Angeles's weather, but there was something special about a rainy day. "What's Newport Beach like?"

He looked down at his hands, intertwined in his lap. "Like LA, only whiter."

The conversation stuttered to another halt. It didn't come as naturally to them as it used to. They both squirmed on their stools, staring at everything except each other.

None of this was going the way Esther had wanted it to. They used to talk so easily. What had happened to that? Had she ruined it all? What if they couldn't get back to where they were? What if she'd broken them irrevocably?

The food was bland and mediocre. But they were both ravenous and grateful for the distraction, so they tucked into it like it was a five-star meal.

When the check came, Jonathan tried to reach for it, but Esther snatched it away. "I asked you out, remember? It's my treat."

"We could split it," he offered, like they were on some sort of business lunch.

She didn't want to split it. She was trying to woo him, and wooing didn't include going halvsies on the check. "Let me do this. Please."

He let her pay without further protest.

Esther's feet objected strenuously when she hopped off the stool and shoved them back into her shoes. Not only did she have blisters on both heels now, but her feet had swelled while she was sitting on that godforsaken stool, making her shoes feel even tighter.

The night seemed darker when they stepped out of the restaurant. Bleaker.

"You okay?" Jonathan asked as they started the six-block trek to the car.

She forced a smile and tried not to limp so noticeably.

"Yep. Fine."

"It looks like your feet are hurting."

"I shouldn't have worn these stupid shoes. I wanted to look nice, but I forgot they give me blisters."

He reached for her hand and gave it a comforting squeeze. "You'd look nice no matter what shoes you were wearing."

Her heart stuttered in her chest, and she squeezed his hand back, holding on tight in case he had any thoughts of letting go again. "Even my fuzzy Chewbacca slippers?"

His face split into a grin. "Even your fuzzy Chewbacca slippers."

Getting to hold his hand made up for some of the pain in her feet, but by the time they got to the car, she was limping like Quasimodo. She sagged into the driver's seat and groaned with relief as she kicked her shoes off.

"Ouch," he said, wincing in sympathy at the sight of her blistered feet. "You want me to drive?"

"No, I'm fine now that I can take these wretched shoes off." She chucked them over her shoulder into the back seat. More fodder for the Goodwill pile.

Traffic was clear on the drive home. Jonathan fidgeted in the seat beside her and stared out the passenger window. Neither of them spoke. By the time she pulled into her parking space, Esther was convinced the whole night had been a failure. This was her chance to win him back, and she'd blown it. Some date she turned out to be.

"Stay right there," Jonathan said when she cut the engine. He jumped out of the car and came around her side to open the door. When he offered his hand to pull her to her feet, Esther assumed he was just being chivalrous. Then he turned his back on her and said, "Alley oop."

She stared at the back of his neck. "What?"

"I'm giving you a lift upstairs. Hop on."

"Are you serious?"

"We can't have you walking barefoot through the parking area. It's unsanitary."

"I'm too heavy for you."

He twisted his head around to roll his eyes at her. "Pu-leez."

"All right, fine." There was only so much protesting she was willing to do when an invitation to mount him like a show horse was on the table.

He crouched down, bracing his hands on his knees, and Esther grabbed his shoulders and clambered onto his back. Straightening easily, like she was light as a feather, he put his hands under her thighs to help support her. His bare hands. On the backs of her bare thighs under her skirt.

Warmth pooled in the pit of her stomach as she wrapped her arms around his shoulders and squeezed her thighs against his waist. For better purchase, of course. Definitely not because she loved the feel of him between her thighs.

"You good?" he asked.

"Mmmmm." She pressed her face into the back of his neck and breathed him in. His hair smelled like rosemary and mint, and it layered exquisitely with the cedar smell of his skin. So many smells, so much goodness. This was the best thing that had happened all night.

He closed the car door, and Esther held on tight as he conveyed her up the stairs, then past his apartment door all the way to hers. It was a genuine tragedy when she had to hop down and let go of him. The loss of contact with his warm body left her feeling chilled.

Once he'd deposited her safely on solid ground, he spun around to face her, stepping back a little. Putting more distance between them again.

The floor of the breezeway was cold under her bare feet, and she shifted from foot to foot like grade-schooler in need of a bathroom pass. "Thanks for the lift."

He nodded, plunging his hands into his pockets. His brows

drew together as his expression darkened.

Esther's stomach did a dive. Pinpoints of light reflected off his glasses, partially obscuring his eyes. The air between them suddenly felt heavy with impending catastrophe. She wasn't ready for tonight to be over. She needed more time to make things right.

"I'm sorry," she blurted before he could speak. "I wanted tonight to be special, but instead everything was awful."

His frown deepened. You could stick a pencil in the furrows of his forehead. "It wasn't awful."

"We missed the beginning of the movie, dinner was a bust, and I spent the whole night limping on bloody stumps because I apparently can't even dress myself like an adult."

Dismay spread across his face. "I don't care about any of that—I mean, I care that your feet hurt—but I don't care about the rest of it." He shifted closer, and the reflections on his glasses cleared, bringing his eyes into focus. The irises were tinged with silver. "I had a great time tonight."

A bubble of hope expanded in her chest. "You did?"

"I was with you. It was perfect."

The bubble in her chest exploded into joy. He moved closer, and lifted a hand to cup her cheek. She leaned into his touch, letting his fingers warm her skin.

His eyelashes lowered as he tilted his head toward her. It took all her willpower not to surge upward. She was desperate to feel his lips again, but afraid to initiate the kiss after the way he had turned his head away last night.

When he was just out of reach, he paused. Their noses bumped. Their breath mingled. He held her gaze as his thumb scraped over her cheekbone. "Esther."

The word dissolved between them, soft as powdered sugar.

"Please," she whispered in an agony of anticipation. Desperation had rendered her pathetic. Her chest constricted as she held her breath, waiting. Dying. His visage dimmed and blurred as her eyes watered.

Jonathan brushed his mouth against hers. Tender. Fragile. The barest of kisses.

A needy whimper escaped her lips, and she curled her hands into his shirt. Pulling him closer. Every atom in her body yearning for him.

"Shhh," he murmured, and kissed her again.

She shuddered a sigh, sinking into him. He tasted even better than he smelled. Even better than she remembered. A hand slid into her hair, then around the back of her neck, deepening the kiss. His other arm was around her waist, his palm flat against the small of her back, holding her close.

Unwinding her fingers from his shirt, she moved her hands over his chest, then his shoulders, finally settling around his neck. As she pressed her body into his, she felt his lips curve against her mouth, and he let out a low huff of air.

She reached up to touch his face, marveling that she was permitted to do so. When her fingernails scraped through his beard, his mouth curved even more and his blue eyes sparked bright in the dim light. She wanted to devour that smile of his and make it her own. Rising on her toes, she angled her mouth against his.

Every muscle in her body quivered as she kissed him. Their tongues met in a slow, wet slide—earnest, intent, and a little frantic. Their teeth clashed and scraped, their breaths reduced to a series of staccato gasps. She put everything she had into that kiss, filling it with promises. She didn't want it to be a goodnight kiss. She wanted it to be the start of something, not the end.

"Esther," he murmured when they finally came up for air. His fingers combed through her hair, his breath fanning her face.

She gazed up at him and licked her lips, neurons crackling. Expectant. Hopeful. Nervous.

The smile resurfaced, lighting up his whole face. "Aren't you going to invite me inside?"

Chapter Thirty-Three

$\mathcal{E}$sther propelled herself at him, heart singing with relief as she crushed her lips against his. Just as his mouth started to open to hers, she pulled back, grinning as she twisted away.

Her keys. She needed her keys.

Behind her, she heard him blow out a breath in—frustration? Anticipation? Something. She dug through her purse, letting out an "Aha!" of triumph when her fingers closed around the elusive metal objects.

As she jammed one of them into the lock, Jonathan stepped up behind her and pressed his body against hers. One of his hands flattened against the door beside her head while the other reached around her waist.

"Guh," she groaned as his fingers spread out over her stomach, holding her flush against his body. Every firm inch of it.

Shivers raced down her spine as he nosed aside her hair. He pressed an open-mouthed kiss to the top of her shoulder, then moved to the side of her neck, leaving a wet trail that tingled in the cold night air. When she felt his teeth graze the flesh between her neck and shoulder, her knees went to jelly, threatening to buckle on her. But his hand on her stomach held her in place, fingers curling into her waist as he continued his delicious assault on her neck.

"I thought..." She trailed off, sighing as he nuzzled into her hair and his mouth found the tender spot behind her ear.

"Hmmm?" he breathed against her. "You thought what?"

Her head lolled forward. It was hard to think about anything other than the nearness of his body and his tongue on her skin. "I thought you wanted to come inside?" she finally managed.

Wordlessly, he moved his hand to cover hers, and they turned the key together. He reached for the doorknob and twisted. The door swung open, and he pushed her into the apartment.

Spinning to face him, Esther let her keys and purse fall to the floor as Jonathan slammed the door shut behind them and threw the bolt home. His expression was hungry as they surged together, meeting halfway in a fierce, open-mouthed kiss.

Her nose knocked his glasses askew in their eagerness for one another, and she dragged her mouth away from his to remove them. She set them on the table by the door as he blinked at her, his eyes slightly unfocused while he adjusted to his uncorrected vision.

Smiling, she reached up to pet his beard. He leaned into her touch and made a purring sound in his throat not all that different than the sound Sally made when Esther scratched her in the same spot. *Note to self: he likes to have his beard petted.*

He brushed her hair back from her face and gazed at her with heavy-lidded eyes. "I've been thinking about kissing you all night."

Her mouth fell open in surprise. "You have?"

His thumb dragged along her lower lip, his expression dark and smoldering. "I couldn't think about anything else. Every time I looked at you, all I could focus on was your mouth, and how much I wanted to taste it again."

Esther's stomach did a pleasant swoop as he bent to kiss her.

His long fingers caressed her jaw, and he tilted her head for a better angle, savoring her like an expensive delicacy.

She was struck all over again by how gentle he was. How careful. She wondered if it was because he was afraid of hurting her, or because he was afraid of being hurt.

A rush of guilt pooled in her stomach. Her hands tightened on his arms, pulling him closer. There was too much fabric between them. Craving connection, she went to work on the buttons of his shirt.

Heat radiated from his skin as her hands smoothed over his torso. She found the steady thud of his heartbeat and pressed her lips to it. As she breathed in the familiar scent of him, affection welled up inside her, burning the back of her throat. She squeezed her eyes shut, wound her arms around his waist, and rested her cheek against his bare chest. Her breath hitched traitorously as she hugged him tight.

"Hey." Gentle hands slid across her back in soothing circles. "What's wrong?"

"I missed you," she said, her voice coming out rough. "Sometimes it felt like I couldn't breathe, I missed you so much." She clung to him like gravity didn't exist. Like he was the only thing keeping her from flying into the empty vacuum of space.

"Shhh." He pressed a kiss to the top of her head. "I'm here now."

She clutched him harder. "I thought I'd lost you."

"You didn't lose me. I'm not going anywhere." He gently loosened her grip, turning her a little in his arms. "Look at me." He put a finger under her chin to tilt her face up.

She blinked at him, overwhelmed by what she read in his expression—but also ashamed of her sudden outburst of emotion, and embarrassed she'd thrown a wet blanket on what had been heading toward being a very hot night.

He bent down and kissed her on the lips, with so much tenderness she thought her heart would burst. "You *have* me. If you want me."

Unwinding her arms from his waist, she reached up with both hands to cradle his face. "I want you," she said, solemn as an oath.

His pulse jumped under her fingertips. He blinked at her through those incredible, glossy lashes, and his lip betrayed the minutest hint of a tremble. "Good."

He was so beautiful. It hurt to think about how much she'd hurt him. How she'd tried so hard to push him away. She threaded her fingers into his hair and pulled his face down to hers so they were nose to nose. Forehead to forehead. "I didn't mean to break your heart."

She felt him shake his head. "It doesn't matter, as long as I get to have you."

"If it helps, I broke my own heart too."

He pulled back, eyes softening, and reached up to caress her cheek. "I don't want your heart to be broken. I just want to make you happy."

"You do."

Uncertainty clouded his face. "Really?"

She pressed her fingers to his brow, smoothing out the creases. "No one's ever made me this happy before." She watched the skin around his eyes crinkle before she kissed him. Slow and deep. Trying to pour everything in her heart into it. *I care about you,* her lips whispered silently. *I need you. I love you.*

They spent a few dreamy minutes just kissing. Enjoying the feel of each other, and the taste. Her hands found their way back to his shirt and she eased it off his shoulders. His bare arms wrapped around her, radiating warmth and security. She sighed happily at the sensation.

His hands roamed over her back until his fingers found the zipper of her dress. She arched against him as he tugged it down. Breathing heavily, he eased her dress off one shoulder, and then the other. She could feel him holding himself back, his urgency evinced by his strained, jerky motions as he worked her dress down her body.

When he got it down to her waist, he paused and exhaled a long breath, his eyes burning brighter as they devoured her. She helped him out by shoving her dress down her hips, letting it pool on the floor at her feet. Her hands moved to his pants, enjoying the way his stomach muscles flexed at her touch. Working quickly, she unfastened his belt and pants, shoving them down his legs.

He toed off his shoes and socks, stepped out of the jumble of fabric at his feet, and grabbed her, pulling her against him. Their bodies sparked with heat everywhere their bare skin came together.

Tender hands caressed her. His palms moved over her breasts, then glided down and around, cupping her backside. Her breath caught as she was lifted off the floor. She twined her arms and legs around him, and he carried her into the bedroom.

Jonathan halted at the foot of her bed, frowning at something over her shoulder. "Move, cat. I need the bed."

Esther laughed as he spun them around and sank down onto the bed with her in his lap. Over his shoulder, she saw Sally Ride dash away as the mattress bowed under their combined weight.

Jonathan buried his face in the crook of Esther's neck, and she sank her fingers in his hair, arching against him. His hands smoothed over her thighs, and his mouth traveled down to her cleavage, exploring with his tongue.

Just when she was starting to get impatient for more, he reached up and unclasped her bra, allowing her breasts to tumble free. He sucked in a ragged breath and cupped them in his palms. Then his hands slid down her body, and he was lifting her up again, laying her down gently on the bed.

Standing over her, he yanked down his briefs. She squirmed in anticipation as he stooped to drag her underwear down her legs. His hands glided over her skin, sending her into a frenzy of desire.

She tugged at him, pulling him onto the bed with her. Needing to feel him. Wanting him everywhere.

He murmured her name softly, drawing moans and sighs from her as his hands explored the planes of her body. As they came together, she gazed into his beautiful blue eyes, defenseless. Overpowered by emotion. Swept away on a wave of bliss.

I LOVE HIM, Esther thought afterward as she lay in the cradle of Jonathan's arms. The knowledge burned in her chest like a supernova. It was both miraculous and terrifying. Part of her ached to say the words aloud, but another, much bigger part of her quaked in fear at the idea. She didn't trust her own emotions, and she certainly didn't trust this new thing that was happening between them. This *relationship*. She didn't do relationships. She didn't even know how they were supposed to work. She had no experience to guide her.

What if she wasn't ever able to say the L-word? Or what if she said it, and it scared him away? What if he didn't love her back? He'd said he loved her weeks ago, but that had been in the face of her rejection. An attempt to win her back. Maybe he hadn't meant it. Or maybe he had, but he didn't anymore. He hadn't said it again since, which could mean he didn't feel that way about her anymore.

"Hey." He nuzzled into her hair, pressing his nose against the back of her neck.

"Hmmm?"

"You got all tense all of a sudden. You okay?"

"Yeah."

He pushed himself up onto one elbow and rolled her over onto her back, studying her face in the soft lamplight. His brow furrows had returned in full force. "No freaking out on me. You aren't having regrets, are you?"

She pressed her fingertips to his forehead, and the creases

melted away at her touch. "No regrets." She didn't want him thinking she was about to bolt again. She wasn't going to do that. If she was going to screw this up, she'd undoubtedly find a new and different way to do it. One neither of them were prepared for.

"Scared?" He knew her too well. How had that happened?

"Maybe a little." It was a big admission for her. She was trying. "But not of you."

"Then what?"

Myself. That she wasn't cut out for this. That she wouldn't be able to give him what he needed. That he'd realize he wanted more and leave her. That she'd open herself up to him and end up alone.

Her eyes skated away from his. "I'm just feeling...overwhelmed, I guess. This is all new to me."

He lay on his side and propped his head in his hand. His fingers interlaced with hers on her stomach. "What is?"

"Caring about someone."

His face broke open. She was never going to get over that smile of his. "Oh, well, it's not that tricky." He brought her hand to his lips. "You've got good instincts. You'll pick it up as you go along."

She could feel her heart stretching as she looked at him. Making even more room. Somehow, he'd crept into her dark crevices and dusted out the cobwebs, filling in her sharp corners with his tenderness. Maybe everything would be okay. Maybe they'd be able to do this together.

She turned toward him and pressed a hand against his face. His eyes fluttered closed as she stroked his beard. *So much like a cat.*

"You look different without your glasses."

His eyes opened again. "Different good or different bad?"

"Good. I feel like I'm getting to see Secret Jonathan. The real you, that no one else gets to see."

He leaned over to brush his lips against hers. "I still can't believe—" He broke off, smiling and shaking his head.

"What?"

"Nothing." He looked smug. Like someone with a secret.

"Tell me. What can't you believe?"

His fingers traced the line of her jaw. "Do you know how long I've wanted to kiss you?"

"How long?"

"Since the very first moment I met you. I'll bet you don't even remember it."

Her mouth opened as her mind reached back, trying to grab onto the memory. But there was nothing there. It felt as if he'd always been around, in the background of her life, ever since she'd moved to LA. She couldn't pinpoint the moment when she first saw him.

"I'll give you a hint," he said. "You yelled at me."

"Of course I did." She shook her head, laughing. "I'm afraid you're going to have to narrow it down a little more."

He rolled onto his back, and she scooted over to snuggle up against his chest. "It was the day after you moved into the building," he said, wrapping his arm around her shoulders. "I'd seen the movers bringing your stuff up, and I must have watched you walk back and forth past my window at least a dozen times." He smiled at the memory. "I thought you were beautiful."

She felt her cheeks heat. "Shut up."

"I did! So the next day, I was sitting out on my balcony when I saw your car pull in below. And I grabbed my keys and sprinted downstairs, so I could 'accidentally' bump into you and introduce myself."

"That's adorable." She wished she could remember it, but she was still drawing a blank.

"I got to my car as you were unloading your groceries, and I unlocked it like I was going out." He played idly with her hand as he talked, running his thumb over her knuckles. "And when you looked up, I said, 'Hi, my name is Jonathan. I live next door to you in six.' And you said, 'You're supposed to park your car between the lines, not on them.'"

Esther burst out laughing. "Oh my god! I didn't!" She buried her face in his chest, mortified.

"You did."

"I'm the worst! How could you possibly like me after that?"

He laid a hand on her hair and kissed the top of her head. "I couldn't help myself. I think it actually made me like you more."

She lifted her head to look at him. "That's twisted. You know that, right?"

He shrugged. "I remember thinking, *Well, I blew it. She hates me now. She'll never agree to go out with me.*"

"And look how wrong you were." She kissed his chest and laid her head back down. His heartbeat fluttered against her cheek. "I didn't *hate* you though."

"Liar. I know you did. You didn't even try to hide it."

Her fingers played with the light trail of hair leading down his abdomen. "That's because—and you may know this about me already—I can sometimes be too blunt. Aggressive, even."

He chuckled, pulling her closer and nuzzling his nose against her head.

"I didn't *hate* you," she said, smiling into his skin. "I just... disliked you."

"Oh, okay. That's so much better." He rolled her onto her back so he could kiss her.

"I didn't know you. Once I got to know you, you were irresistible."

"Yeah, right." He dipped his head to kiss her neck.

"It's true." Her fingers curled into his hair. She loved his hair. She loved that she could run her fingers through it whenever she pleased. "I didn't *want* to like you, but I couldn't help myself. You make me helpless."

He tilted his head, gazing up at her through his long lashes. "I can't imagine you ever being helpless about anything."

"I am when it comes to you. You wouldn't believe how I pined over you. *Me.* I don't pine. Ever. But I did over you."

His mouth curled into a smirk. That infuriating, sexy, irresistible smirk. God, she loved it. "Seriously?"

"Yeah. It was pathetic."

He kissed the tip of her nose and flopped onto his back again, tugging her into his arms. "Is it wrong that I like the idea of you pining for me?"

She rested her head in the perfect cradle of his shoulder. "No, I don't think it's wrong."

His arms tightened around her. "I was pining for you too, you know."

"We were both pathetic."

"What are we now?"

Her fingertips found his heartbeat. "Happy."

"I like the sound of that," he said, yawning.

She snuggled closer, soaking up the sense of contentment. She wanted to exist here forever in the protective circle of his arms. Listening to the gradual slowing of his breathing as he drifted off to sleep. Counting every beat of his heart.

This was where she belonged. It was everything she'd ever wanted.

It wasn't a disaster, it was a miracle.

Chapter Thirty-Four

*W*hen Esther woke, she was alone. Dust motes danced in the grayish-yellow light stealing in through the blinds. It was morning. For a fleeting moment, she genuinely believed last night had been a dream. In the disorientation of half-sleep, her brain tried to parse fantasy from reality. Had they really spoken? Had they even gone on a date? Had her imagination concocted all of it to torment her?

She heard a cabinet close in the kitchen and her mind defogged enough to identify the smell of coffee filling her apartment. Coffee and...something else. Whatever it was, it smelled heavenly.

Throwing back the covers, she grabbed an old T-shirt and wandered into the kitchen.

Jonathan stood at the counter in nothing but his glasses and his underwear, whisking something in a bowl. It wasn't a dream. It was better. For a few seconds, Esther stood silently and watched, taking in the sight of him. Memorizing the moment, in case it didn't last.

He glanced her way, and a smile stole over his features. "You bought a real coffeemaker."

She walked over to him, rose up on her toes, and pressed her lips to his mouth. "I did."

His arm banded around her waist, holding her against him. The smile on his face got wider. "Good morning." He gave her a soft, lingering kiss. Smiling the whole time.

"Good morning to you too." Esther couldn't remember ever smiling this much in her whole life. Her cheeks ached as muscles that had atrophied with disuse came to life.

His smile shifted into a smirk. "It's not as good as my Chemex, of course."

"Of course."

"But it's pretty good for a beginner."

"I'm glad it has your seal of approval. I'll let that beginner comment go unremarked."

Still smirking, he let go of her and turned back to the bowl. It was full of thick batter. Butter sizzled in a nonstick pan preheating on the stove.

"You made awkward pancakes," she said, delighted.

Bemused furrows sprouted across his forehead. "Awkward pancakes?"

"That's what I used to call it when a guy I'd slept with tried to get me to have breakfast with him the next morning."

Jonathan's eyebrows lifted. "Is that so?"

"Yeah, but these aren't authentic awkward pancakes because I actually *want* to be here, eating your pancakes."

His mouth quirked. "Is that a euphemism?"

"No, but it definitely should be. Oh, wait!" she said, suddenly remembering the hat she'd knit him weeks ago. "I have something for you."

She dashed back into the bedroom and dug through her dresser. When she came back into the kitchen, Jonathan had his head stuck in her refrigerator. "Do you have syrup?"

"Pantry."

He emerged from the fridge, and his eyes alighted on the knit hat in her hand. "What's that?"

"I knit you a hat," she said, holding it out to him.

"You made this?" Admiration glowed on his face as he turned it over in his hands.

She took the hat from him and pulled it down over his head, tucking his hair back, off his forehead. She was right—the gray yarn did look good with his eyes.

He bent down and kissed her. "Thank you for making me a hat."

"You don't have to wear it if you don't like it."

"Are you kidding? I love it. I'm going to wear it every day."

"You definitely don't have to wear it every day."

"Nope, my girlfriend made me a hat. I'm never taking it off." The word *girlfriend* caused her stomach to drop as he turned back to his bowl of batter. "How many pancakes do you want?"

She recovered quickly. "Will you think poorly of me if I say four?"

He grinned at her as he poured a scoop of batter into the pan. "Nope."

"Then I want five."

Laughing, he reached for the spatula. "Coming right up."

It was almost too much to bear, how much she loved him, how she'd never stood a chance without him. The words spilled out of her before she'd made a conscious choice to say them: "I love you."

The hand holding the spatula stilled. "Because I made you pancakes?"

"No. I mean, I also love that you made me pancakes—but no. I love you with or without pancakes."

The eyes he turned toward her were bright and shining. "You love me?"

"I do," Esther said, feeling a weight lift off her shoulders. "I love you. I've loved you for a while, but I was too scared to say it."

Jonathan set down the spatula and pulled her into his arms. "You shouldn't have to be scared to tell someone you love them."

"Yes, but you see, the thing you don't know about me is that I'm pretty broken."

His nose rubbed against hers. "Believe it or not, I'd actually figured that out already."

"To be honest, you may want to reconsider getting involved with me. You don't know me all that well yet, and I'm not sure you realize exactly how—"

"I love you too," he said.

A starburst of affection exploded in her chest, and her face split into a grin. "Well, you're screwed now."

"God, I hope so." His hands tightened on her ass, and he hiked her up onto his hips.

She laughed, feeling dizzy as he spun her around and plopped her onto the counter, sending measuring cups flying.

"I love all your broken pieces," he said. "I love everything about you. I even love the way you argue with me."

"You realize telling me that is going to backfire on you big time, right?"

He locked eyes with her, running his hands up the outside of her thighs. "I love how opinionated you are, and that you act like you're not afraid of anything when on the inside you're afraid of everything. I love the frowny face you make when you're bossing me around. I love how much you care about your friends, and the way you try to take care of them. I love you, Esther Abbott, every bonkers bit of you, and I want to take care of you the way you take care of everyone else."

What had she ever done to deserve him? She reached for his face, holding it in her hands like it was something precious and fragile. "I love you, Jonathan Brinkerhoff."

He captured her lips in a kiss that was impossibly sweet and tender. He tasted like coffee and security. Like unconditional love.

Goose bumps shimmered over her skin as his mouth traveled

to her pulse point. She tipped her head back, exposing her throat to him.

The smell of smoke intruded on her happy moment. "I think the pancake's burning."

"I don't care about the pancake," he muttered into her cleavage.

"What if I do?"

He lifted his head enough to raise an eyebrow at her as his fingers moved up the inside of her thigh. "Do you care about the pancake right now?"

"Nope, definitely not," she said, shuddering with pleasure. "As long you promise to make me more pancakes later."

Without letting go of her, he reached a long arm out to turn off the stove. "I will make you all the pancakes you want. I will make you pancakes every single morning. I'll make you pancakes for dinner, I'll bring them to your office for lunch, I'll—"

"Okay, that's enough pancakes. Sex now, please."

He lunged forward to bury his face in her neck again. Her hands slid down his torso, and he let out a shaky breath as her fingers dipped inside the waistband of his underwear.

"Fuck," he said, freezing against her.

"That is what I'm trying to do."

His head sagged heavily against her shoulder. "I have to go to my parents' today."

Esther took her hand out of his underwear. "When?"

He straightened, sighing. "Soon. My mother wants me there for lunch, and it's a long drive."

"Oh." He looked so glum at the prospect, it made her insides clench. She pulled his head down to kiss away his distress. "We can take a rain check on the sex."

"I don't suppose..." He bit his lip, suddenly shy.

"What?"

His eyes glimmered with guarded hope. "You'd want to come with me?"

"To your parents'?" She hadn't expected that.

A cloud passed across his face. "I know, it's too soon. I shouldn't have asked."

"Do you *want* me to come with you?"

"I always want you with me."

Her knees tried to go all melty but she shook it off. There were more pressing matters at hand. "Yeah, but to meet your parents? Are you ready for that? Are they?"

"Are you?"

She smoothed a hand over his shoulder. "Will it make it easier or harder for you if I'm there?"

"Easier. Definitely easier."

Her hand stroked up the side of his neck, pulling him in for a kiss. "Then I'll come."

"Really?" His sigh of relief tasted as sweet as cotton candy.

"Of course. I'm happy to do it." Anything to keep him from being sad. She would wrestle a bear if it would put a smile back on his face. Staring down a couple of Orange County WASPs was nothing.

His pulse fluttered against her fingers. "Are you sure? Because my parents are no picnic. And I'm miserable company when I'm around them, so it's not going to be any fun for you."

"I'm not going for fun. I'm going to support you. That's what friends are for."

He arched a very sexy eyebrow. He was still wearing the hat she'd made him, and he'd never looked more adorable. "Friends?"

"Friends in love." She reached up to pet his beard. "That's the goal, right?"

The corner of his mouth quirked. "That's the goal." Behind his glasses, his eyes were soft and bottomless.

Her lips found his, needing to taste his sweetness and vulnerability. Maybe, if she kissed him long enough and hard enough, some of it would wear off on her.

His fingers dug softly into her spine as he leaned into her, opening his mouth to hers. She could have absolutely stayed there all day, kissing him like this. But if she was going to meet his parents today—soon—she had other priorities.

Esther pulled away, ignoring his moan of protest. "What should I wear? Are they casual people or formal?"

Jonathan's mouth turned down at the reminder of their impending social obligation. "They are definitely not casual people. We'll probably go to the club, so you should dress up a little."

She traced his frown with her fingers until it dissolved into a smile. "There's a club?"

"There's a club."

"I've never been to a club before."

He turned his head to kiss her fingertips. "It's not that exciting. Neither are my parents."

Her heart was glowing so brightly in her chest, it felt like it could light up the world. "I don't care. As long as I'm with you."

Esther wrapped her arms around him, and promised herself she'd never let go again.

Acknowledgments

As always, the first people who need to be thanked are my family: my husband, Dave, and my daughter, Emma. Their love and support made this book possible.

Special thanks must also go out to:

My marvelous editor Julia, for her impeccable guidance and attention to detail, and for liking my jokes.

Nicole, who explained very patiently to me what an aerospace engineer actually does. Any inaccuracies are my bad and not hers.

Joanna, who catches the mistakes that slip by everyone else; Lisa, the best cheerleader and Los Angeles fact-checker an author could ever want; and Jeny, who answered all my Seattle questions.

Mer, Jaimie, Kat, and Bethany, who told me what I needed to hear to make this story better.

Genie and Jen, for going above and beyond to support my last book.

And last, but definitely not least, my ever-supportive friends Mikaela, Lisa, Dena, and Tammy. I love you all to the moon and back.

About the Author

SUSANNAH NIX lives in Texas with her husband, two ornery cats, and a flatulent pit bull. When she's not writing, she enjoys reading, cooking, knitting, watching stupid amounts of television, and getting distracted by Tumblr. She is also a powerlifter who can deadlift as much as Captain America weighs.

www.susannahnix.com

Also by Susannah Nix

I and Love and You: A Romantic Short Story Collection

Chemistry Lessons Series:

Remedial Rocket Science

Intermediate Thermodynamics

Advanced Physical Chemistry (coming soon)

CPSIA information can be obtained
at www.ICGtesting.com
Printed in the USA
LVHW080801141120
671715LV00035B/586